D0919847

York's Moon

York's Moon

Elizabeth Engstrom

FIVE STAR
A part of Gale, Cengage Learning

Detroit • New York • San Francisco • New Haven, Conn • Waterville, Maine • London

Five Star Publishing, a part of Gale, Cengage Learning.

Set in 11 pt. Plantin.

LIBRARY OF CONGRESS CATALOGING-IN-PUBLICATION DATA

Engstrom, Elizabeth.
York's moon / Elizabeth Engstrom. — 1st ed.
p. cm.
ISBN-13: 978-1-59414-928-3 (hardcover)
ISBN-10: 1-59414-928-3 (hardcover)
1. Tramps—Fiction. 2. Bakery employees—Fiction. 3. Murder—Investigation—Fiction. 4. Municipal government—Corrupt practices—Fiction. I. Title.
PS3555.N48Y67 2011
813'.54—dc22 2010043411

First Edition. First Printing: February 2011.
Published in 2011 in conjunction with Tekno Books and Ed Gorman.

Printed in the United States of America
1 2 3 4 5 6 7 15 14 13 12 11

This book is dedicated to Al Cratty, my sweet, exceedingly patient husband.

ACKNOWLEDGMENTS

A book is the culmination of inspiration from so many. I'd like to thank John Saul, Mike Sack, Susan Palmer, Karen McGowan, Bob Kccfcr and Maggic Doran for starters. Students, friends, family: you have no idea how far the wind carries the seeds you sow.

First Day of the Full Moon

It wouldn't be right to say that the whole thing began when Clover found the dead guy in the weeds. Clearly, malfeasance had been afoot long before, but up until that moment, life in Yorktown was as it had been for years.

"Shhht. Here she comes." York leaned his head back against the dirt and gravel hillside and felt the low vibration. He loved that vibration. It brought back memories of being young and adventuresome, of being light of spirit and easy of conscience. Those were the days when a young man could ride the rails in relative safety and earn himself a life. "A couple miles off yet. She's late." He pulled back the frayed cuffs of his layered coat, sweater, shirt, and thermals and consulted the battered watch on his thin wrist. It had stopped two years earlier, but York, being blind, didn't know that. He had to keep up appearances, so he consulted the dead watch and repeated himself. "Real late."

"Stupid government," said Sly. He rubbed his long gray hair out of his eyes with a frustrated hand. "Trains are the key to our salvation, and the government's ruining them. The government's going to ruin this country. Atlas is just gonna shrug and we'll all be in for it."

"Yeah, yeah, shut the fuck up," said Denny.

"Hey," York said. York didn't like that kind of language. He wished they would be quiet so he could enjoy the vibration and the anticipation of the train yet again. As long as the trains came by, as long as York heard them, felt them, remembered them, he wasn't dead yet. "I toil in a garden of souls, Lord," he said raising his sightless eyes to the sky, "and though my back grows weary, the harvest remains meager."

"Yeah, yeah," said Denny. He poked a square forefinger out of a hole in his too-small knit gloves and felt around under the square of canvas he was lying on. He, too, felt his heart pump a little harder when the train came by. No matter how many trains had come down those tracks in the years he'd lived with York, the wonder of the giant machinery making its way always brought out the little boy in him. He recognized that feeling in the others, too. "Wonder where Clover is," he said.

Nobody answered him because just then the Western Express blew its customary three blasts on the horn. York smiled, a snaggletoothed, raggedy-faced smile, and raised his hand in a return salute. The train rambled by on its early-evening run, kicking up dust and sparks from the tiny fire it was Sly's job to tend.

"Idiot!" Sly screamed at the huge metal wheels as they ground by, their rails rocking loosely. He scrambled around to find something to shield the fire, but, of course, by the time he grabbed a nasty, crumpled old sheet of corrugated tin, the train was long past and whistling on down the road. "Trying to make up the time," Sly said. "Blow us off the planet on its way. Stupid government." He kicked at the coals and threw the tin back onto a pile of junk. "Coffee's ready, York."

The smart thing would have been for Sly to make a permanent shield for the fire out of the sheet metal, but Sly wasn't smart, York didn't see the problem, and Denny didn't care. One day Clover would fix it, Sly would find something else to scream about, York would never know the difference, and Denny still wouldn't care. Their system worked.

And it had worked thus far for York and the ever-changing landscape of his companions for a dozen years or more. Yorktown was known in the rail riding community as a safe place, where you kept your weapons to yourself and your foul language inside your mouth. Where there was a pretty girl, sometimes, who would talk about girl things in a girl voice and bring back memories of different times and different places and women that had been of those times and places long past. But you kept your hands to yourself. You shared your food and others shared theirs with you. You didn't steal, you knew right from wrong, and you behaved yourself.

Not like most of the hobo camps around the country, where any one of the denizens would slit your throat for the price of a jug—or these days, a fix. Where rats would chew holes in your clothes while you slept. Where keeping your hands to yourself wasn't an issue; you were more likely to be beaten and raped as you slept.

Yorktown was safe from the prying eyes of those walking the street above, with its barrier of tall tangle of blackberry canes. A slim path wound down through those towering brambles, down the hill from the street to their little city, walled with stack and stacks of newspapers pilfered from the mission donation box by the gas station. These newspapers, over the years, with the rain and the sun, became solid walls, tough as brick, and as the bottom layers composted away, the walls sank and eventually had to be fortified on top with fresh bundles. Yorktown was a maze of walls about three feet high. Each citizen had his own bedroom, a not-so-private latrine had been dug off to the west, a jug of water dripped into the dirt not far from the fire pit and the coffeepot, and a guest area was available for the occasional visitor. A half dozen old, cracked white buckets littered the yard and were available as seats for visiting dignitaries.

Yorktown was safe all right, and men dropped in on a regular basis, but they didn't stay. It was too much like home. Or church. These folks were on the road because they wanted their freedoms, and most of them would never understand that their kind of freedom was also its own kind of prison.

York, Sly and Denny were the only true free ones, or so York liked to think. They had government, they had laws, they had punishments and disciplines. York looked upon Sly and Denny as his children, and he tried to do right by them. He was their father, their mentor, their governor, their teacher, judge and landlord, all in one. Just like a dad.

And they were young enough to be his boys, too. York had lost count of the seasons, but he reckoned he was nearing his seventies, if not already among them. His sight had begun to dim twenty years previous; too many years in the California sun had burned his eyes right through.

Sly was the first to join York on anything resembling a permanent basis. A man disappointed in life, who one day set down his wallet and his car keys and walked away. His anger had changed from volatile to showmanship over the years; he still acted angry because it was the only way he knew how to act, but York didn't think Sly was really all that angry anymore. He had nothing to be angry about. Sly was middle aged and healthy, tall and thin, with dark, dark eyes and a swarthy complexion that took kindly to the hot sun. His hair, once dark, had silvered, and his once-handsome face had hardened until his nose seemed beaked and his lips too thin. Sly adored his conspiracy theories, and wasn't above spending his evening making up new ones, though he was still able to go out and work a day job now and then when they needed something serious. Sometimes he just did it to prove to himself that he still could. He'd go up into town and sign on for a labor crew for a day, and come home with a fistful of cash and, like as not, a fresh smell, having found himself a bath and haircut. Nothing makes a man feel like a man more than bringing home the bacon. And when Sly got to crying, which he sometimes did,

York would gently suggest that he go do a little work for some boss somewhere and rekindle his appreciation for his freedom. It always worked.

Denny showed up half a dozen summers ago. Denny was a young rat yet, seemed like so many of the rail riders were young'uns. Maybe that was because York had outlived most of his cronies, maybe because life didn't have much to offer the young ones anymore. Denny never worked. Sometimes he came home with things, and sometimes money, and York knew that Denny stole, but he never stole from York or Sly, and so he didn't cross any boundaries set up in Yorktown. Denny was a young stud, sturdily built, with lots of thick, light-brown hair and a beautiful set of naturally white teeth. Girls gravitated to his easy smile and his shy demeanor, but Denny wasn't the settling-down type, and so he mentioned that to every one of them almost as soon they met. It kept life less complicated.

Clover liked Denny, and they'd been something of an item for the past year or so, although Clover had a lot of good common sense and wasn't about to do anything permanent with one of the losers who lived down by the tracks. She had a job and she kept her own place in town. She never let any of them into it, though, and kept pretty closemouthed about who she was and what she did. Sometimes York's heart ached for her. He'd never seen her with his traitorous eyes, but she was as pretty a soul as he'd ever come across, giving him a part of her paycheck every week, making sure they all had toothbrushes and vitamins and something to eat besides roasted rodent. They were pretty self-sufficient, but sometimes they were so lonely it even made York want to cry along with Sly. Then the girl would come tripping down the trail through the berry bushes, her gait unmistakable, and the air would lighten up, and they would encourage her to read to them, or to tell them stories, or just talk in her sweet girl voice.

If York had a wife, or a daughter, or a granddaughter, he'd want them all to be like Clover. They all loved her, and they all dreamed about her, but Denny was the only one who ever touched her. Maybe because he was allowed. York had never tried; he didn't know about Sly. They all tried to concentrate on other things while Denny and the girl sneaked off for some privacy together, but it didn't work. Those were perhaps the loneliest of times. But then they'd come back, and the girl would be bubbly and giggly and they'd all imagine it was them that made her that way, and that lightened the mood considerably.

York wasn't alone in his ministry. He'd never have been able to do all he had done in this place without the girl, God bless her.

Life was good, stable, sweet, and freedoms were assured.

Until the afternoon that Clover found that dead guy. It was a full moon, of course it was a full moon, it had to be. Full moons were always trouble. York knew a full moon without having to see one. Full moons tugged on the tide of reason, and nobody was quite in their right mind during a full moon. It was the first evening of the July full moon when the Western Express screeched down the rails and that guy hit the ground and rolled to within a hundred feet of Yorktown.

He wasn't quite dead at first. He moaned, and that's how she found him.

She'd just come down the hill, still wearing her pink donut-shop uniform, hair tied up in a ponytail, worn-out sneakers and bare legs, toting a bagful of day-old, when she stopped mid-step and said, "What's that?"

"What?" Denny said, rousing himself at the sound of her voice.

"You didn't hear that?"

"C'mere with them donuts," Denny said.

"Over there," the girl said, pitched the bag to Denny and

stomped through the weeds.

A low moan wavered across the dry litter, and this time everybody heard it. Then he coughed, and it was a jelly cough that put Denny right off the raspberry-filled donut he'd been about to bite.

Sly was up and running ahead of the girl the minute he heard it. Somebody in trouble. Somebody in bad trouble. "I've heard dead guys before," he said, leaping over trash and stumbling up and over the pile of old railroad ties. "I've seen lots of them in Vietnam, both the dead and the dying. This one's almost there."

York sat up and listened, his nose twitching in the wind. He smelled trouble, and it reached farther than the man who lay dying in the weeds. "Tell me what you find," he commanded in a whisper that only Denny heard. "Crushed chest, broken bones, mashed-up face."

Denny dropped the jelly-filled donut into the bag and tossed it aside. He sat up, stood, and brushed dust off his ragged Levis and ran his dusty fingers through his hair.

"Thrown from the train," York said. "By a big man wearing a red-and-blue-plaid shirt. I seen it. I seen it all in a dream."

"He's dead," Sly yelled. "Dead as hell."

"Full moon," York whispered.

"We need to call an ambulance," Clover said.

"He's way past an ambulance," Sly said. "Dude needs a hearse."

"York?" Denny asked, worried. Somebody needed to get control of this situation before it controlled all of them.

York reshuffled his stack of old sofa cushions, lay back, and sighed. "Hold on to your hats, boys," he said. "We're in for a ride."

Sly and Clover came stomping back through the weeds. "We need to put a sheet or something over him," she said. "His face is all mashed up. There's flies."

"You know about dead people?" Sly asked nobody in particular. "They're so quiet. They're so still. I don't think I could ever get used to dead people."

"I gotta see," Denny said, and wandered off.

"Maybe I should just go call the cops," Clover said.

"No, no, God, no, fuck no," Sly said.

"Your *language.*"

"Yeah, sorry, York, no, no cops," Sly said. "Don't call the cops. They'll start files on all of us. I don't want to be in a government computer."

"He's got family somewhere," Clover said. "They need to know about him."

"It's what they've been waiting for," Sly said. "There's always someone just sitting around waiting for one of us out here to screw up so they can arrest us and clean out our place here and put in a parking lot or some kind of a development or something."

"Yeah, this is really valuable land," Clover said with a smirk. "Right next to the railroad tracks."

"You know they don't like us," Sly said. "You call the government about that dead guy, and we're all as good as locked up in jail forever. They'll blame it all on us. Murder One, kids."

"No, they won't," Clover said. "We don't know anything about that guy."

"Doesn't matter."

"Call the cops," York said.

"What?" Sly said. "You're kidding."

"We didn't kill him. We don't know anything about him. Call the cops, they'll come investigate, and everything will be fine," York said. He knew the chances were slim that they'd be able to escape the moon that easily, but it was worth a try.

"Yeah, Sly, we can't just bury him," Clover said. "People will be looking for him."

"Who?" Denny asked from the field. "Why would they look here?"

"The people who killed him know where they dumped him," York said. "And they don't know that he is dead."

"Bringing in the cops is a bad idea, York," Sly said.

"What about the people who love that guy?" Clover countered.

"Love," Sly scoffed. "I say we bury him and shut up about it."

"*We* think we should call the cops," Clover said, crossing her arms over her chest defiantly and moving to stand closer to York.

"Sly's got a point," York said. "Let's sit on it for a while. He ain't going nowhere. We don't even need to say we knew he was there until we all start to smell him."

"In a while it'll be dark," Clover said. "You just going to leave him there by himself all night long?"

"There's footprints all around him," Denny said, standing at the top of the pile of ties. "Pretty obvious people have been looking at his dead ass. Look what I found."

In his hand was a roll of cash with a rubber band around it.

"Hey," Sly said, tripping over himself to scramble up to see the money. "Let me see."

"Back off," Denny said.

"Oh, no," Clover said. "York . . . ?" But as she turned to look at him, to beseech him to help the boys deal with their jealousies and greed, she saw something that disturbed her even more. "Hey," she called to the guys who were squaring off at each other at the tie pile. Reluctantly, they looked down at her. She pointed with her chin, and they all looked.

Ed, a toothless, smelly, alcoholic transient was headed their way, bedroll on his shoulder.

Denny shoved the wad of cash into his pocket and then

shoved Sly as he hopped down off the stack of creosote-soaked lumber. "Hey, Ed," Denny said, then grabbed Clover and pulled her down onto his canvas with him.

Ed looked as though he didn't hear. He was short and thin and nervous. "York?" he said when he got close enough. "Hey, York?" He dropped his bed into the dirt, then stood humbly, wringing his black knit hat.

"Hi, Ed," York said.

"Kin I stay a while?"

"You sober?"

"Not exactly."

"Got the law after ya?"

Ed was silent, twisting and twisting that poor hat. He was dirty, and hadn't shaved, but somehow, his thick white hair looked clean and shiny.

"You can't be drinking and puking around here, Ed," Sly said. "Last time you were here you puked on my bed. And then the law came down here and hassled us. You can't be bringing the law down here anymore."

"York?" Ed said, trying to ignore Sly.

"We live clean, Ed," York said.

"Just one night please? I got no drink. I need to sleep, just one night where I don't hafta keep an eye out."

"One night," York said, and Sly moaned his disapproval.

Ed, his head down, not making eye contact with anybody, scuffled around until he'd cleared himself a little space, then threw down his bedroll, took off his shoes and climbed between the layers. He looked like a little gray-haired dog, snuggled down in his dog bed.

Clover picked up the bag of day-old and disentangled herself from Denny's amorous advances. "No," Denny protested, trying to snag the bag away from her. "Not the gooey ones."

She parried him efficiently, stood up, brushed the dust and

weed seeds from her uniform and walked over to Ed. "You probably shouldn't eat much more sugar, Ed," she said. "But I think there's a bagel or two in there."

A grimy hand slipped out of the blanket and snatched the bag. The girl never saw his face.

"Bless you, Clover," York said.

She smiled at him.

Sly knelt down next to York and whispered harshly, "What about the . . . the . . ." He gestured toward the body and then toward Denny, his gestures falling, of course, on blind eyes.

"Shhht," York came back just as harshly. "It'll all wait until morning."

He was wrong.

When the moon was full up, Denny slipped out of his sleeping bag, pulled on his boots and then made for town, that roll of cash hot and urgent in his pocket.

He felt free and happy and light as a hummingbird. He was putting one over on that stupid Sly, thanks to Ed's intervention, and he was putting one over on that dead guy by taking his cash, and he was putting one over on God, for finding a windfall when God had never seen fit to give Denny anything worthwhile before. Ever.

Except maybe the girl. Denny had lucked out on that, but he knew it wouldn't last. She had a job and an apartment, and though she slept under his blanket with him some nights all night long, it was just because she was lonely and he was clean. Some nice girl like that was going to find herself a real boyfriend someday, and then she wouldn't come around him anymore the way she did with her soft skin. But, hey, while it was handy, he would help himself.

But, right now, there was only one thing on Denny's mind, and it wasn't quiff. It was steak. A big thick one, red inside and oozing juice with a baked potato dripping with butter and sour cream and a frosty Heineken he could suck right out of the bottle. Oh, yeah.

He passed by the low-down no-name bar where most of who he knew hung out, and headed uptown—not too far, just far enough to get himself a good meal. Tomorrow night he'd start earlier, and he'd bring York. York could use a good steak dinner. York and the girl, yeah, he'd treat them both.

Just before he opened the door to the steakhouse that had the dark, low-lit lounge where he could eat at the bar, Denny stopped to smell the night.

He loved the night. He loved the fact that he, and others like him, were alone in the night while almost everybody slept. There was less mental static in the atmosphere. Heads were clearer, senses were heightened. He breathed in deeply through his nose and as he did, his eyes rested on the moon, smaller now, and higher up than when he first awoke. It wasn't exactly full—tomorrow night the moon would be solid round—it still had a little flat spot on the upper right. Denny loved the moon. The moon was the main reason he slept outside—always had, even as a kid. When he turned over in the night, and his eyes flashed open for that instant, if he could see the moon, or the light that flowed from it that turned the world black and silver, he felt safe.

It was a good omen indeed that there was a big moon tonight. He had money in his jeans, he had a nice rare steak in his immediate future, he had adventure in his soul, and he had a moon to watch over him.

Life was sweet.

In the men's room, he washed his hands and face, finger-combed his brown hair away from his face, and then went into a stall to count the cash. The rubber band broke as he tried to slip it off the roll, the money unfurled and he almost dropped half of it into the toilet. So he sat down and counted it out into his lap.

Six hundred and forty dollars in twenties.

That was good, and that was very good.

It was good because it wasn't thousands. A man could have and lose six hundred bucks, no big deal. The dead guy could lose it, and Denny could have it. No questions, not like the questions that would be asked if the dead guy had five hundred thousand dollars on him or something like that. That would be serious business indeed. But six hundred and forty dollars? Nothing more than a solid week's paycheck.

So it was good because it wasn't serious money, and it was very good because it was Denny's.

He folded the bills, stuffed them into his pocket and went in for his feast.

The restaurant was closed, the lights dim and the chairs up on top of the tables. The lounge was still open but quiet. Two women sat at the end of the bar, smoking and talking intently. Two cowboys played pool at the far end of the room. The air in the place tasted foul.

The jukebox was silent, and the rolled-and-tucked black vinyl booths and matching, low-wheeled chairs around small round tables spoke of a hundred affairs and a thousand heartbreaks.

Denny looked at the two women, who were surely talking about men, and the two men, surely wishing they were with women, and he thought this was perhaps the loneliest place on the planet.

He sat at the bar, ordered his meal, then swiveled around and leaned against it with his Heineken in his hand. He watched the men play pool until they didn't want him to watch them anymore. They were very clear about that.

Denny didn't want any trouble, so he turned back around and began watching the women. They didn't even notice him.

They weren't old, but they had been used. Denny guessed that any women smoking and drinking alone together in a bar around midnight had problems he couldn't even imagine. And they all revolved around being used and being tossed aside. He knew the feeling. He'd been tossed aside a few times by a few women, and he had learned. Do the tossing. Don't never put yourself in a position to get tossed aside again.

He reckoned that someday a woman would blindside him and hit him so hard and so fast that he didn't see it coming, and when that happened, he'd fall deep into love and put himself at risk. And that would be fine, but until that happened, he kept his distance. The girl, Clover, she was starting to get under his skin a little bit—she was so damned cute!—but he could still walk away, no problem.

The food came, and with it, a fresh beer, and he sliced into that rare beef and put the first heavenly bite into his mouth.

He never got to the second one, nor the baked potato that was awash with butter, sour cream, chives and bacon bits, or the steaming fresh green hunk of broccoli that looked like something he'd been longing for, but hadn't realized it until he saw it. No, Denny only got one bite of steak before the door opened and the shouting started.

The door opened, and the first indication Denny had that trouble was about to erupt was when the worn-out blonde whispered to her companion, "Oh, shit." Denny swallowed his steak and turned to look.

A rangy-looking guy in a tank shirt, jeans, and a huge belt buckle, with long gray hair pulled back into a ponytail, came in. He had a couple days' growth on his chin and a storm brewing behind brown eyes.

"I ain't talkin' to you no more, Norman," the blonde said. "I'm done cryin', and I'm done beggin' and I'm flat-out done with you."

"You come on home now, Christine," Norman said in a very low voice. It was a voice Denny knew well. It was the voice of violence being held in control by the tiniest of fraying threads.

"No, I told you."

"Come on, Christine. Stop all this now and come home to your children." He moved slowly toward her, and Denny watched the man's fingers curl.

"She *said* she ain't going," the redhead said.

Norman ignored her. "Christine?"

"Go away," Christine said.

Denny looked at that lovely slab of meat on his plate and said good-bye to it. He knew that he couldn't stand by and have this woman go home with this man, nor could he watch whatever steps that man was about to take in order to make her go with him. Whatever was going to happen, the steak and the potato and the broccoli wasn't going to taste nearly as good when it was all over.

Denny turned toward the situation. "Go home, Norman," he said. "Cool off. She'll come home when she's ready."

"This ain't about you," Norman said, never taking his eyes off his woman.

"You bring it into this place, you disturb my meal, you make it about me."

Christine flashed him a smile of gratitude, and that was just exactly the wrong thing for her to do.

The cowboys, pool cues in hand, moved in closer. The girls huddled. Norman spun on his heel and gave Denny a punch in the side of the head that knocked him off his stool. One of the cowboys cracked Norman over the head with the cue, and got tossed onto the pool table for his trouble. The girls started screaming, the bartender came out from the back, took one look and skedaddled out of sight.

Denny, eyes not working just exactly right, stood up. "Go on home, Norman," he said again, and thought that was perhaps the wrong thing to say under the circumstances. Norman picked up the broken pool cue and came at Denny with it.

Denny, younger and healthier, with adrenaline running hot, ducked and parried and danced Norman around a little bit, at least until the flashing red and blue lights shone through the small tavern windows.

"Cops!" Christine yelled. Denny looked at her just at the wrong moment, and that fat stick of wood caught him square in the forehead.

Vaguely, he heard sound swirling around him, mixed in with the thick black air, and he felt himself slowly falling through it. Someone was touching him, someone was pulling on his clothes, and he tried to speak, but his tongue was fumbled and there was cotton in his ears and everything seemed so far away. Oh, yeah, and his head hurt in a way it had never hurt before. This wasn't like a headache; this was like a pain so large he saw it instead of feeling it. And he could feel the sounds. Too many sounds, too loud, echoing in his head until he thought he would puke. He had to get up. He had to get out of there. He had to get outside where it was cool, God he was hot, he had to get away from the noises, from the activity, he had to get out. Out under the comforting influence of the moon.

Getting out was not as easy as he thought. His legs didn't work right. He squirmed like a bug on the floor.

Then a cool hand was on his head, and a rag so cold he thought it would burn him was on his forehead, and a soft voice cut through all the rest and it said, "Shhh, just relax."

He followed orders well, Denny did, and he was happy to follow these.

A few minutes later, he opened his eyes and saw the redhead looking down at him. "Hi," she said. "You going to be all right?"

Denny didn't know the answer to that.

"Boy, you got a knot the size of a suckling pig up there where Norman cracked you."

A trembling hand found the knob on his forehead, and it felt as big as a handle, and it made him go weak in the knees again, even though he was lying flat on the floor, his head resting on something soft.

"He stole your money," the girl said, "and ran out the back. Christine went with him, the silly bitch."

Denny didn't remember having any money worth stealing.

"Cops said if you want to make a complaint, to call them."

Money. Money. *The money!* Oh, man. . . . No dinner, no money, no nothing but a doorknob in the middle of his forehead. He wanted to get up. She helped him.

"I said I thought you ought to go to the hospital," she kept talking, breathing bourbon breath into his face, "but someone said you lived by the railroad tracks and that you weren't gonna die, so they just left you. Is that true? You live down by the tracks?"

"Now I can't pay for my meal," Denny said, feeling the emptiness in his jeans pocket. He stood on unsteady legs, the redhead helping him. He felt like crying. "I wanted to pay for my meal."

"It's okay, hon," she said. "I paid for it, and I'll get Christine to pay me back."

"I want to sit outside," he said, and he leaned against her like an old drunk as they walked between the tables and out the door into the night.

It wasn't cool, it was still and kind of sticky. But it didn't stink; at least it didn't stink like cigarettes and stale beer. It stunk like the refinery and diesel fuel, but at least it stunk like outside and not like inside. He sat on the curb and she sat next to him for a few minutes until his head cleared and all that was left of the incident was an empty pocket and a severe headache.

When he felt better, she walked with him to a pancake house, and they settled under the bright lights in a corner booth. She ordered coffee for both of them, then, as if she owned the place, walked behind the counter, got a damp cloth, filled it with ice, and brought it back to him for his forehead.

The cold made him see floating globes of light for a moment, but then it felt good.

"You're kinda young to be living down by the tracks," she said. "And cute. I bet you clean up real good. You've got that Tom Cruise thing going on about you, with that hair and that smile."

"I'm twenty-eight."

"I thought only old, has-been guys lived down there."

He had no answer for that, so he sipped his coffee. It made his headache worse.

"Where'd you get that kind of money, living down by the tracks?"

"Off a dead guy," he said, then wished he hadn't.

"Yeah, okay, I'm just trying to be nice to you."

"You are nice. And pretty." That made her smile shyly and look down at the pattern in the Formica. It was true, he realized, if she wouldn't put so much dark red in her hair, she'd be prettier, but she was probably not yet forty, and she had a smile that lit up her whole face. "I mean it. A real dead guy. Fell off the train."

"No shit?"

"No shit." That's enough talk about the dead guy, he thought. He should never have mentioned it. He wasn't going to mention it again. "What's your name?"

"Brenda."

"I'm Denny. You married, Brenda?"

"Not anymore."

"Got anybody who's likely to come in here and bust my head again over having coffee with you?"

She smiled, that fine smile again. "Nope. Nobody."

He looked at her with mock suspicion. "You're not seeing anybody?"

She shook her head.

"Pity," he said, then picked up his coffee cup and clinked it with hers.

"You're young."

"Not that young." He smiled with all the enthusiasm he had, which wasn't much, considering the drumming that was going on inside his skull.

"I liked that you stood up for Christine when you didn't even know her."

"No good deed goes unpunished," he said, then the drummers took a break to let the tubas in. They began a melancholy tune that soured his stomach. "I think I better go home."

"Come back to my place. I'll make you cozy on the couch."

"Is it close?" Denny wasn't sure he was up to walking far, maybe not even as far as his nest in Yorktown. But if he was alone, he could fall down or sit down and nobody would think anything but that he was drunk. But he didn't want to make an ass of himself in front of Brenda, the nice redhead with the Crest Kid smile. On the other hand, he wouldn't mind having a woman tend to his wounds for a day or two, either.

"Two blocks," she said.

"I'm yours."

She left two bucks on the table next to the soggy bar rag, and Denny leaned on her all the way back to her place, where he collapsed on the couch and was asleep before she could put a pillow under his head.

Brenda got a small bag of frozen peas from the freezer and put them gently on the scary-looking lump on Denny's forehead. Then she went into the bedroom, feeling kind of hyper and excited, and called her friend Suzanne to tell her about Christine, Norman, the pool cue, Denny, and especially about the wad of money and the dead guy down by the train tracks.

Suzanne called her brother, who worked the midnight shift at the railroad. The brother thought this might be just exactly the right information to get himself promoted. He took a cup of coffee in to his supervisor, and they sat for a while, talking. The supervisor called security, and they all had a meeting about the politics and timing of when to call the police.

Denny woke up, achy and disoriented with something warm and gushy on his face. Panicked, he ripped it off, and it hit the wall with a dull thwap. He sat up slowly, the thundering inside his head making his stomach queasy. After a moment, he remembered the redhead, and her kindness. He touched the egg on his forehead and wondered that his skull hadn't cracked with the blow. Maybe it had.

The moon shone through the lace curtains, casting thick shadows on the woman's cheap furniture, and he thought of Clover, and what she would think if she saw him coming out of the redhead's apartment in the morning while she was on her way to work. Women were funny about things like that. She'd never understand, despite his injured head, and he would find himself in a lose-lose situation. The redhead was too old for him, and he'd lose the good thing he had going with Clover.

He stood up, waited for the dizziness to pass, then walked out of Brenda's apartment, down the hall, down the stairs and into the night.

He felt bad, like he ought to have left her a note, or some kind of a thank-you.

Then he thought about the dinner he had been going to buy for York and Clover with that money, and about the other little things he'd thought he'd do for other folks, not to mention himself, with a windfall wad of cash like that, and he lost the nausea and dizziness in a rush of anger.

York needed a new coat. Brenda needed—Brenda needed something, Denny was certain. Clover could use some new shoes. As long as he'd known her, she'd always worn those same sneakers, and the heels were worn down to the black. He hadn't realized how much he planned to do good with that money for those who had done good for him in the past—how good he felt about himself with that six hundred and forty bucks in his jeans—until it was gone. Gone to Christine and Norman and their sicko, self-destructive ways.

Well, dammit, stealing was nothing new to Denny, only he always stole stuff to support himself. This time he'd get a few things for some other folks for a change. The thought made his heart swell.

He took a deep breath of the warm air, figured the time to be early morning by the taste of it—at least two hours to daylight, and decided if he was going to do something, he better get on with it. He willed the headache to take a hike, and then he headed uptown, toward Sears or one of those places like that, to do a little off-season Christmas shoplifting.

About the time Denny busted through the skylight of Walmart, York's useless eyes snapped open.

He listened with heightened awareness, ever alert to intruders of both the human and the animal persuasion, creatures who could invade his territory and do harm to a bunch of defenseless old men. He heard nothing out of the ordinary, save the wheezy snoring of Ed getting his good night's sleep.

Must be that, York thought to himself. Ed's here. That's what's different.

He listened for a while longer, and heard Sly's breathing. He didn't hear Denny or Clover, but that didn't surprise him.

Clover was at her place, probably, and Denny usually slept with his head down inside his bag. It was a burden, being the protector of these souls, but somebody had to look out after them, and it might as well be him.

He lay there for a while, feeling the adventuresome tug of the moon. He wanted to get up and wander around, but his wandering days were long behind him. Besides which, his internal calendar told him that a check would be waiting for him at general delivery, and he had to conserve his strength so he could walk all the way to the post office in the morning.

He thought about that check and the good dry goods he could buy with that money: beans, and rice and corn and some dried meat and cheese.

Money. He remembered Denny with a wad of money in his hand.

The dead guy.

Oh, yes, the dead guy, dammit all to hell. York, being the unofficial mayor of Yorktown as well as Father Confessor and all the rest, was going to have to deal with the dead guy sooner or later.

He sighed.

It seemed that challenges like these ought to be reserved for the young. He turned his sightless eyes to the heavens and implored the gods to grant him a little peace, a respite from all these moral decisions and challenges, from all these actions he had to take. He was old and it was time for him to rest. Wasn't it enough that he was spending his time ministering to the restless ones?

He'd spent his whole life ministering to restless souls. The first had been The Right Reverend Tecumseh Gittens, who stopped by the farm when York was just a boy. His mother had been dead for a year or so, and his father wasn't getting sober anytime soon, so when the reverend asked him to come along and aid in the ministering, York didn't even bother to close the front door behind him. It felt like the simple thing to do.

Over the next couple of years, they worked together, the middle-aged preacher and the young farmhand, holding tent revivals and preaching gospel in the homeless missions and the hobo camps. Eventually, York began to believe the things they said, could see some of the fruits of their labors, and the ministering became a passion.

One night, as they camped by a river somewhere in Ohio, the reverend lay down, put his head in York's lap and told him that he loved him. York was surprised at the action, but not at the sentiment. He responded in kind, and then Tecumseh Gittens sat up, took York's young face in his hands and said, "No, boy, I don't think you understand. I mean I've fallen in love with you. I can't deny it another minute."

York was too surprised to do anything but look at him, and then the reverend kissed him, full on the lips, with tongue and all. York endured it because he didn't know what else to do, and when the reverend pulled back to gaze into his beloved's eyes, York stood up, grabbed his bedroll and walked off. Behind him, he heard the reverend calling his name, and then he heard the reverend sobbing, but York never looked back. If there had been a door to walk through, he would have left it open, just like he had at his father's place.

He just kept on traveling, ministering, spreading the Good News, but kept himself to himself. He didn't seek out the ladies—didn't much have to, as they all sought him out—and certainly learned not to give the wrong impression to any man who liked his small-boned physique. He tried to resist the women—sometimes he could and sometimes he couldn't—but he never settled down with one, something that he regretted on the occasional lonely night.

When the weariness settled into his bones too harsh to ignore,

York got off a freight train, threw his bedroll down and sat on it, saying to himself that he was going to stay put for a while. And he'd been in West Wheaton ever since. He kept waiting for Tecumseh Gittens to step down off a freight one of these days, but by now, of course, he was long dead.

Still, the remembrance of that time and of his mother and of his inconsolable drunken father and the farm and his childhood gave him regrets and a simple restlessness that he tried to pray away.

But imploring the nameless, faceless force that twirled the heavens didn't help. Never had, never would. York figured that he kept doing it just so that God didn't forget that he was down here, living in the dirt next to the train tracks. He might be easy to overlook, there in the shadows, not much trouble, when there were so many others out making a real name for themselves. God must spend a lot of time and energy on those folks, because they surely needed it. York just needed the minimum of attention.

And the minimum was all he got.

That was just fine. He didn't mind. He had all he needed, and he spent some good time alone with his God, trying to hear the answer to the riddle.

He closed his eyes, listening to the night and hoping for the sound of his creator's voice, dozed again, and he waited some more, but never got any closer to wisdom. Seemed he'd had a lot more wisdom, knowledge, and the firepower to use it all when he was younger.

He kept up the dozing and the praying and the listening and the regretting until morning came, and Denny showed up rustlin' like some damned walking rosebush with a half dozen plastic bags full of stuff, and not five minutes later, the law came wandering on down the road in a pack, looking for a dead guy and not happy at all to be finding one.

Sly had been dreaming about sailing.

He'd grown up in a sailing family, all preppy-looking people with white-toothed smiles. They wore red, white, and blue and spent evenings at the Yacht Club. His father had dark, Armenian blood, silver hair and eyes so deep brown you couldn't see the pupils. His mother was tall and thin, with the palest of blue eyes and blondish hair she kept collected at the back of her neck with a ribbon. Young Sylvester and his baby sister Darla sailed dinghies in regattas when they were but tiny, and vacationed on yachts when they were teens. They wintered on the Italian Riviera and summered in the Hamptons. Sylvester went to prep school, but made the mistake of taking a year off to get some real life under his fingernails between prep school and college, and the Department of Defense wasted no time snagging him.

While his friends at home were drinking martinis and boffing their tennis instructors, his real friends were with him in Vietnam, dying from snakebites, bullets that blew their eyes out, self-inflicted gunshots, and fear. When it got too much, Sly closed his eyes, ducked down in the mud and went sailing. While artillery shells exploded, raining flesh all around him, limbless men screamed, napalm exploded the jungle in the wake of the airplanes, and babies were sawed in half with automatic fire from his superior officers, Sly hoisted the main and let the wind carry him out into the bay.

There was a certain feeling Sly had every time the boat left the dock. No matter what was about to happen, whether it was a week-long vacation with his family or a quick turn around the lake or a good-natured Hobie Cat competition, as soon as the boat left the dock, something inside the boy sighed, "Aaah. At last." It was as if his body had ached to be floated, only he didn't know it until it was happening. Floated and rocked. It was a natural feeling. It was a "way things are supposed to be" feeling.

He came home from Vietnam wrecked. He had attitude, and had no reason to give it up. He never slept a night through. He hated everybody and had contempt for everybody else. All he wanted to do was smoke dope and watch television, a sneer being the only facial expression he had left. He didn't know why he had to be one of the guys to live when such good guys died in his arms. He hated God and was going to devote his life to exactly that endeavor. He gave his sister her first joint, took her out to get drunk on her twenty-first birthday and she died of a heroin overdose five years later. His father died of a massive coronary the following year, and his mother died of loneliness, tranquilizers, and vodka a year after that. Their attorney sold everything, per Sylvester's instructions, and put the family money in the bank, where it sat, untouched and accumulating, unless somebody was stealing it. Sly didn't care. He didn't want anything to do with it. It wasn't his. Sly told the attorney he was going to the west coast, and that he'd be in touch, but his car broke down outside of West Wheaton, and he stayed in an ugly motel by the refinery until his pocket money ran out and then, as he was walking toward the tracks, thinking of hopping a freight, he found York. He still thought of himself as being "at the beach." He was in California, after all. It wasn't the Chesapeake, but, hell, it was . . . probably not much more than a day's drive to the ocean.

He felt responsible for the dissolution of the family. Three more deaths that God had caused. God should kill him instead of the good folk. That would make more sense. Even less sense was leaving him with all that money. It was ridiculous. Taking care of the family wealth was far more responsibility than he could live with.

At York's, Sly was only responsible for his own self.

He never told anybody about his history. He never told anybody about his family, his money, prep school, or Vietnam. Well, he told people he was a veteran, and that's about all, and that seemed to explain a whole lot to a whole lot of people, and he never could understand all of that. He felt as though people thought he'd been squeezed through a cookie press—that Vietnam had reduced him to some common denominator along with everybody else who came through that same experience. "A Vietnam vet, oh yeah, okay, now I get it." And they looked at the lines in his face and the length of his gray hair and the attitude in his aura and nodded knowingly. "Now I get it," they'd say.

Get what?

But he learned to hide within that guise, and then it was fine. People left him alone once they began to look at him as just another damaged, disturbed, and disposable Vietnam vet. He intimidated them, and that was just fine.

The night terrors were the worst, when he would startle himself awake time after time after time, sometimes for hours before falling into a twitchy sleep just before dawn, flashes of antipersonnel mines exploding through his head.

But the morning of the dead guy, just before the police poked him awake, he had been dreaming of sailing, something that happened every month on those three nights of the full moon. The sun was hot, the water was cold, the spray invigorating. He hauled in the main and leaned out over the side, tiller feeling strong and steady in his hand. The bow bounced on some chop left over from the water-skiers, and he grinned into the wind, feeling free and alive. He laughed out loud.

And then a boot poked him in the shoulder.

Oh, yeah. Real life.

Dead guy.

Second Day of the Full Moon

"Lookee all them Walmart bags," was the first that either of the lawmen said.

"I got a receipt," Denny said back.

"Yeah, I just bet you do."

"Leave it," Sheriff Goddard said to his young deputy, a kid with too much testosterone for his own good. The kid, Travis was his name, was always looking to turn a conversation into a confrontation, a situation into an event. He was spoiling to use those big muscles he acquired in the gym; he was itching to pull his gun, and one of these days he was going to, and that would be the end of Travis. Sheriff Goddard had told him more than once to cool himself, and he figured he would be telling the same thing to Travis in another ten years. Kids like that just flat-out don't cool down until they're in their forties.

"Nasty bruise you got there," the deputy said to Denny, ignoring his superior's comments. "How'd you get a bruise like that?"

"Leave it," Sheriff Goddard said again. Travis was going to burn himself out. Or maybe the sheriff would end up pulling his gun on him before it was all over. Damned punks watching all that gun-happy television with all those macho big-city policemen shooting people in the streets gives kids ideas that even the police academy can't wash 'em clean of. It was a problem. It was a problem for Travis, and that made it a problem for the sheriff.

The sheriff walked down to where York was yawning and

stretching and climbing out of his bed. "Morning, York," he said. The two other men in suits followed him, leaving Travis to try to stare Denny down.

"Morning, Sheriff. What brings you down here so early?"

"Hey, yeah," Sly said, sitting up and rubbing his eyes. "How come you guys ain't out eating your weight in donuts?" He looked the other two suits up and down and was about to ask what it was that they ate, when the sheriff spoke again.

"Heard tell of a dead guy, York. You know anything about a dead body around here?" The radio on his belt squawked and he turned it down.

"Can't say as I have, Sheriff," York said. "Dead guy? Think I'd have heard about that."

"That's why I come to you first, York. You and me, we've always been square with each other."

"Always will be, Sheriff. This here's a clean place. No dope, no booze, no crime."

"Awful lot of Walmart bags here," the deputy said, and poked one of them with his shoe.

The sheriff looked around, nodding, and smiling. York did run a clean camp, and Sheriff Goddard took all the credit. "These here guys are from the railroad."

"Nice to make your acquaintance," York said, and took his time standing up, his old joints creaking, his bones aching. Once he was upright, he held out his hand, and each of the two men shook it in turn.

"Samuel Greening," one said, and his handshake was firm, dry, and crisp.

"Mark Tipps," the other one said, and his handshake was too brief, as if he didn't want to touch York. Mark Tipps was not to be trusted, but the Green one was a-okay. So was the sheriff, but York knew that one of these days that idiot deputy would come on down here and make big trouble if he didn't get his hand slapped hard enough and often enough. That Deputy Travis was the type of kid who'd never been spanked. And should have been. Regular and furious.

"You boys hear about any deceased neighbors?" York called out to his camp mates.

"Nope," Sly said.

"Nope," Denny said.

"What's this?" the deputy said and poked a toe at the wad of blankets that was actually Ed.

"That's Ed," Sly said. "He's tired."

"Is he dead?"

"Nope," York said. "He snored all night long."

"*There* you are," Clover said, and all heads turned to see her, makeup perfect, hair glossy and pinned back behind her ears, smiling and carrying two bags of donuts, wearing a fresh pink uniform. "Missed you this morning, Sheriff. This here is day-old, but I believe there might be one of your favorites in there."

Her eyes naturally went to Denny, and her mouth fell open as she took in the knot on his forehead and the bruise around it that was sliding down and blackening both eye sockets. She gasped and put her hand to her mouth.

Denny smiled at her, winked, and just nodded slightly as if to say, *It's okay—we'll talk about it later.*

"Why, thanks, Miss Clover," Sheriff Goddard said, reached into the bag and pulled out a maple cruller. Clover tore her eyes from Denny and handed the sheriff a napkin.

"Bring coffee too?" the deputy said, pulling a chocolate donut out of the bag.

"Sly here'll make you a good cup of coffee," Clover said, giving Deputy Travis a disdainful look. Clover didn't like the deputy any more than anybody else did. He was always trying to touch her with some sleazy sleight of hand.

"No thanks," the deputy said.

"No thanks," Sly said.

"You men here to see about the dead guy?" Clover asked.

Old Ed wasn't as asleep or as tired as everyone assumed, because as soon as Clover said that, there was a flurry of activity under that hump of blankets, and then it rose up on itself and took off running, that dirty gray blanket flapping behind.

He needn't have run; nobody chased him, but he never looked back. They all just watched. Deputy Travis didn't even twitch his gun hand.

"Ed have anything to do with the dead guy?" Sheriff Goddard asked.

"No," York said. "Dead guy fell off the train yesterday."

"He was pushed," Sly said. "Murdered."

"Now how come you didn't come to me with this news yesterday, York?"

"Didn't want no trouble," York said.

"Well, too bad, old man," the deputy said. "You just made yourself a whole new package of trouble by not reporting this."

The sheriff shook his head in disgust. The deputy always acted as if he were in some kind of a movie. The sheriff looked at Sly. "Want to show us?"

Sly led the way around the little walls built up of stacks of old newspapers that defined their camp, over the heap of ties and along the tracks, following the mashed-down trail in the weeds where they'd all gone to gawk at the deceased intruder the evening before. Poor weeds hadn't even had a chance to recover before Sly, Denny, two cops, and two railroad guys tramped over them one more time on their way to gaze at the corpse. Soon there'd be the medical examiner, ambulance guys, doctors, more cops, more railroad guys and only God knew who else.

Clover stayed back with York. She didn't need to see it all again; she was fairly certain any change in the guy's condition had been for the worse.

"Looks like Denny went shopping," she said casually. "Wonder what he bought with all that cash. Wonder how he got that bump on his head."

But York had his mind on other things, one of them being the parade of people through his little personal hometown and how he, as unofficial mayor, was going to receive them. How does a hosting dignitary act? Ought he put out some red carpet, or haul up a banner? "Welcome to Yorktown," it would say, "home of the dead guy." Maybe there ought to be a wine tasting and craft fair to boot. Jeez. Just exactly what he didn't need.

And more of what he didn't need was about to show up in the person of the mayor of West Wheaton, California, the real town that Yorktown was unofficially attached to. That mayor was all about big business, and there was no doubt in York's mind that he and his little crew of unsightly good guys was a burr beneath the saddle of Mayor Milo Grimes. The mayor had his fingers in lots of real-estate-development pies, or so York had heard over the years, but the mayor was way too crafty to let any of his conflicts of interest show. Digging for dirt was one thing; pushing it in the faces of the townspeople was another thing.

And one of the things all his soccer moms would like would be for him to get rid of the damned bums living down by the railroad tracks. They were crazed on drugs and ate babies for breakfast, the diseased, vermin-laden scum. The white-toothed, sandy-haired, clean-cut children of West Wheaton had to give that nasty area of town a wide berth, but of course, all kids were curious, and the moms were forever worried that one of their precious ones would be overcome by their own lack of good sense someday, and go on down there by the tracks to see what all the fuss was about. Everybody knew that those kids would never be seen alive again. It hadn't happened yet, in all the decades York had been at his camp, but somehow, generations passed in town and the rumors, true to their nature, never got smaller.

And now it had happened. A dead guy had been found in the hobo camp.

Life was about to get messy indeed.

"York?" Clover said.

"Hmmm?"

"Think y'all're gonna have to move?"

"Hope not, missy," York said, impressed again with her intuition, but he did indeed think they were all going to have to move. He'd been meaning to go down to the county records place to find out just exactly who owned this property so that he could get permission to camp on it, but he had never got around to it. Probably belonged to the railroad. He never really thought he'd still be here, all these years later. But as his sight failed and his world narrowed, well, all that was left for him was to go on the public dole and live in some old fart's home. That wasn't for York. He had to be out under the moon until the day he died.

"It wouldn't be so bad, you know," Clover said, as if she sensed his mood of impending doom. "We could get us a house together, all of us. Ed could even stay there when he came through town. Sly could work now and then, and with my wages and your pension . . ."

York knew she meant well, but it sounded like death to him. Worse than death. Torture. Her voice trailed off as if she thought about the reality of it and it didn't sound all that great to her, either.

"I know what," Clover said. "Let's go to the post office. It's time for your check."

"We ought to wait to see what happens over yonder," York said.

"They'll be at that all day long, York. C'mon. Get yourself up. Get your blood moving. Let's go shopping. That always makes you feel better."

He didn't jump at the offer, but he didn't refuse it, either, and Clover knew he just needed a little coaxing.

"I'll help you put your shoes on." She reached into the bag, pulled out a reasonably fresh cinnamon-raisin bagel and handed it to the old man while she rooted around looking for his boots. York had a sturdy pair of lace-up leather boots that still had most of their soles on. He didn't do a lot of walking. His socks had holes in the toes. "After all these folks are out of here," she said, watching him munch the bagel with his store-bought teeth as she laced up his boots, "we'll do some laundry. Your socks are about to knock me out."

"Don't know what I'd do without you, girl," York said around a bite of bread.

"You'd get by, just like you always have," Clover said, "but there's no need to be thinking along those lines, because I'm here today, and today's all we've got."

She grabbed him by both hands and planted her feet next to his boot toes, and hauled on him until he stood full up. He would never stand straight again, but he could get vertical. She smoothed over his hair in the back, and tugged at his clothes to make him look a little more presentable, then she grabbed his arm and got him moving up the path toward town. York was sliding backwards, health-wise. Seemed as though he had lost a little of his will, and was content to just sit and shout orders, but if he didn't move, he would die. Sly and Denny never seemed to figure that out, so it was up to Clover to make sure York stayed healthy.

"Laundry and a bath, York," she said from behind him, a hand on his back. She didn't exactly push him up the path, but she kept him leaning uphill.

"Yeah, I know," he said between wheezing breaths.

Clover had to be very careful about where she drew the lines in her ministry work with these hobos. She was tempted to take them back to her place, and cook for them and do their laundry and let them use her shower, but that wasn't a good idea. It was bad enough, according to her mother, that she took vitamins, dental floss, and day-old down to them. "That's a bad element down there, Clover," Eileen would say while she squirted raspberry filling into those donuts. "You're wasting your time."

But Clover didn't see it as a waste of her time at all. She liked these guys, and they needed her. Maybe she was wasting something by sleeping with Denny all the time, having that deliciously slurpy sex like they did, but that couldn't be bad—it only made her feel pretty.

"Someday you're going to wake up and you'll be forty years old," her mother said. "You'll be used up and have nothing to show for it but a drawer full of dust rags that used to be donut-shop uniforms."

Clover thought her mom ought to know about those things, in that that's exactly what Eileen had to show for her life. Never married, one illegitimate daughter, and worked in the same damned donut shop almost her whole life. First as early-morning cook, then as a waitress, and now she managed the bakery in the back. The shop had changed hands twice in the five years since Clover started working there right out of high school, and had been sold more times than her mother could count since she'd been there right out of high school, but even new owners knew good workers when they saw them. And every time the minimum wage went up, they each got a raise.

Clover wasn't doing anything important at the donut shop, besides flirting for tips. But she was doing important stuff down by the railroad tracks. It didn't matter to her what the future held. That was something for the old people to be thinking about. She knew she'd never end up living down by the tracks. Not when she could waitress as good as she did.

She made small talk with York as they walked slowly, laboriously, up the hill. The path was only wide enough for single-file walking, so Clover put her hands on York's back and kept up the steady pressure, alerting him to any rocks or holes that might make him stumble. On both sides of the path, blackberry brambles rose up much higher than Clover's head. York kept an old pair of rusty garden shears and throughout the summer, somebody—Sly or Denny or Clover—would grab those shears and go whacking on the brambles, but it was a never-ending job. Tendrils were always trying to bridge the gap and trip anybody who ventured down to the tracks.

Clover and York made it to the top of the hill, waited a moment for York to catch his breath, then moved slowly toward town, stopping frequently to rest. Clover chattered on about the shop, catching him up on all the soap-opera news of her coworkers. Then she moved on to thinking about what they were going to buy at the store that would keep, and not be too heavy to carry, and would be healthy and yet a little bit of a treat for the guys. Clover always threw in five or ten dollars a week to help tide them over between York's monthly pension checks.

York, Sly and Denny were her project, and it was a work in progress.

"You're going to have to see a doctor pretty soon, Daddy," she said. She only called him Daddy when it was just the two of them, privately together. It made her feel good to be able to call somebody Daddy, and York didn't seem to mind. In fact the first time she did it, it just popped out natural-like, and it stopped York in his tracks. Then he smiled, and that was all there was to it. Now and then she called him that, and it was a nice little thing they shared that made them both feel good.

Once in a while Clover wondered if York had any daughters,

but if he wanted to talk about that kind of stuff, he would. She didn't want to ask. One of the reasons they lived the way they did was because they wanted to erase their histories, and Clover was a bright-enough girl to have figured that out first thing.

"No doctors for me," York said. "When the lord wants me, I'll just go."

Clover didn't know too much about much, but she figured he had bad lungs, probably a bad heart, and it wasn't going to be long before York couldn't make it up the hill at all. She wondered if he'd make it through the next rainy, cold winter, and she got a shiver at the thought of tripping down that trail some morning and seeing that the dead guy with flies on his face was York.

They picked up his check at the post office without any fanfare. Clover made a mental note to find out what it would take for her to pick up his government check when he was no longer able to do that. Then they went shopping, but they were only able to do a little bit before York was ready to give out. He grew faint in the produce section, so she left the cart mid-aisle and walked him out of the store. She sat him down on the sidewalk, feet in the gutter, and though she didn't like to see him there like that, she needed to finish her business inside and get back to him. When she had more than she could comfortably carry, she fetched him and they began the slow walk back toward the tracks, York complaining between wheezy breaths that he ought to be shouldering the load instead of making the lady carry his stuff.

"I'm going to the Goodwill to get you some new clothes," she said. "I'll take Denny. And maybe we'll get you a new cooking pot to boot."

He nodded, and bumped up against her in appreciation. That was all the pay Clover needed to keep her going for another season.

The coroner's car was sitting at the top of the hill when they rounded the last corner, along with a couple of other cars. And a local television news van.

York was beginning to see black globes float around the dull gray of his vision, and he wanted to make it down to his bedroll before he passed out, fell, and hurt himself permanently. He took it slowly and carefully, despite his impulse to hurry and get down there, and he made it down the path to his great relief. Maybe next time he wouldn't go to the store. He'd get his check and have somebody else do the shopping. Or maybe he'd fashion up some kind of a mailbox and get the mailman to deliver that damned check. Or something. He had a month to figure out something.

A lot could happen in a month.

A lot had happened in the hour or so that they were gone. Pieces of yellow tape with black lettering on it were strung up around the place, and suits with walkie-talkies wandered around.

York didn't have the energy to deal with it. He slowly lay down on his bed, instead of collapsing on it as he'd like, listened to Clover stash the food, and concentrated on breathing. It was all he could do, damn this worn-down body anyway. Even when Sly came running up, jumping over the railroad ties and all, out of breath with excitement, York had no energy to give to him. He lay quietly breathing and listened as Sly filled Clover in on all the details of what they'd missed.

And York was right. The mayor was there, supervising the removal of the dead guy's carcass. The mayor was not smiling in front of those TV cameras.

York closed his eyes and watched the colors swirl around his oxygen-starved brain as he tried to think of a Plan B. He had no Plan B. If he was evicted—and sure as the sun rose in the east he would be—he had nowhere to take his merry band of freedom-loving friends.

"They're leaving," he heard Sly say, and he heard the slamming of car doors, and the starting up of engines. Then he heard footsteps, big footsteps from two big men, coming down the path, and he didn't even have the energy to open his sightless eyes as a courtesy.

"Going to have to ask you to take your show on the road, York," the sheriff said.

York had no answer for that.

"He okay?" the sheriff asked someone.

"We just got back from town," Clover answered. "He's pretty worn out."

"Can you get him up to the mission or something for a couple of days? The mayor and the railroad guys aren't happy about a murder down here, and, well, I'd just like it if you all found another place to be for a week or so. I don't want anybody to get hurt, if you know what I mean."

York knew exactly what he meant, and it wasn't a threat, it was the truth. The railroad guys who weren't thugs knew a few thugs, and they could definitely do some midnight harm to three bums living in the weeds, and nobody would ask any questions after, either.

"I'll try," Clover said.

"The mission," Denny said, and spit in disgust. Nobody liked the mission. It was dirty.

"I'll hear a little respect out of your face," Deputy Travis said, "or I'll take a look at all those Walmart bags there under your blanket. Something tells me that you, that lump on your head, and that broken Walmart skylight all have something in common. So don't give me no lip, you hear, ace?"

Denny didn't respond.

"We'll vacate," York said. "Might take me a little while." Just saying that made the colored globes float around again.

"Take your time, York," the sheriff said. "I've got no trouble with you. But there's bound to be some vigilante talk in town. Besides that, whoever killed that guy might be back to make sure there weren't any witnesses, and I'd like you to be well gone before that happened."

"I'll see to them, Sheriff," Clover said, bless her heart.

There was a long pause, long enough for York to open his eyes and look around out of habit. He couldn't see anything but vague shapes in the grayness. "Walk me up to the car, Clover," the sheriff said, and one pinkish shape moved toward the two brownish shapes and they all disappeared behind the wall of brambles.

"The mission," Denny said again.

"I ain't going to no mission," Sly said. "I hate that fucking place. It's full of fools and assholes. The food's bad, the preaching makes me itchy, and the beds are lumpy. I'm not going."

"Whatcha got in those bags, Denny?" York asked.

"Presents for you guys," he said, "but there ain't no joy in it anymore."

"You steal that stuff?"

"You don't ask me that, York. You never ask me that."

"See what's happening here?" Sly said. "We're suspicious of one another. You know that Denny steals, York, you don't have to ask. Don't be asking. Don't be knowing. It's these people, casting all kinds of suspicions around, left some lying here on the ground. Don't be picking them up, neither one of you." He looked up the path, knowing the sheriff and Clover were having a conversation at the door of the cruiser. "I wonder what they're talking about."

"Her virtue," Denny said, and spit again. "What are we going to do, York?"

"We could move on down the line," Sly said. "Or maybe I'll just go to the beach for a while. I've been marooned here too long as it is."

"That'd be just like you to abandon York and me when the shit hits the fan," Denny said. "Fuck, my head hurts. This whole damned thing makes my head hurt."

"Shhh," Sly said. "Here comes Deputy Dawg."

Deputy Travis was escorting the girl back down the pathway, and he was talking and gesturing, but the words didn't reach, just the sounds of emphasis.

York put his head down and closed his eyes. He didn't want to know what the deputy had to say. He never had anything worthwhile to say.

"Hey, York," the deputy said.

"He's tired," Sly said.

"I'll kick his ass until he's tired," the deputy said. *"Hey, York."*

York opened his eyes.

"Move on out, you hear? This is a warning, and it's the last one you'll get."

York nodded and closed his eyes again, worried. Worried.

"You getcherself home now, Miss Clover, and don't be trucking with rail rats like these."

Footsteps receded.

"I'll kick *his* ass until *he's* tired," Denny whispered.

"You better listen to him," the girl said. "I don't trust him. Not at all."

"What did he say to you?" Denny asked, grabbed her hand and pulled her down to sit on his blanket.

The girl was silent enough to make York really nervous. "Just don't trust him," she finally said.

"Don't trust nobody during the moon," York said. "People ain't what they normally are."

"So, York," Sly said again. "What are we going to do?"

"Stay and fight," Denny said. "We ain't done nothing. They can't run us out of our home and off our land for no reason."

"Ain't our land," York said. "Probably belongs to the railroad."

"So what?" Sly said. "I think Denny's right. We should stay and fight. We've been here long enough to have rights. Squatter's rights. We should secure the perimeter. We could plant a few antipersonnel mines, get us some firepower, and just fucking hold the line."

"You're nuts," Clover said, and touched the blue bulb on Denny's forehead.

"No," Denny said, pulling away from her feminine touch. "He's right."

"Listen," York said, sitting up and fixing them with what he hoped would be a riveting stare, only he wasn't exactly sure where they were, so he had to kind of imagine where they were and take an average of their various positions. "The good lord has a plan for our lives, and the book is already written. We do what's asked of us to do, no more, no less. If it's time for us to up and vacate this terrain, that's exactly what we'll be doing. We're innocent men, we know that in our hearts, and God knows that, too. We do what he asks of us and that's that."

"I buy that, York," Sly said, "but I don't think Sheriff Goddard and the railroad guys are speaking for God. I'll do what God says, but I'll not do what Deputy Travis says."

"Yeah," Denny said. "I'd like to kick his skinny ass."

"You're the one with the skinny ass," Clover said, then laughed. And she was right, of course, Deputy Travis's ass was pumped full of steroids. His muscles threatened the seams of his uniform.

"The key to life is accepting what comes down the chute," York said.

"Not from those assholes," Sly said.

York felt his face growing flushed. He felt his blood pressure rise. All his life, he'd spent going with the flow, as it had been said, accepting life on life's terms, never asserting his will over that of others.

And what has that got you in the end, old man? Stinking socks and a dirt bed by the railroad. What have you got to lose by putting up a bit of a fight?

"Some things are just worth standing up for, York," Sly said. "I learned that in the Army. There are things to fight for and things to let pass on by. This may not be our land, but by God, it's our home, and we live clean, upstanding lives here. I work now and then, and bring home a fair wage for my work, you deserve the pension you get every month. Denny's the only one who doesn't have a legitimate way of earning a living, but I haven't seen anybody down here arresting him, so I guess he's discreet. Anyway, that isn't the point. The point is, we've done nothing wrong, and if it was okay for us to live here before the dead guy, then it should be okay for us to live here after the dead guy."

"What about guys like Ed?" Denny asked. "What would happen to him if he came down here and you weren't here to feed him and preach the good kind of stuff to him—not that Bible-thumpin' shit you get at the mission—think he'd be okay?"

"Ed's not the only one," Sly said. "Think about the guys who bunk here on an annual basis. Hundreds. It's your ministry, York, it's your calling. That's what God wants you to do, not to dance to Mayor whatshisass's whim."

The boys had a point.

"I'm tired," York said, lay back down and closed his eyes against the smoggy glare of the sun.

"I'm going to draw my line in the sand," he heard Denny say, and then there was some scuffling about as Sly did the same, and for all York knew, the girl drew a line, too. But York was too tired to fight, too old to mix it up with the powerful men in town. He was just a sick old bum, and he didn't want to spend the last of his God-given energy on some ridiculous fight that he could never win.

Maybe he ought to move to the mission, and add a little common sense balance to the hellfire and brimstone preaching the poor guys who lived there had to endure for their soup.

Not that he could stand that for more than a minute. He had to be outside. It was in his nature.

Maybe they ought to move on down the line.

But the thought of hauling his old carcass up into an empty freight car one more time was too much. Riding the rails was for the young. York and Ed were too old for that game anymore, only nobody had told Ed that yet. He was still clinging to an old way of life, and it was just about to catch up with him. York doubted he'd ever see Ed again.

If York moved away, then for sure he'd never see Ed again.

There were a lot of people who depended upon York's hospitality, his good sense and mild advice. What would happen to them? Well, they'd be cared for, just as they'd be cared for by somebody after York was dead. When York first threw down his bedroll on this land, he knew he'd live like the lilies in the field, just like the promise in the Bible. The lilies didn't have to grapple for their sustenance, neither did the birds nor the gophers. Nobody did, and he had been proving that all these years. He got what he needed, and if he wasn't there to help God give to the others what they needed, somebody else would. God had a plan for those needs after York was dead, didn't he?

But York wasn't dead yet, because that wasn't God's plan. He still had work to do, and if he wasn't going to do it here, then he was going to do it somewhere, but here is where he'd always done it, and he saw no good reason to move.

Denny was right. They hadn't done nothing wrong.

And yet, what if they fought the system, and won the right to stay there, but God's plan would have them on down the line, to meet up with some unforeseen destiny? What then? What opportunities would York miss? Would his life turn to gristle because he was rubbing on the outside edge of the container of God's grace?

It was a horrible problem, a decision of unimaginable consequences. He couldn't begin to figure what would happen by simply acting or not acting.

He was too tired.

The concepts tumbled around in his head like laundry in a dryer while he vaguely listened to the sounds of the young ones talking. Their voices were conspiratorially low, and York knew that they were including him in whatever plan they were making. He could always bow out, but the truth was, Denny and Sly seemed to have more on the ball than he did at times, and certainly more than Deputy Travis did. Add Clover's smart compassion to the mix, and he was certain that everything would be all right. He heard himself begin to snore, and dropped right into rest.

When he woke up, he was ready for a battle. It just might be God's battle.

The Western Express breezed by, sounding its horn, and York opened his eyes. He smelled fresh coffee. "Sly?" he called, sometimes disoriented at first, a little bit afraid because he couldn't see who was there and what was happening.

"Sly's in town," Denny said.

"What did you all decide?"

"To hold fast."

"I'm with you," York said, with a strange certainty that made him suspect that work had been taking place in his mind while he slept. Holding fast was indeed the higher road to take, and so for better or worse, for the greatest good of all concerned, he was going to stand fast with them, and see if the righteous would indeed win out. How could he imagine that he could do anything other than God's will? He wasn't that strong. "Hold on to your hat," he said.

"We're all holding on to our hats," Denny said. "Want some coffee?"

"Yeah," York said with the excitement of a new adventure growing in his belly. "I don't want no conflict, though."

"We'll take what we get," Denny said, and York thought that was pretty true about life in general.

"They're harmless," Sheriff Goddard said. "They're relics from another time. I know York, he's been there since I was a curious kid. There's never any booze or drugs down there. He runs a clean camp."

"I want them gone." The mayor stood in the sheriff's office with his legs spread and his arms folded across his chest. He meant to be taken seriously, and if anybody held the keys to the sheriff's reelection campaign, it was the politically hefty mayor. He wanted to summon the sheriff to his own office, but thought that might be a little bit too heavy handed. Goddard didn't like to be pushed around.

"Sit down, Milo," Sheriff Goddard offered. "Let's talk about this for a minute."

The mayor was no fool, and knew that it would be expedient to turn Goddard's mind around until cleaning up that homeless dump was his own idea. Then he'd be motivated. If it was just taking an order from the mayor, there was no telling if and/or when the task would be accomplished, and Milo wanted those bums out of there, right now. He sat. "I don't know what there is to talk about, Sheriff."

"They had nothing to do with the murder of that sleazeball, and you know it as well as I do."

"But the townspeople . . ."

"The townspeople will know it as soon as you and I tell them."

Mayor Grimes decided to take a different tack. "That place down there is a disaster waiting to happen, Steve."

The mayor hardly ever used the sheriff's first name, and the ingratiating effect of it was not lost on the sheriff.

"I've got my priorities," the sheriff said.

"I need you to rearrange them. Cleaning up the scene of a crime and its scummy, disease-ridden neighborhood should be one of your top priorities."

"There's no disease down there."

"Where do those guys shit, Steve? Can you tell me that? When was the last time this blind friend of yours took a bath? You know that whole place is a major health violation, and for the life of me I can't imagine why you're giving me such a hard time about this."

Steve Goddard knew all about the effective latrine system Sly had designed, dug, and maintained down there, but there would be no telling the mayor about it. Steve Goddard had learned a long time ago to pick his battles, especially with the mayor, and this was not one he was going to win. He only had a certain amount of political credits in his account and as much as he liked York, he didn't want to spend all his political cash on him. He looked at the stack of paper in his in-box and sighed. "Give me a couple of days, okay?"

"What's the big deal? Go down there with a bulldozer and give them thirty minutes to vacate. Need a dozer? I know a contractor—"

Sheriff Goddard stood up, ending the meeting. "I'll take care of it, Mayor Grimes, but I won't do it with any bulldozer. Keeping the peace is my job. Now, you can just cross this item off your list and let me handle it the way the townspeople elected me to handle things like this."

"I know you will," Milo Grimes said. "Thank you for your time."

The two men shook hands, and Grimes left, leaving a bad taste in Sheriff Goddard's mouth. He didn't like the mayor, didn't like his politics, didn't like his sleazy way of lining his pockets at the public expense, just flat-out didn't like his way of doing business. But politics makes strange bedfellows, and both of them had to compromise their would-be steadfast positions in order to serve the people of West Wheaton.

Goddard would move the hobos. But he hated like hell to do that, especially at York's advanced age, and he wondered what kind of a dangerous element would take their place down there in that hole. Or would a new railroad shopping center go up on that land, owned by one of the corporations that seated Milo Grimes on its board?

What the hell. Maybe it was time York went to an old-folks' home, where he'd be cared for anyway. Regardless, it seemed to be out of Goddard's hands.

He looked out the window at the nice park across the street and all the kids who were playing on its bronze dinosaur sculptures. Milo Grimes had donated that land, and one of his corporations maintained it. Nothing there for the townspeople to pay for; they just had to enjoy it.

The mayor was a wily one for certain.

Everybody liked Grimes's big-budget way of running the city. He funded all the social programs, kept taxes down to a decent level and showed up at all the fund-raising events for all the school kids. Parents liked that, and they didn't care that his behind-the-scenes personal financial structure was fueled by their tax dollars as well. They turned their heads, and chose not to see, electing him over and over and over again. Some people talked of paving his road to the state legislature, but Mayor Milo was no fool. His bread was buttered right nicely right there in West Wheaton, and he wasn't about to take his show on the uncertain, ungreased highways of Sacramento. Nope, he'd fight his little battles and fill his little savings account right there in town.

Steve Goddard looked back down at his stack of paperwork and decided he needed caffeine fortification to tackle it. He picked up his coffee cup and walked out of his office, just in time to see Milo Grimes shake hands in the lobby with Deputy Travis.

That was not a good sign. Whatever they'd been talking about, it wasn't good.

Just before Grimes turned to leave, he glanced back and saw the sheriff standing there, watching, coffee cup in hand. Their eyes met, then the mayor left the building.

The gauntlet had been thrown. The sheriff had been challenged. *Take care of this, or I'll have your deputy take care of it for you.* Doing business that way didn't set well with the sheriff. He didn't like being given that type of covert ultimatum.

Don't fuck with me, Milo Grimes. Don't make me do something I don't want to do.

Deputy Travis swaggered in, and Goddard hated the sight of him. He filled his coffee cup and went back into his office, closing the door behind him.

It's just about three bums, he told himself, trying to believe it. *This is nothing to jeopardize your career for. Not worth bringing down City Hall over. Relax, take care of today's work today, and think about York and his buddies tomorrow.*

But the finely tuned intuition of a more-than-competent lawman told him that Grimes was setting a lot of metronomes, pendulums, and ticking bombs into motion as he swept through town, and the sheriff better be either following along behind diffusing them, or else taking care of the mayor's business, and on Grimes's timetable, at that.

He looked down at the big calendar on his desk blotter and filled in the four of the date, July fourteenth, with his pen. That's when he noticed. Tomorrow was the full moon.

Great, he thought. *Just what I need. Full-moon lunacy on top of it all.* He doodled a few arrows around the full-moon symbol and then threw his pen down in irritated frustration.

He had been proud indeed when first his eldest, and then his second son left for the University of Oregon to major in criminology. Troy-the-idealist wanted to be police commissioner in some crime-ridden sewer of a city, where he could make a real difference. Zach-the-realist was studying criminal law, and would probably end up a rich trial attorney. Regardless, they had both been inspired by their dad's ethics, and his belief in the system.

But that pride in his boys had slowly turned to pressure. When there were certain things Steve could do to expedite matters, he kept thinking of those boys, and what opinion they would have if they were to discover his not-quite-above-board actions. And how that opinion would shape their love for him, and how they would one day sit around, the two of them and their baby sister, all grown up, and they would talk about their dad, the sheriff, and the way he dealt with things. Would they be proud of his entire record, or would one tiny black mark overshadow all the good he'd done, the way those things sometimes unfairly happened?

This was just exactly one of those situations. He could do as the mayor insisted, infringing upon those men and their civil liberties. Their freedoms. The owner of the land had no complaint; the men weren't doing anything but camping. There was no reason for them to be uprooted like that, especially since York . . .

Well, especially since York had been there for so many years. He was practically an institution.

Steve and York had had some pretty intense, in-depth conversations when Steve was a youngster, and York, although not yet blind in those days, had seemed just exactly as old as he was today.

York was the one who got through to Steve that he ought to be treating people the same way he'd like to be treated. His mother had tried to tell him that a million times or more, but when that concept came from York's mouth, Steve heard, and he understood. Years later, it was York who told Steve that a gentleman always wore a condom. No lectures on morality or sexually transmitted diseases or the life-ruination of an unplanned pregnancy with a high-school girl. A gentleman always wore one, period. Plain and simple.

Steve heard that in a way he'd never heard his parents talk about such things, on the rare occasions that they did talk about such emotionally charged things.

One night, when young Steve Goddard had been restless with hormones and wanderlust, he climbed out of his bedroom window and by the light of the full moon, wandered around town until he found himself down by York's place. A freight train was slowly screeching itself on by, and a little fire was lit under that dented and bent-up coffeepot that York still used to this day. They sat together, Steve and York, in comfortable silence until the train passed on by, and the two of them talked about the wildness of the world and the untamable human spirit while some blanket-covered soul snored and more stars looked down on them than Steve had ever remembered seeing.

That night, York talked of hopping freights, and the danger and the peace. He talked about the freedom and how addictive it was until it was its own prison. He talked about the fence of morality that contained behavior and gave life meaning, direction and rules to abide by. When the sun came up, Steve was foggy from lack of sleep, but he had a completely different view of the universe and his small, yet not insignificant, part in it.

And now what would his sons say if they found out that in the interest of being reelected, he'd thrown York out of his home? Just because he could.

Power corrupts, that's what they'd say.

Unless it was for York's own good. York was old. York had been old thirty years ago.

Steve wondered if his wife would let York stay in their behind-the-garage apartment for a while.

Probably not.

He ran his hands through his bristly gray crew cut and thought about going down and having a little chat with York and the boys and see what they could come up with together. York had always been a fair-minded guy. He might have an answer that Steve could hear.

But then going to York for his advice was a stupid thing to do, particularly since York had a serious interest in the advice he would give, and not only that, but Steve already knew the right thing to do.

Shit.

"Stupid government's got their fingers in everything, know that?" Sly opened with that announcement as he came down the path toward camp. "You got to go to one government agency to find out one thing, and another agency to find out another. You think about the fact that all the schoolteachers are government employees, and that ought to make you sick to your stomach. Teaching all those little kids. It's no wonder the world's in a pickle."

"So what'd you find out?" Clover asked as she brushed Denny's hand off her breast. He was feeling frisky, and she was interested in just exactly what "holding fast" meant.

"I found out that the railroad owns this land we're on."

"That's all?" Denny asked. "Jesus, we all kind of figured that."

"What else was I supposed to find out? Who owns the railroad? Probably the government. They own everything. Besides, I didn't want to get too nosy. Soon they'd be asking for my ID, and saying, 'Your papers, please,' like in the old Nazi movies and then they'd start a file on me. I don't want a file on me, least not anything added to the file they've already got. I don't know how you expect to beat those—"

"Shhht," York said. "Someone's coming."

A long pair of legs, too old for the tiny shorts at the top of them, and too long for the high heels at the bottom of them, were stepping gingerly down the path. Above the blue shorts was a red-and-white-striped top full of boobs, and on top of that was a face too full of makeup and hair that was too red and too fried at the ends.

"Denny?" she said when she saw them all looking up at her.

Clover felt a red-hot flush come up her chest, over her neck and fill her face. She moved a little bit away from Denny, but not before he moved away from her.

"Hey, Brenda," Denny said, stood up and brushed off his jeans. "What are you doing here?"

"I came to see about your head," she said.

"Oh, thanks, it's okay." Denny fingered the bump on his forehead. He felt uncomfortable, and it showed.

"Introduce me?" she asked.

"Oh, yeah, sure. That's York." York smiled and waved. "That's Sly."

"Hi," Sly said.

"Hi." Brenda felt shy, or coy, or something. She hoped she didn't look it.

"And this is Clover." Clover stood up, brushed dust off her uniform and gave him a look that would kill. "Clover's my girlfriend," he said.

Clover smiled and held out her hand.

"This here's Brenda," Denny said as he watched the two women shake hands. "Brenda saved me the other night when I got whacked by a pool cue."

"We owe you thanks," Clover said.

"Wasn't nothing. He was trying to help a friend of mine when her old man came in and started giving her grief. It was the least I could do for a Good Samaritan."

"And I still owe you for that dinner you paid for," Denny said. "I ain't forgot."

Brenda smiled at him and nodded.

There was a long pause, as nobody seemed to have much to say about anything to each other. Clover looked directly at Brenda, not with a challenge, but with the territorial stare of a vixen, and Brenda looked at Denny with a desperate, help-me-I'm-out-of-my-element-here look, but Denny was looking at the ground. Sly was grinning as he viewed the situation, and York's brow furrowed as he tried to grasp the psychic vibrations of the situation at hand.

Finally, Brenda said, "Denny, could I talk with you for a minute?"

"Sure," he said, and together they walked up the path.

"Nice to meet y'all," Brenda said over her shoulder.

Clover stood still, watching them go. At the top of the hill, they stopped and faced each other. Brenda spoke while Denny kicked dirt. Then Denny talked for a minute, looking intently up at Brenda. Then Brenda spoke, and Denny nodded. Then she kissed him on the cheek, turned, and walked away. Denny kicked dirt some more, then turned and came back down the hill.

Clover never moved, not knowing who she was anymore. She didn't know what she thought, or what she felt, or what she wanted. The identity that Clover considered hers had up and vanished, and in its place stood a stranger. A scary stranger. The intense jealous rage that flared up in her and made her want to strangle the redhead was as foreign an emotion as any she'd ever had. She had no idea she felt that way about Denny. But she knew one thing, and she knew it suddenly and for absolute certain: She had given Denny the power to hurt her, and to hurt her in a big, bad way.

"Brenda's brother works for the railroad," Denny said when he came back down. "Railroad guys are fixing to evict us."

"What else did she say?" Clover asked.

"That Christine and her dumbass husband, the one who cracked me on the head, they took the six hundred bucks they stole from me and sucked it right on up their noses. Or something."

"Anything go on between you two?" Clover asked.

"Did it look like it?" Denny was secretly a little bit pleased that this was getting a rise out of the girl. He didn't mind having two women square off over him.

"I don't know."

"I introduced you as my girlfriend," he said.

"Yeah," she said, stifling a smile. She sat down on his blanket and pulled him down with her. "That was kind of nice. You've never done that before."

"Evict us?" Sly said. "What does that mean?"

"Well, you are," Denny said to Clover, and poked at her playfully. "Aren't you?"

Clover giggled. "I guess."

"What did she mean, evict us?" Sly asked again.

"She meant baseball bats under the dark of night," York said. "I seen it in a dream."

Sly looked over at Denny, panic rising, but Denny was smooching with the girl, and Sly knew that once a man's whanger got the best of him, there was no talking with him until it had had its way with him.

"We need weapons, York," Sly said, and visions of his creepy lieutenant came back into his head. He crouched down next to York and whispered urgently to him, while out of the corner of his eye, he saw Denny pull the girl up and take off with her somewheres on down the track. "We need to secure the perimeter, stand watch, defend ourselves. We could use a couple of semi-automatic weapons, some booby traps, some intelligence about the movement of the enemy troops."

"Don't want no conflict," York said. "Don't want no violence."

"Well, conflict is just exactly what we got, and violence happens if they start it. We're just standing fast. Holding the line."

The good thing was that Denny wasn't much for basking in afterglow, and in about ten minutes, they were back. He kissed the girl long and hard, then whacked her on the butt and sent her off to home. The men had work to do.

"I'll be back in a little while," she said. "In case you need me for something else." He lunged at her, and she parried, giggling, then tripped on up the path.

"Did that woman say when the railroad guys were coming?" Sly asked.

"Nope," Denny said.

"We've got to prepare."

"With what? How?"

"No violence," York said. But over York's head, Sly looked at Denny, Denny looked back at Sly, and they both smiled.

As Clover lightly made her way uptown, she idly wondered how a day could turn so dark and stormy and then so beautiful, all within the space of a few moments. She felt in love with the world, and for the first time, started to think about someday maybe putting on a white dress and standing with Denny in front of a preacher.

Her mother would like that, and then she could move out of her dinky apartment, and they could set up housekeeping in a sweet little house. Maybe her mom could live in the attic, or over the garage or something. Clover would fix nice, healthy food, and maybe York and Sly could sleep over sometimes. They could come for a good, hot meal occasionally, and they could take a bath now and then.

Or maybe Clover would want to move Denny away from there, away from her mother, away from York and Sly.

But then that's the kiss of death, isn't it? Marrying a man and then being determined to change him. All the women's magazines said so.

Nope, Denny wasn't all that good a deal, as husbands go. Clover was a good deal, because she was bright, shiny, loyal, a good worker and a devoted friend. She was sympathetic and nice and not too emotional, for a girl.

But Denny. Denny was a bum, that's all there was to that. And Clover needed to watch herself real careful so she didn't get knocked up and end up like her mother.

Maybe York knocked her mother up when they were both about twenty-four years younger, and he really *was* her daddy. That's why her mother didn't want her hanging around down there by the train tracks.

By the time Clover got to her apartment, her nether parts were all sticky, her panties smelled like Denny had just had a go at her, which he had, and she was ready for a bath, not marriage.

She was glad she'd the good sense to reason these things out instead of acting on them.

Still, it was nice to feel loved. And Denny loved her, she knew it.

She walked around the back of the house where Mrs. Fine lived with Charlie, her Down's-syndrome son. Clover had her own little yard, but the yard man mowed it for her, so she only had to take care of what flower beds she chose to keep and tend, and make sure all the birdfeeders were full.

It was a hot, dry July, and the grass looked tattered and

exhausted, though the flowers, well mulched, were abundant and glorious. Clover promised the lawn some water after she took her bath, and promised herself some cut flowers for the coffee table. She checked the feeders and found they were all still full, so the birds weren't having a problem staying fat and sassy this year.

Her apartment, though tiny, was its own separate building. It probably used to be some kind of a shed or something, but it had its own bedroom with a twin bed, a nightstand and a dresser, a living room with a couch, a television, a Formica table, a teeny stove and fridge, and a bathroom with a little plant area next to the tub that got both morning and evening sun through well-placed windows on both sides. She started the tub water running, threw in some Mr. Bubble, and then turned the radio on low to listen to some soft country music.

It felt good to get out of that uniform. She smelled like donut grease, burnt coffee, and Denny.

She lowered herself gently into the hot, sudsy water with a sigh, and started going over the mental agenda she had worked out for herself.

First: laundry. She'd take care of that right after her bath, because she only had one clean uniform left, and Clover didn't like to be that short on things. She could spill something ugly on it right away on her next shift, and then she'd have to look trashy all day long. Second: her mother. Clover worried about Eileen, the way she drank and smoked and ran around at night. If Clover had behaved that way when she lived at home, she'd get a slap for her trouble. But that had never been necessary, because Clover behaved herself. But Eileen—that was how Clover was beginning to think of her, instead of as Mother—was looking older by the minute, and Clover was certain she'd get herself either sick or into trouble soon.

Eileen was due at the bakery at three A.M. every day; Clover's shift started at five. Most times, Eileen looked as if she hadn't even gone to bed yet. Clover thought she'd pop on by Eileen's apartment to see if she could do her mom's laundry while she was doing her own. Maybe that would be a good time for them to talk. Clover was beginning to feel like the adult, and that was a shame, because her mom wasn't even forty yet.

Something ate at Eileen, something Clover couldn't even begin to imagine, but someday, she'd find out what it was.

Okay. She'd pop by her mom's apartment, offer to wash her uniforms, and see where that took her.

Denny. Nothing to think about there. He was on her agenda automatically, because she liked thinking about him, about his shy smile and his nice hazel eyes, his brown hair and his reddish eyebrows and beard.

Clover smiled and dunked herself down in the soapy water. He would not be the father of her children, but she was certainly becoming fond of him. One of these days she'd give him up, she supposed, but she really hoped he'd change from his own wanting to, and then they could make a life together. That weird jealousy was not something she was interested in experiencing again, but that had been her own fault; Denny was blameless. *And* he'd called her his girlfriend.

Clover grinned into her soapy washcloth. She was somebody's girlfriend.

Okay. Last agenda item: Railroad guys evicting Denny, Sly and York. She didn't like the sound of that, and she didn't like the sound of those guys fighting back. That bump and bruise on Denny's forehead had scared her half to death, and maybe it would even be worse with those tough guys. They'd break him like a twig, probably.

Okay, Clover, she thought to herself, *you're so clever, figure something out.*

She closed her eyes and lay back in the warm water, feeling

the anxieties of the day soak out of her as Clint Black crooned softly.

Maybe Eileen would have an idea.

Maybe Clover could go talk to Deputy Travis. Deputy Travis seemed pretty interested in whatever Clover had to say, as long as the top button of her uniform was undone. Maybe Clover should put on a pair of short-shorts and a tight T-shirt and go pay a little visit to Deputy Travis.

The thought made her blush. *Shame on you, Clover,* she scolded herself, *for thinking like that even as you're washing your boyfriend's essence from your body.*

She felt like a sexy little thing, there was no doubt about that. And that was Denny's fault.

And she was doing this for Denny, right?

Right.

She dunked her head back into the warm water, then began to lather up her hair.

With a cigarette in her mouth, and hair that looked as though it might have mice living in it, a scruffy, worn-out-looking Eileen opened the door. "What are you doing here?" she asked, her makeup-free face looking gray and haggard instead of fresh-scrubbed as it ought to look. It had been over a year since Clover had seen her mother without the thick makeup she wore, and the aging that had been taking place in that time was amazing.

"Just came to visit," Clover said. "Is this a bad time?"

Eileen sneered, and Clover thought she might be sneering at her daughter's youth as much as anything. She stepped aside, and Clover stepped up into the trailer that was coated with a thin patina of nicotine and smelled like food gone bad. "Why do you live like this?" Clover asked as she pushed up her sleeves and began running hot water in the sink.

"Why do you come over here?"

"I came over to talk, but you make me worry about you."

Eileen snorted. "Don't waste it." She adjusted her bra, then flopped down onto the worn cushions in the settee. "What did you want to talk about?"

"Where's your dish soap?"

"I'm out."

Clover sighed in exasperation, then decided that a sink full of dirty dishes wasn't going to spell the end of her mother, but she could spell the end of their relationship if she didn't ease off. She turned off the water, dried her hands, and sat down on the orange chair with a blue-striped beach towel covering the seat.

"You got man problems?" Eileen asked. "I can help with those."

Yeah, right, Clover thought, as if she'd take advice from her mom about men. Eileen, the queen of relationship disasters. "How's your love life?"

Eileen smiled in spite of herself, stubbed out her cigarette. "Ain't bad. I'm seeing someone. Someone cute, who treats me nice."

"Good, Mom, I'm happy about that. He work?"

A cloud came over Eileen's face. "Smart mouth, of course he works."

"Sorry. I didn't mean anything." Clover picked at her cuticles and noticed that her bath had failed to get her nails completely clean. "Everything okay for you at the shop?"

"Why are you here, Clover?"

"I'm going to do laundry. Thought I'd take yours along."

"It's in the hamper."

Clover thought she could smell it from where she sat. "Okay, I'll do it for you."

"Good," Eileen said, then stood up in dismissal. "I've got other things to do today besides laundry."

"What?"

Eileen lit up another smoke, took a deep drag, and then struck a pose, looking down at her daughter. "What's this all about?"

"I don't know," Clover said. "Life is just confusing, that's all. Sometimes I wish we were closer."

"Life is confusing, sweetheart. That's why it's life. We're not supposed to understand it, we're just supposed to do it. And keep on doing it, day after day after goddamned day until something happens."

"Like what?"

"Fuck if I know, sis. I'm still waiting."

"Waiting for what?" Clover felt as though there were clues here, but it was difficult, pulling out the tiny fibers of wisdom from Eileen's experience.

"Either to be saved or to die, I guess," Eileen said. "Between here and there is just daily stuff, you know?" Eileen sat back down and leaned forward, elbows on her knees. "What's happening in your life, darlin'? You got mysteries? You got problems? You want to confess and make it all go away?"

"Not really."

"Good, because that doesn't do anything. Confession just makes everybody feel bad. Just keep your knees together and be a good girl on a daily basis." Eileen snorted again and took another drag on her cigarette. "Why am I telling you all this? You're the most perfect little twit I know. Don't drink, don't smoke, pay your rent on time—the only thing I know about you that's weird is that you hang down by the tracks. That's mighty weird, Clover. Why don't you go to school or something? Make something of those good looks and big brains?"

"I will," Clover said, but that plan was floating farther off into the distance.

"Deputy Travis stopped by today," Eileen said, then hauled herself out of the little sofa and took the two steps it took to get into the kitchen. She poured two inches of vodka into a dirty jelly glass and added a short splash of orange juice from the small refrigerator. "Want one?"

"No," Clover said, and then waited. There was no pushing Eileen in any direction for any reason. Eileen had a mystery, she had a secret of her own, and left to her own devices, she'd eventually spill all knowledge in order to impress her daughter.

Eileen leaned against the counter and gulped half her drink, then closed her eyes as it went down. Clover watched her face very carefully, and it didn't look as though Eileen liked the taste, nor did she like the way it went down or the way it fell into her probably-empty stomach. For the first time, Clover realized that her mother was an alcoholic, and she wondered how she had managed to avoid that knowledge all these years.

That thundering realization and all the ramifications, responsibilities, and puzzlements that the knowledge brought with it almost caused her to miss the next few things her mother said, and she had to stop and rewind the unconscious backup tape that her mind always made when she was distracted.

"He said there was going to be trouble down at the hobo place because of some murder and that you ought to keep clear," Eileen said.

"Travis came here?" In no way did Clover want to know how Travis knew where her mother lived.

Eileen smiled around her cigarette. "Yeah. I think he likes you."

Clover grimaced.

"You could do worse, missy. He's got a job. With benefits."

"What kind of trouble, did he say?"

"You involved?"

"No," Clover said.

"I don't know who's got bail money if you are."

"I'm not."

"Then take the deputy's advice and steer clear."

"They're my friends," Clover said.

"You need a higher class of friends," Eileen said, then sucked that cigarette right on down to its filter.

You could use some better friends yourself, Clover thought, but didn't dare say. "Well," she said. "I better get to the laundry."

"Yeah, thanks. You know where the key is hid."

"You going out?"

"Got a date."

Clover smiled. "That's nice. Yeah, I'll put your clothes away."

"Pick up some dish soap while you're out?"

"I'll try."

"Thanks, kiddo," Eileen said, pecked Clover on the cheek, then went into the bathroom and closed the door.

Clover lifted the lid on the clothes hamper in Eileen's tossed bedroom and almost closed it right back up again. Instead, she stripped the bed, dumped the hamper full of moldy towels and stinking uniforms into the middle of the sheets, and hauled the bundle out the door without saying good-bye.

Clover's heart was heavier than the bundle of laundry, though. Her man was in trouble and so was her mother. Something had to be done, and it was probably going to be up to her to do it. For both of them.

While the three washers were going, Clover realized that being a man and being a drunk absolved people of their responsibilities, and that wasn't fair.

While she folded the fresh clothes, she wondered if girls were always the responsible ones. That seemed to be the way it went, women running around cleaning up after their men. Maybe that was the natural order, and those who kept doing it stayed married. Those who refused, got divorced.

Did that mean that she'd have to clean up after Denny?

Did that mean that her mother needed somebody to clean up

after her? Who would? What would happen if nobody signed on for that job and her mom grew old and sick by herself?

But that wasn't something Clover needed to think about today. Today she just needed to finish the laundry.

After she put away her mother's clean laundry and washed the sink full of dishes and then picked up around the place a little bit, feeling weird about being in her mother's trailer alone, she realized that while she was there cleaning up after her mother, she didn't really *have* to be there, and perhaps she wouldn't do it again. She didn't have to be responsible for either her mother or Denny. If she had to choose, she thought she just might go to bat for York above everybody else. York seemed to be pretty self-sufficient, and so was Clover. Needy people ought to hang together, and self-sufficient people ought to hang together, but maybe that isn't exactly the way God made the world. Maybe he meant for opposites to attract in that way as well, so there was always somebody to look after the needy ones.

Ugh.

Oh well, Clover thought, *there's nothing to do about all of that today.* Just do the laundry and be as good at life as she could. That lightened her mental load, and doing the laundry lightened her physical load. She felt ready for some adventure, and decided to go on back down toward Denny's place and see if anything interesting had developed.

She looked around for a piece of paper and a pencil so she could write a little "I love you" note to her mom, but she could find neither pencil nor paper.

Cleaning the place up is a love note all in itself, Clover, she told herself. With a sadness she was afraid to define, she closed and locked the door, and replaced the key under the pot of plastic geraniums.

"The time will come," Tecumseh Gittens had said to his protégé, "when God will test your mettle as a man. You'll recognize that time, too. There will be no doubt. It will come in one swift and devastating realization, and you will know, just as will God, forever after, whether you are a man or a coward. You won't see that moment coming, son, so prepare yourself, and make every decision a courageous one."

York found it hard to believe that it had probably been some fifty years since he'd left behind a heartbroken Reverend Tecumseh. At times, when the evening was coming on and the dust was settling after a long day of busyness, doing whatever it is that dust did to justify itself, that York thought about him, thought about that particular pronouncement that York could recite to the word, with every inflection intact, where they were when he'd said it and the profound effect it had had on himself as a lad. They used to have some talks together, about things that mattered, usually just about twilight.

But York had just about decided, all these years later, that either the reverend had discovered that he, himself, was a coward, and placed way too much significance or blame on whatever it was that helped him come to that conclusion, or else he was just flat-out wrong. No life-determining, profound moment had ever had its way with York, not that he had always paid attention, but if it was to happen the way Tecumseh said it would, then it hadn't happened yet. Unless it was that moment that he walked away from the reverend, but that didn't seem all that courageous.

But then again, he was still alive, so maybe it was yet to come. Maybe that's why he was still alive—the jury was still out on old York's internal mettle, and when it had been determined once and for all whether York was a man or a coward, well, then God could have him or not.

All of this was moving around through York's mind as the day dwindled and York became concerned about the next few days. He'd always been in charge of the camp before, but now he wasn't. Forces greater than he had taken control, and those forces were called Ego, Fear, and Pride. This was Denny and Sly, two loose cannons, against the railroad guys, and nobody had a clue as to their agenda or who was poking them in the back with long pointed sticks. Deputy Travis probably had a hand in it, a loose cannon hisownself, and York wouldn't be one bit surprised if Mayor Grimes held the spear that was poking Travis in the back. Travis was a suck-up, and might go to great lengths to impress the mayor, when the truth was, the mayor was just a small-time politician out for his own gain who would think nothing of slapping Travis away if he got to be too pesky after this whole thing was settled.

Obviously, York never read the newspapers or watched television. He wasn't political, and he wasn't in on the community affairs of West Wheaton, but a man couldn't be breathing within the city limits for as long as he had without having at least a passing idea of its politics. Besides that, Clover brought the news of the day down to them more frequent than not.

Yep, this was a political problem, and York felt on the verge of war. He wished he had someone pretty, soft and nice smelling to talk it over with, but then, that had been a wish of his for many years. It had never come true before, mostly due to York's lifestyle. Women came through camp now and then, but they were roughened and hard and not the type of woman that York would like to unburden himself to. The soft, sweet-smelling type would never live in the dust. Maybe the women York knew started out that way, but the dust got into their pores and their souls and solidified them into crusty, brittle creatures that were unafraid and therefore unresponsive to the miracles of life and the majesty of its details.

He worried about that happening to Clover. Now there was a sweet one, and she always smelled good, even after a sweaty shift in the hot donut shop, when she smelled like raw woman mixed with powdered sugar and scorched coffee. But, of course, all the men lifted their noses when she came trotting down the hill after a shower, when she smelled like powder and perfume and little-girl sweet. That Denny. He had no idea what he had.

Then again, maybe he did. He seemed to treat her with great respect, and that's the only reason York allowed their dalliance to continue. If Denny ever raised his voice or his hand to that girl, York would kick his ass all the way to the other side of the Mississippi and make sure he never came back. But Denny had never mistreated Clover, and York discovered that aside from a personally felt twinge of envy, he had no objections to their young love. He hoped for Clover's sake that Denny stopped the stealing and became a righteous man, but York held out little faith that that would happen. More likely, he'd knock Clover up, get arrested for grand theft, and go off to prison, leaving Clover destitute and heartbroken.

Wasn't much York could do about that, if it happened.

And there wasn't much York could do about what was about to happen to himself, either. This land belonged to the railroad, and if they wanted him evicted, well, they would flat-out evict him. York felt bad about his prospects, but he didn't want to dwell on any bad news until it actually came about. A pot of coffee was a far better idea.

"Sly?"

"Yeah."

"Coffee?"

"Yeah, okay."

York heard him pour water from the big jug Denny or somebody filled up every morning from the hose at the gas station up the road, shake the last of the coffee out of the can and set the whole works on the fire. York could see the low flame grow a little brighter as Sly fed it some bits of fuel. York pulled a bag of beef jerky from under his pillow and broke off a piece to suck on, his teeth being store-bought and not much good for things like jerky, though he loved the taste of it, and offered the bag to Sly.

Sly sat down next to York, took the beef, and they both chewed in silence while they listened to the poor coffeepot begin to boil, and then, to perk.

"Denny thinks we ought to fight them off," Sly said.

"He's a hothead," York said. "I'm saying no violence."

"You want to just lie down and let them beat us to death with baseball bats?"

"If they come down here bent on violence, then I guess we ought to try to defend ourselves," York said. "Sometimes I think turning the other cheek isn't prudent in this day and age. But if they say 'get on out,' then I think we should get on out. It's their land, after all."

"We didn't do nothing. It's just a farce. They're just throwing their weight around. Government-like."

"Don't matter. We've been living here rent free for a lot of years now, and that's more than we're entitled to."

"Seems to me that if we've been here this long that we ought to have some rights."

Footsteps sounded on the path, and York knew by the cadence that it was the girl. "Ask her," York said. "She's the one with the library card."

"I'll ask around," Clover said when she heard their idea. "It's sort of like common-law marriage. You live long enough on a piece of land, it ought to be yours." She poured coffee.

"But that don't help us tonight," Sly said.

"It might," York said. "You better go on home, girl. It's getting dark."

"I'm staying."

"There's going to be trouble, and you oughtn't be here."

"I've gotta be here, otherwise it'll get ugly."

"You being here ain't going to keep it from getting ugly," Sly said, and bit off another hunk of jerky.

"We'll see."

Denny showed up about an hour later, with a high-powered slingshot in his hand and a pocket full of ball bearings. He let Sly inspect the weapon, kissed Clover, accepted the cup of hot coffee she poured for him, and the piece of jerky that York handed him.

"Man," Sly said, handing him back the slingshot. "That'll do damage."

Denny frowned at him and tipped his head toward York, who pretended not to have heard.

"I ought to have something," Sly said, and he got up to go look for something he could use to defend himself and his territory. He came back moments later with a hefty, evil-looking splinter from one of the black, creosote-soaked railroad ties.

"You shouldn't be here, honey," Denny said to Clover.

"Too bad," she said. "I'm staying."

"No women in combat. It ain't right," Sly said. "The kid there will be thinking of you instead of tending to business."

"No *combat,*" York said.

Sly nudged her, but she crossed her arms and held firm.

Denny wished she'd leave, but admired her grit. On the other hand, maybe somebody fixing to do them harm would think twice when they saw that a woman was among them.

"Ain't nothing going to happen anyway," she said.

"You work tomorrow?" Denny asked.

"Nope," she said. "So I can stay all night long."

"Good," he said. Then he scraped a little hole in the dirt by the fire and emptied his pocketful of steel peas into it.

"I'll take the first watch," Sly said. "You all get yourselves some rest."

Denny nodded and scooted around until he was lying down, his head on a stack of old newspapers they used to kindle the fire on the rare occasion it went out. He wanted to be comfortable enough to nap, but not comfortable enough to sleep sound. Clover lay next to him, her head on his shoulder. But there was no sleep in the camp. Sly might be taking the first watch, but it was early, and Sly was overly dramatic anyway, military history and all. Denny still had an aching leftover in his head from the crack of that pool cue, and wasn't eager to repeat any sort of a performance that could get him hurt. Or Clover. He didn't want anything to happen to Clover while she was under his care. Nobody would hurt York, and Sly could take care of himself. Denny had to worry about himself and this woman, and that was plenty.

He looked down at her. She looked like a child, her hair over her eyes, her little orange sweatshirt glowing in the fading firelight. She'd taken off her sneakers, but had her jeans on, and her socks had little kittens on them, he'd noticed earlier. He felt an astonishing surge of affection, and kissed her forehead. She smiled and nuzzled his shoulder.

Silently, the four of them sat thinking about their pasts and their futures, as they awaited their destiny.

"Gotta go, babe," Travis said. "C'mon."

"No," she whined. "More."

"Later, you insatiable wench. C'mon. Get up."

Reluctantly, Eileen reached for her drink on the deputy's nightstand, plumped up a pillow, and sat up to drink and watch him dress. She liked seeing him in uniform, but she liked seeing him in those tight, faded jeans even more. It was hot, and he wore a cotton plaid shirt that had the sleeves ripped out of it, a few ropes of tangled threads hanging down the back of his bicep. He tucked the shirt in and hooked a wide belt with a big buckle. "C'mon, Eileen. Get dressed."

She knew she better hustle, or he'd turn on the light, and she wasn't certain how old she'd look in this light, but didn't want to chance it. Deputy Travis was a good fifteen years her junior, and she knew he was a little lusty for her daughter. Clover need never know Eileen was having a fling with him. It was nothing serious, of course, it was just one of those things that made her feel like a woman every now and then. Travis had been kind of a steady lover, if infrequent, and if Eileen thought about it, she could get mad at the idea that he was using her for sex when he couldn't find somebody else. So she didn't think about that. She chose to consider their relationship in other terms. She chose to believe he liked her company. She certainly liked his. He needed someone young, like Clover, and she needed someone more mature. But for now—well, for now, he always seemed to carry her brand of vodka in his cabinet, and he usually had some type of flavored drink or fruit juice that hadn't gone sour, and he had a cock that would not quit. She liked all of those things.

"You talked to Clover, right?" he asked from the bathroom as he inspected himself in the mirror.

"Yeah," Eileen said as she hoisted her breasts into a bra. "How come you're not wearing a uniform?"

"This ain't official. This is unofficial. A favor to the mayor and my friends at the railroad." He turned out the bathroom light and came out to fit his off-duty .38 in the back of his jeans, then threw on a light jacket to cover.

She didn't want him to watch her dress, but she had dawdled too long, and now she had no choice. She stepped into panties quickly, to cover her sagging stomach, and as she did, she saw his eyes travel the length of her in the dusky light. Then he turned away, and with a woman's intuition, she knew that he hadn't liked what he saw.

Maybe she'd join a gym.

Anyway, while he was looking the other way, she stepped into her pants, and pulled her cotton sweater on over her head. Then she made a couple of quick steps to the bathroom.

While sitting on the toilet, she saw that there wasn't any toilet paper. A roll of paper towels stood on the floor beside the filthy tub. She ripped off a sheet, moistened a corner of it in her mouth and rubbed at the skin under her eyes to remove mascara smudges. Then she poked at her hair with her fingers, finished on the toilet and that was about all the time Travis was going to give her. He was understandably edgy; he had a mission tonight, and he wasn't sure how it was going to go. She admired the fact that he was brave enough to venture into territory like that.

"Don't forget," she said as she exited the bathroom. "Clover dates that guy."

"I would never forget that," Travis said. "C'mon, let's go."

He preceded her out the front door of his house, then looked both ways, up and down the street, to make sure nobody was going to see them.

"See ya," he said, and skipped down the stairs, leaving her there, no good-bye kiss, no idea of when they'd talk or see each other again. It was a small point to her, as she knew he'd be at the donut shop in the morning, puffy-eyed and ready for caffeine, but it would have been a nice gesture to give her a kiss or at least the promise of a date in two or three days. Or something.

But that wasn't the shape of their relationship, and Eileen had to staunch that little drop of blood that leaked out of her heart as he dismissed her so readily. She was just a convenient lay for him, and she knew it, and to think anything else was to set herself up for certain disappointment.

Still, a girl could dream, couldn't she?

"Bye," she said, and resisted the impulse to touch him. They got into their respective cars and drove off, she to her cold, lonely, stinking trailer, and Travis to his side job for the mayor.

Eileen wondered if she should stop and check on Clover, to make sure she was home safe.

Nah, she thought. *Clover's probably in bed, tired after doing all that laundry.* And Eileen needed a shower and an early night to bed, too. The bakery never slowed down, and her three A.M. shift seemed to come earlier and earlier. Before shower, before bed, she also needed a good, stiff drink, made with something other than grape Kool-Aid, which was all she could find at Travis's place. She needed to get right with herself about the way that Travis treated her. Either that, or dump him. Maybe it was time to give that some serious thought.

Who else would she get to bed her, if not Travis?

Somebody, certainly. If she joined a gym.

She started the car, trying not to attach significance to the fact that Travis never touched her in public, ignored her at the donut shop, sped off into the night before she got her rattletrap car started, and didn't stick around to make sure that it did start, never mind seeing her to her door, and . . . and . . . and he always went first out the door, and if someone was on the sidewalk, he pushed her back in and closed the door until the coast was clear.

She knew. She was no dummy. But all those fantasies she entertained about the two of them making a future together were just that. Fantasies. No basis for reality, no possibility of coming true. They gripped her the strongest after they'd made love, when she was awake as he slept next to her. She'd resist the temptation to touch his face, to smooth his hair, to stroke the muscles in his back or on his arm. She'd want to kiss him with affection, but he hated that, and he'd brush her off. So she learned not to do that, but to just look at him with affection and heartfelt desire and wish things were otherwise. She wished she didn't drink as much or smoke, so he could respect her a little more, she wished she were a widow or something honorable, rather than having never been married, yet owning up to an adult daughter.

A daughter that was only a couple of years younger than her lover. And someone her lover had his eyes on, too.

No, Eileen and Travis were not to be for long, but for now it was okay. It was good, sometimes, even, when they'd had decent sex and sometimes Travis forgot himself and wanted to cuddle her afterwards. That's when she felt like a woman, small, soft, and feminine.

Those times were worth all the rest. She ignored all the bad stuff—Travis was a jerk, after all, and everybody knew it.

Life included lots of tradeoffs. He was one of them.

Her trailer was dark, but when Eileen turned on the living-room light, she noticed that Clover had cleaned the place up. And hung fresh uniforms in her closet.

That Clover. Wasn't she something?

Eileen had done something right in raising Clover, although she had no idea what it was.

She poured herself a glass of vodka, splashed in a little bit of orange juice and gulped down half of it. "I'll shower in the morning," she said to nobody, took off her clothes, put on the T-shirt she'd stolen from Travis a few months ago, and slipped into her bed. She picked up a paperback that was on her nightstand, opened it to the mark, but she couldn't remember the characters or what they were up to. She'd have to start reading it all over again, and she had no patience for that.

So she put the mark back in the book and the book back on the nightstand, turned out the light and sipped her drink.

She thought about calling Clover and thanking her, but decided instead to thank her in the morning.

If morning came.

She drained the glass and set it on top of the book.

Morning would come. Life was too cruel to cancel morning and let her off the hook.

Just about the time Travis met Sonny Topolo, the Samoan heavy he planned to take with him down to the hobo camp as extra insurance, York was thinking about the man who had died not twenty yards from where he lay, Denny was thinking about the fact that he had introduced Clover as his girlfriend, and what exactly that meant to her and more importantly, to him, Sly was beginning to panic and think about sailing, and Clover was busy picking names for their third child, the first son being Denny Junior, the second one being York, and the third, sure to be a girl, would have a name a little less strange than Clover, but something equally as old-fashioned. She enjoyed being a Clover. Maybe her daughter would be Violet. Or Lily. These were thoughts she'd keep to herself, though, because they were certain to scare Denny away. There were some thoughts that she had to keep to herself: Thoughts about children, of commitment and marriage, and the thoughts that came right along with them about Denny sleeping indoors in a bed with her, and especially the biggie: the job Denny was going to have to get to support her and the three little ones she wanted to lavish love upon. Nope, there would be time for all of that, because they were young yet, and as things they wanted became as apparent to him as they were to her, he would move in those directions. She just had to be patient.

Introducing her as his girlfriend to another woman was a big leap. Things were progressing.

She sighed the contentment of a woman with an unencumbered mind.

Denny heard her sigh and wondered if what he was doing

was fair to her. It wasn't, he knew it wasn't. She ought to be finding herself a man she could settle down with, a man who could give her the kids she wanted, someone stable, with a job and a house and all the rest. Denny was probably going to be a roamer, footloose, for the rest of his days. The fact that he hadn't moved from this one spot in the last two or three years didn't mean anything to him. He still felt like a transient, and lived a transient's life, with no roots, no belongings, and no ties. Sometimes he caught himself in a daydream, where he and Clover had a bunch of rug rats running around the yard, playing on the swing set, and he read bedtime stories to them, and she had her own donut shop and he spent time . . . doing what? Nothing legal, for certain; he could never toe the line for some boss. He knew what the right thing to do would be, and that was to stop building up Clover's hopes. He wasn't good for her.

But every time he thought about her coming down that path, smelling so nice and giggling like a girl, and bringing donuts and seeing to York the way she did, and he thought about not touching her, or worse yet, having to know that somebody else was touching her on a regular basis—Deputy Asshole, for example—it made him a little bit crazy, and he knew that he'd never be strong enough to break it off with her.

Nope, she'd have to be the one to end it, and he hoped she'd do it soon before he had to feel guilty about sucking away her best years.

He felt her little head on his chest, and listened to her girlish little breaths as she floated on the edge of dreamland next to him, and his mood turned surly. *Being responsible is the shits,* he thought.

Before the clouds came to cover them, the stars appeared, and Sly looked at them and thought they looked mighty tropical. There wasn't any jungle vegetation around him, but in the warm dark he could easily imagine himself in Vietnam. His nerve endings told him he was preparing for a raid and a firefight, and he was wound tighter than he had been in thirty years. He kept reaching for his M16, always within reach, but it wasn't there, of course it wasn't there, they weren't in Vietnam, they were in California, *for Christ's sake, Sylvester, get a grip on yourself.*

But he was no child, and he knew that life had its ups and downs, and that it had been too much of a cruise for him lately. For the last ten or twenty years, in fact, and it was time for some shit to hit the fan. There was nothing too fun about life; it was serious business. Even living like they did was serious business. Most people had no idea. Life was just the same, whether you were on the corporate fast track or living in a hollowed-out dump by the train tracks. You still had to find food to eat, and maintain a latrine, and deal with the weather and all kinds of people in the process. All the time dealing with people. Must be a part of the divine plan, because it was fucking inescapable.

Well, if everything he heard was accurate, they'd be dealing with some people this evening, and it would be no joke.

Stand firm, he told himself, *and be there for your buddies.* This was not a time that Sly could go sailing and either live or die by the hand of God and the Viet Cong. This was not a time where his foxhole mates could cover for him or take a bullet for him or continue the firefight whether he had been hurt or put out of commission in some way or just flat-out went sailing and left them all to their own devices. No, these buddies were damned near helpless. This was York, an old blind man who might as well be Moses or Buddha, as far as Sly cared. He loved York as much as he loved any other human being. York would give no resistance, York would not defend himself. And Denny was still young: the little rat had his whole life ahead of him. Nope, this was Sly's job. He was the one who had been combat trained, had at one time been a fine-tuned fighting machine, though his mind went to the brisk and balmy Caribbean breezes every time the fight came his way. Still, he knew how to do all those things, and this, the fatalist in him reasoned, had been the reason all along for that wretched experience. He needed to defend York and their perimeter. Well, he could do it. He would do it, and he would do a good job of it. It might redeem his soul for the cowardice he had displayed in real combat. Nobody knew about any of that but him and his God, because the rest of the platoon sure as shit never talked. He was the only one who'd survived.

He reached his hand down for the M16.

It wasn't there, of course.

Travis and Topolo drove to the railroad yard, which seemed eerie and uncharacteristically abandoned in the night. The two railroad guys waited there, smoking and shuffling their feet. Travis parked in the dark lot, and wordless except for a quick greeting, the four of them got into a green van owned by the railroad. In the backseat were two baseball bats. Travis tried not to balk when he saw them, their polished wood illuminated in the harsh interior lights. He and Sonny climbed in the backseats, and the railroad guys climbed in the front for the four blocks or so to the place where they had vermin to eliminate, exterminate, or otherwise induce or persuade to thrive elsewhere.

This was not Travis's favorite job, and he hoped to almighty God that the bums would go quickly, quietly, and without a problem. He knew he could trust himself, but he didn't know about these railroad goons. He resisted the temptation to look more closely at those two baseball bats, to see if they had blood on them or anything.

Maybe one of their kids was on a Little League team.

Maybe not.

York was worried over the dead guy. He knew that the mayor

and the railroad wanted him off their land, but that was nothing. There was something else afoot. Someone had been murdered, and that was a far more threatening thing to have been brought into their world than a little dispute over squatters' rights. There was a murderer at large.

He felt an unfamiliar agitation over the approaching evening. He wasn't worried about Sly; Sly was a lot of talk and no action. York had been hearing about Sly going to the coast for ten years, and nothing like that had ever really approached happening. York had no doubt that Sly had been in the military, because occasionally he traded on his veteran status, and always to good advantage. But all that talk about defending the perimeter was a lot of hokey. York was glad that he didn't need to depend on Sly for much of survival value. He came through at the right times with the right stuff, though, like medication when York needed it, and the occasional paycheck when there was too much month left at the end of the money. But battle? Never. Not Sly.

Denny. Denny was the impetuous hothead that had York worried. Denny and that slingshot. Those ball bearings could probably kill a man if powered out right and hit in a crucial spot.

But even Denny's arrogance and disrespect for the law and those men who were coming to evict them tonight weren't the real thing that worried York. It was whoever killed the guy and pushed him off the train. That guy wasn't going to be finished with his business until he knew for certain that nobody could finger him.

York hoped that Sheriff Goddard was keeping Deputy Travis busy with that part of the investigation, and leaving to the railroad the whole question of whether York could stay put. Those guys had other, more important things on their minds than a couple of old guys living harmlessly in their weeds. But that Deputy Travis. He was another hothead who acted before he thought.

Travis and Denny going toe-to-toe would be something to see. They were both too ornery to let their fight flash to an instant conclusion. More likely, it would be like a giant anaconda fighting a gator, a slow-motion grind to the death of them both.

Denny and Sly both knew how York felt about violence and disturbing the peace of their little village. If they wanted to beef, they needed to take it somewhere else. York was in charge here, as far as that went, and he, in accordance with his heartfelt beliefs, would do what the powers asked of him, rather than initiate any nastiness.

If they wanted York to move, he would. He just hoped to hell they moved him to a nice place, with good-smelling women and not where he'd have to worry about getting his throat slit in the night by an icy-eyed killer on the train.

Sly had the watch, whatever that meant to Sly. To York it meant that Sly had something to keep his mind occupied, and York could relax. Sly had a tendency to go off the deep end when it came to military stuff sometimes, and his actions and reactions worried York a little bit. But Sly wasn't a young man any longer, and those fighting hormones tended to diminish over time.

Everything seemed quiet and peaceful. York could hear Clover's soft, girly snoring. Insects sang in the weeds, and a minimum breeze blew the smell of those creosote-soaked ties over York's face. All seemed right with the world.

He relaxed, settled his head down on the sofa cushion he used for a pillow, and let himself drift off to sleep.

Next thing he knew, there was a hand squeezing his foot.

"What?" he said. Adrenaline shot through him as he remembered that they were anticipating some kind of nastiness, and that Sly was on watch.

"Shhh," came the whisper from Sly. "Enemy approaching."

York's heart began to pound big and strong, and he found it heard to breathe. He tried to calm himself, to tell himself that there was nothing to worry about, there wasn't going to be any trouble, but to be wakened in the middle of the night by someone who was himself scared, well, that just put too much tension in the air.

York was happy his heart worked so well, but he wasn't so sure about his lungs. He kicked away from Sly's hand, and heard Sly move around. Denny and the girl were no longer snoring; York felt them wide-awake.

He heard footsteps coming down the path, only one set of light footsteps. He knew that walk, that shuffling cadence. "It's Chris," York whispered.

"Hey," Chris said in his pre-puberty voice.

"What the fuck you doing out here this time of night?" Sly said.

"Came to see York," Chris said. "Why?"

"This isn't a good time, Chris," York said. He sat up and found it much easier to breathe.

"What's going on?" Chris sat down on the edge of York's sofa cushions and lit up a cigarette.

"You shouldn't smoke," Sly said. "Kid like you'll ruin yourself by smoking."

"I can't sleep," Chris said.

"It's the full moon," York said. "People get restless under the moon."

"Can't see no moon," Chris said. "Clouds."

As long as York had lived under the stars, youngsters had come around. He never put them off, or put them down. Kids, mostly, who needed somebody to listen to them, and York guessed he could listen sometimes better than their parents, and different from their friends. They rarely came in a crowd, although sometimes two came together for the first time, kind of daring each other, egging each other on, and then acting embarrassed and giggling and shuffling their feet, not knowing what to say. Within a couple of days, though, one of those boys would be back, just to sit and be in the company of men. Men who were different. Men who were free.

Sometimes York had company, and on the occasion when a traveling man came through, a man with not such a great reputation, York would chase off the young'uns. Last thing he wanted was for something bad to happen to one of the kids who was seeking out his company, his counsel or just a safe place to smoke a butt pilfered from his parents, and watch the stars. As long as York had been a bum, there had been kids coming around to talk to him about life.

Chris was one. Clover was another.

"There's been trouble, Chris," York said.

"Yeah, I heard about the dead guy."

"We think they're coming tonight to try to evict us," Sly said.

"Evict you? At night? What kind of—oh, I get it."

"You ought to be home," York said. "It wouldn't be good for somebody to find you down here."

"It isn't even late," Chris whined.

But before he could finish that cigarette, before he could stop whining, before he could stand up, give his good-byes and get on his way, a van stopped at the top of the hill. York heard the two doors and the sliding door slam, and he knew they'd come.

"Get out of here," he whispered harshly to Chris, and the boy lost no time scampering off down the tracks.

The first thing Sly noticed was that they had baseball bats, or at least two of them did. The third was Deputy Dawg Travis Twit. Asshole Supremo.

Sly stood up, and as he did, the clouds parted and the moon shone down on the whole scene. For a brief moment, in the black-and-silver light Sly saw their camp as everybody else must see it. It was a dump. It was a roofless house with little rooms, the short walls separating them made out of found materials, newspapers, chunks of concrete and dirt. The ever-present campfire glowed in the common area, and that's also where York slept, without walls. It looked like trash. No wonder the railroad guys and the city fathers wanted them out of there. Who was in charge of policing up this area?

Just before one of the intruders spoke, Sly had a flash of gratitude that his mother wasn't alive to see him live like this.

"Thought you were going to be vacating these here premises," one of the guys said, and he swung his baseball bat like a pendulum by his side.

The other one had his bat resting gently on his shoulder.

"I'll handle this," Deputy Travis said. "C'mon, York, we don't want no trouble, do we?"

"York's got nowheres to go," Clover said, and stood up.

"Clover? What the fuck you doing here? Why aren't you home? Didn't your mother tell you to stay away from here tonight?"

"She did, but I'm here anyway. Let one of your gorillas there take a swing at *me* with that big honkin' bat." She took a taunting step out. "C'mon, tough guy."

"Hey, hey," Travis said, stepping between them. He took her arm and handled her back toward Denny.

"We don't want no trouble," the other guy said. "We just need you to vacate the premises, and we need you to do that nice and quiet, and right now."

"Or?" Sly asked.

"Why does there have to be an 'or'?" the other one said. "This is railroad land, and you're trespassing. It's our legal right to shoo away trespassers. It's our right to defend our land." He let his bat swing down and crunch into Denny's bedroom wall.

"Hey!" Denny jumped up and lunged at him.

"But we don't want to have to do no defending. Right, guys?" Travis was quick to jump in front of Denny and put a hand on the offending bat. He turned back to York. "Help us out here, York. Can you guys find somewhere else to live?"

"Right now? This minute?" York said. "Doorway at City Hall."

"We ain't hurting anybody," Denny said. "Y'all can just leave us alone and we'll leave you alone, and we'll all just live in peace."

"The way it's been for the past twenty years," York said. "I don't know what all the fuss is about. I don't know why suddenly, after all these years, you want to evict us."

"Because we can," one of the toughs said, wound up and took a swing at the coffeepot. It was a direct hit, and that little pot sailed into the dark, trailed by sparks from the poor fire. The clouds moved back over the moon again, plunging everything into relative darkness.

"It's the mayor," Travis said, and York heard the desperation in his voice. Travis didn't want violence, either. For the first time, York felt a kinship with the guy. "The murder. It's just flat-out trouble, and we don't want any more of it."

"That wasn't our trouble. Not our fault, and we shouldn't be punished," Sly said.

"Take that up with the mayor," Travis said. He walked over to Clover. "You oughtn't be here, honey."

"Don't honey me," she said. "You go on home and leave us. We ain't hurting nobody."

"Okay," Travis said, positioning himself in front of the two dudes with the bats. He was taking charge, and because he had a badge, he could. "This is the deal. Consider this fair warning. Tomorrow night, I want this place empty. Bulldozers are coming in the morning after, and we're cleaning up this place. Tomorrow night, we'll be back, and you best not be here, because all three of us will have these persuaders greased up and ready for evicting." He spread his legs and put his hands on his hips. "Don't make us use 'em." He turned to Clover. "And you, little lady, you keep out of this. You have a nice mama and a nice apartment. You go on home and take care of that stuff and leave these here bums to the law."

"You ain't no law," Clover said. "Not with those clothes on. Not with baseball bats. You're just a bully for hire, and you ain't fooling anybody, Travis."

For a second, Sly thought Travis was going to raise his hand to Clover, and he tensed, ready to jump on the asshole the second he did it. But apparently, Deputy Dawg thought better of it because he took a step back toward the goons.

"You need help finding a place, York," Travis said, "I'll send social services down. You want me to do that?"

"No, he doesn't want that," Clover said. "And he doesn't need any help from you. You just get your ass out of here. We'll figure out what to do. Just go."

"You got some mouth on you, girl."

"Go away, loser," Clover said.

Travis tore his eyes from her and her hurtful words and laid them back onto York, the pitiful old man. Along the way, he surveyed the sad little domain he had been sent to dismantle. "Tomorrow night," he said. He jabbed Sonny Topolo in the ribs, and they turned and filed back up the pathway. He turned back, just to make certain he got the last word in. "Tomorrow night," he said. "Be gone."

Nobody said anything until the van doors had slammed. The van started, flashed its headlights, and drove off.

"Fuck you," Sly said to nobody and everybody.

"We got rights," Denny said.

York was quiet for a long time. "Clover?" he asked quietly.

"Hmmm?"

"Would you call social services for me tomorrow?"

"Sure, York," she said.

Sly kicked at things and cursed under his breath. Denny remained quiet. York thought his life had ended, and reminded himself that it had been a long, wonderful ride, and maybe it was time. Clover started to cry.

And then it started to rain.

Bully for hire. The words echoed through Travis's head all the way back to the railroad yard, and then he wordlessly shook hands with the toughs, got into his own car, and headed home.

Bully for hire. That wasn't who he was when he was in uniform, but that's exactly who he was when he was working his nose up the mayor's ass, that was for certain. He pulled into the driveway of his house, turned off the ignition and sat there, his guts burning.

Is this who he intended to be? Is this what he wanted for his life? To strong-arm old men out of their well-worn rat holes? To push little girls around? To threaten harmless old fools with a baseball bat? He hadn't carried one, but he might as well have. And now what was going to happen the following night? He'd given them an ultimatum. Now he had to follow through. He and the railroad guys with their baseball bats. He *had* to follow through.

He didn't want to follow through.

He rested his hands on the top of the steering wheel of the Pontiac muscle car he couldn't afford and he looked at his house. It was a typical, no-personality, cookie-cutter ranch house that he couldn't afford. No furniture to speak of inside. No food, no dishes. No pots and pans. One sofa, one coffee table, one television. In the bedroom was a cheap bed and an even cheaper dresser, and the only thing on any of the walls was a poster of Janis Joplin in his bedroom. If he remembered right, he was still out of toilet paper, and the roll of paper towels he had been using for the task was about empty as well.

His life was headed the wrong way. He didn't have enough money to make his car payment and his mortgage payment. He was bullying the innocent guys down by the railroad, and he was doing it for some future favor from the mayor, not for any immediate gain, but immediate was exactly what he needed. He was in deep trouble, borrowing from his credit limit on his credit cards to cover his ass every month. Sure, the mayor would probably back him when it was his turn to run for sheriff, but that wasn't anytime soon, and the mortgage company wasn't patient.

Bully for hire. Loser.

Boy, she'd nailed it right on the head. He was a loser.

Raindrops started dotting the windshield as he sat in his driveway.

Funny thing about Sheriff Goddard. He was a man that Travis had always looked up to, but Travis was acting exactly the opposite way that the sheriff would. It was as if Travis was still a teenager, with that authority thing—that pissy, don't-tell-me-what-to-do thing. He thought he'd gotten over that a long time ago, left it behind him when he left home and joined the force, but he still felt that way about Sheriff Goddard. Maybe because Sheriff Goddard was so much like his dad. Smart, authoritative, respected, right. He was right. He was always right, and Travis rarely was right, and that's what pissed Travis off. So he kept pushing it, waiting for a time when he'd be right and the sheriff would be wrong, and then he'd feel good about himself.

Maybe.

He wasn't feeling so good about himself at the moment.

He needed something and he didn't know what.

Yes, he did. There was one thing that made him feel good about himself, only it was just a surface bandage and he knew that. Still, it worked. She liked him, she liked him a lot. She made him feel like a king at times, and if the light wasn't too bright on her aging face, and she didn't breathe cigarette breath in his face, for a few minutes, he could make her sigh and squirm and he could pretend that he was king of the world.

It was late. She'd be mad.

He looked again at the solitary porch light over the door to his house, his albatross, then he punched in the clutch, turned the key, and backed out of the drive.

Steve Goddard watched the slatted light from the moon slide across the sheet that covered the contours of his sleeping wife. He sat up, pillow against the headboard, knee raised, sweaty and sleepless, and worried about York and the boys down by the tracks. He had a bad feeling about Travis and those railroad guys and that slimy mayor, and he wanted to go down there just to check on them, just to make sure that one broken-necked dead guy didn't turn into a blood bath on his turf.

He had watched the red digits of the clock click by for over an hour, and there was no way he was going to sleep without going down there to make sure things were all right.

He slid his hand along Athena's muscled rump, up across her back, felt the "Hmmm?" of her sleepy question as to why he was waking her up while the full moon was still high.

"Honey?" Married to a sheriff, Athena was used to being roused in the night, but it was always prompted by the ringing telephone. "Baby?" He rubbed harder until she began to make a little whining noise. "Honey, I'm going to go out for a while."

She opened her eyes and looked at him. "You okay?" she asked, her voice clear.

"Yeah, but we've been having trouble down by the train tracks, and I'm worried about York and those guys."

"They can take care of themselves," she said, and reached an arm around him. He slid down the bed and she fit snugly into the space that God had made for woman next to man, under his arm, her soft hair on his chest.

"I can't sleep," he said.

"Want to make love?"

"I think I better go check on those guys. Travis and the mayor are up to something, and I don't like the sound of it."

Athena's muscles tensed a little bit as she came more into awareness. "Maggie Sweeney's son Chris hangs down there a lot, and it worries her."

"I used to hang down there a lot," Steve said.

"I know, but I think Chris is more . . . malleable, maybe. More easily influenced than you were."

Steve doubted that.

"Anyway, she's going to get up a petition or something to get those guys out of there."

"Well, that's the way to do it. Nice and legal and safe. York needs to go to a place where he can get medical care." He moved her arm away. "Anyway, I'm going to take a run down there."

"Hurry back," she said.

"Okay," he said and kissed her cheek.

Everything was quiet when he got to Yorktown, but it looked as though there was a little town meeting going on. The fire was blazing in the drizzling rain and he could see people sitting up around it. He donned his rain slicker and carefully walked down the hill toward them. For a moment he felt like a little boy again. He wished he could be Chris Sweeney, young and innocent, trying to figure out what made a man a man. At forty-six, Steve Goddard wasn't old, but he felt creaky and jaded. And he hated like hell to do what he felt he had to do.

"Guys," he announced as he tripped down the path.

"Sheriff," Sly said, jumping up and throwing off the sheet of polyurethane that he'd wrapped around himself. "Travis was just here with railroad guys and baseball bats. They gave us until tomorrow night to be gone, or they'd be back to beat us all to death. Isn't there something you can do about that?"

Steve wasn't surprised to hear it, but he was saddened just the same. Tomorrow night. Next to Denny sat Clover, who sat next to York. They all shared a plastic sheet over their heads. "Miss Clover, now what are you doing here at two o'clock in the morning?"

"I'm going to take York to social services in the morning, Sheriff," she said.

Steve nodded. If York were safely out of the way, well then Denny and Sly could do whatever they wanted to. It might be best if they went back on the road and settled someplace else. "You okay with that, York?"

"Hell, no, he's not okay with that," Sly said. "York in some old fools' home? Can you see it, Sheriff? Huh? Can you see it? He'll die of suffocation in a week. York needs to live out here with us."

"York?" Steve said again.

"I'm old," York said. "Not much fight left, so I'm paying attention to the signs. And they all say to go."

"Ain't there something you can do about Travis, Sheriff?" Denny asked. "He's turned into a goddamned goon." He scuffed his foot in the dust and then spit. "Goddamned goon."

"I'll handle the deputy," Sheriff Goddard said. "You just make sure you don't give him reason."

"Gonna handle the railroad guys, too?" Denny asked.

Steve Goddard looked at the little group around their little campfire in the night, the stars breaking through the clouds in the dark black night, the train tracks behind. *The moon ought to be coming out of the clouds soon,* he thought. *Another full moon and here I am, witnessing the end of an era. Wild things become extinct because civilization encroaches. It's a cryin' shame.* "C'mon,

Clover, I'll take you home."

Clover stood and dusted off the back of her jeans.

"The rest of you ought to get a little sleep," he said. "Looks like the rain is stopping. Tomorrow might be a big day for all of us."

"Thanks for looking in on us, Sheriff," York said. "Good night, Miss Clover."

"Good night, guys," she said. "York."

The men chimed their good-byes, and Steve walked Clover up to his truck. *Might want to drop her by Eileen's place,* he thought. *Clover needs to have a chat with her mother.* The hour was late, but knowing Eileen, she'd be up. She'd be up getting ready for work, if she had even been to bed.

"Don't be wasting your life," he said as they got their seat belts buckled and he started up the truck.

"I know," she said. "But, Sheriff, they need somebody to look after them. You know they do."

"Yes, honey, I know that, and everybody knows the contribution you make to their health and well-being, but it doesn't have to be you. There are agencies for that type of thing."

"Useless," Clover said and crossed her arms over her chest.

"I'm worried about you and that Denny," Steve said. "You're not going to go and do something stupid, are you?"

"Like what, get pregnant like my mama?" She snorted. "I don't think so."

"He's not the settling-down type, Clover," Steve said, feeling like a father. It was a good feeling. He and Athena should have had a few more kids. Maybe they'd have had a little girl. "You need yourself a good man who will treat you right and feed and clothe and educate your babies."

"I know," she said, sounding a little petulant. "He tells me that all the time. But I'm young. I've got time. I can devote some money and some energy to those poor guys down there. I don't need no husband and family just yet. Hey, where are we going?"

"Thought I'd drive by your mom's place, see if she's up to talking with you about this whole mess."

Clover snorted again. "I don't need her advice. Look at her. Who'd take advice from her?"

Deputy Travis, that's who, Steve thought as the deputy's muscle car came into view, parked big as day, right in front of Eileen's trailer. A quick glance at Clover showed him that she was looking at her hands, and he made a quick U-turn.

"What?"

"It's too late to be knocking on anybody's door. I wasn't thinking."

"Good. I'd just as soon go home."

"Working tomorrow?"

"Day off. You?"

"I work all the time."

He pulled up in front of her house, cut the lights, put the truck in park and turned toward her. "It's not going to be pretty down there, Clover. The railroad doesn't want the boys down there anymore, and the mayor is going to see to it that all evidence of their camp is erased, and soon. Please steer clear, okay?"

"York . . ."

"I know, and I think it's wonderful that you're going to take York in to social services tomorrow. But then let things shake out as they will, okay? Sly and Denny will probably go on down the line a bit, and that'll be good for everybody."

He heard the ragged breath she took, but didn't back down in the face of female emotion. "I want you to promise me, Clover. Let those guys do whatever they will. It's time you started thinking about Bonita Community College anyway, and putting your extra time and money to better use."

She nodded, and wiped her face, then opened the truck door and hopped out. He waited, watching in the dark, until she disappeared into her dark cottage, then he put the truck in gear, turned on the headlights, and slowly idled into the street and back toward his warm bed and his willing wife.

York had just settled down on his rearranged and soaking-wet couch cushions, wondering if he'd be sleeping in a real bed the following night, one with sheets and a pillow. He wondered if he'd be taking a regular bath and eating regular meals. Maybe he could get some spectacles of some sort that would help him see, and maybe he could get himself some better store-bought teeth. There was no use in dreading the future, he'd learned long ago. The good lord had a strange plan in mind for everybody, and it was best to just go along with it. Fighting the lord never got nobody anywhere.

Denny was still rustling his Walmart bags or something, and Sly was muttering to himself some type of obscenities, when York heard footsteps on the train tracks. He listened quietly. Coyote, probably.

"York?"

It was Chris, whispering too loudly.

"You better get on home, Chris," York said.

"Can't," Chris said. "My mom threw me out."

York sat up. "What?"

"I've got no place to go, York. I thought I'd stay with you tonight."

"You know what's going on here?"

"Yeah," Chris said. "I heard." He sat on the end of York's cushions and lit up a cigarette. York heard the strike of the match, smelled the sulphur, heard the inhale, heard the burn of the tobacco as the fire consumed it, then smelled the smoke on the wind as Chris breathed it out.

"Smoking get you kicked out of home?" he asked.

"Partly, I guess."

"School?"

"Stupid. I stopped going."

"That's what's stupid, Chris," York said.

"I thought you'd understand. I thought you would be the one person who didn't judge me."

"I'm not judging you, I'm judging your actions, and they're stupid. Dropping out of high school is just plain dumb. Smoking will ruin your health. You want to do something good in your life? Quit smoking, go back to school, become a productive member of society. Hanging out in places like this isn't good for a kid."

"What about you, York?"

"I'm not the brightest pup in the basket, boy, and neither are the others who hang out down here. But you are. You're a smart kid with a good brain. You've just got a little teenage rebellion, is all. You could have a wonderful future. You could be rich. You could have beautiful women looking at you all the time, but not if you're down here. Look at us. We're bums, and we're getting throwed out of here tomorrow. They'll put me into one a them places where I'll have to pray and sing gospel for my food, and who knows what'll happen to Denny and Sly. What's the attraction, anyway?"

"I like you guys. I like your freedoms."

"Ha! Freedoms. Listen to me, boy. Freedom is where you can do what you want, and you know who has freedoms? Those with money. We've got no freedoms down here. We can't go anywhere, or do anything. I can't get to a doctor; I can barely get to the post office to pick up my disability check. We don't have freedoms, Chris, and don't you ever forget that. Education buys you freedom. You go on back to school now, and you make something of yourself."

"Can I stay here the night?"

"You going back to school tomorrow?"

"Maybe."

"Well, that's better than a no," York said. "I think there's some extra blankets under a tarp over there by Sly. Help yourself."

The boy rustled around until he was settled, but York's blood was hot and getting hotter. "You'd have to be a lunatic to want to live this kind of life, boy. It's nothing but heartache and more heartache." He felt his fists ball up and the sandy grit grind between his toes, and he felt a scowl etch itself into his face so deep it would probably be permanent. "You go on back to school, and you go on back to your mama, and you go on back to church and make something good of yourself."

"You wish you had?" the boy whispered in the dark.

"We all have our paths," York replied.

Soon he heard a little snuffling, and he knew the boy was crying for his youth, even though it was not yet lost.

I ought to be the one cryin', York thought. *But cryin' only fixes things for women and little kids. Cryin' never did a damn thing for a grown man.*

York lay quietly listening to the rustle of the breeze in the weeds, listened to the boy trying to disguise his heartbreaking confusion, listened to the voice of the moon that seemed to call him. He listened to the blood run in his veins, pumped there strongly by a case of righteous indignation that initiated the squeeze of his tired, old worn-out heart. He felt the flush on the inside of his face, felt the cool of the moon on the outside of it, and he tried to put all other feelings and emotions aside and concentrate on what it was that the moon was trying to tell him.

Instead, he kept hearing his own words over and over again. "We all have our paths," he'd said to the boy. *We all have our paths.* Including, presumably, Deputy Travis and the railroad guys.

And just exactly what is my path? York wondered. He thought he'd known, all these years, being out here, ministering to lost souls, but to end up in an old-folks' home run by county money just didn't sound right. The good lord always seemed to provide for York's minimal needs, and while he thought this nursing home nonsense could be just a little bit more of the same, he couldn't reconcile himself to that thought. *If the lord was going to put me inside,* he thought, *he'da done it long ago.*

Then again, maybe paths change. Maybe he was to be outside with the lost ones, with the travelers, the wanderers, and to learn his trade. Maybe now he was to be inside with the sick ones, the old ones, those ready to meet their maker.

Nope, he thought. *It ain't true. That ain't the way. That is not where my path lies, and that is not the path I will tread.*

"God," he whispered out loud, "my work is too important here. You know it and I know it, and I ask that you look out after us and help us find a way to keep this ministry afloat. There's evil people in this whereabouts, Lord, and while I don't want to fight them, I will, if that's what you've got in store for me. Me, and Sly, and Denny and Miss Clover, and maybe this here Chris, too, and the sheriff, if he's the good-hearted man I believe he is. Draw them all to our side, Lord, and help us find a way. I believe with all my heart and soul that this is your will. If it is not, then tell me now, or tell me soon, before we all make fools of ourselves or end up in jail."

"You mean it, York?" Sly's voice came across crisp and clear.

"I'll look out after them, God, and keep them all in line. Nobody's going to get hurt, but we will fight, if that's what you want, because that sure is what I want. I'm too old to end up in some bedpan place. Let me die out here in my own hometown, please, Lord."

"You ain't never gonna die, York," Sly said.

York tried to concentrate to hear God's message back—he always tried to hear the answer to his prayers, but by the time Sly disentangled himself from his bedding, and Chris sat up, sniffling and wiping his nose and eyes on his shirt sleeves, and then Denny was banging on the coffeepot, trying to fit the dented lid back on the caved-in body after it had taken such a heroic whack from a ball bat, York couldn't concentrate on any message that might be coming through from above.

"What are you doing?" he asked.

"There's no time for sleeping now," Sly said. "We've got work to do. Strategy to plan."

"We're going to kick ass," Denny said. "And this is to help us," he said, laying something on York's stomach.

It was a box. York sat up, smelling the coffee as Sly threw a handful in the pot to boil. He fumbled open the box and inside were a pair of shoes. Tennis shoes. Nice shoes.

"Here, York," Denny said, and handed him a fresh pair of socks, still with the sticky paper wrapper around them.

"Thanks, son," York said, touched by the gesture. "I'd surely like to bathe before putting these on."

"No time for that," Sly said. "We've got work to do."

"Can I stay?" Chris said.

"Shit, yeah," Sly said. "We need foot soldiers. Cannon fodder. Ha!"

York wasn't entirely certain that foot soldiers or cannon fodder was what they needed, but he let Denny take off his old boots and socks and wipe his feet clean. Sometimes the girl helped him to the Mission where he took a bath, and when that happened, she found him some fresh clothes, shaved him, trimmed his toenails and such. He reckoned that wasn't more than two weeks ago, so he was okay with putting on some new socks and the new shoes. And they felt good on his feet. Felt gooood on his feet. He wanted to walk around, but figured that could wait. For now, he was content to wiggle his toes inside fresh cotton and a nice cozy envelope of fresh shoes. They even smelled fresh.

"Fine gift, Denny," he said.

"Compliments of the dead guy," Denny said. "Sort of."

Third Day of the Full Moon

The last thing Steve Goddard wanted to see so early in the morning, before he'd finished his first complete cup of coffee, was the insolent face of his deputy. What he had to say, however, couldn't wait even a half hour.

"Listen to me," Sheriff Steve Goddard said to Travis's smug face, "I don't care who you sleep with on your time off, and I don't care who you do so-called security work for on your time off, but you goddamn well better remember that you're a deputy of the West Wheaton police force twenty-four goddamn hours a day, which carries with it a certain moral responsibility."

Travis didn't flinch.

"You want to tell me you're in love with Eileen in her broken-down trailer, I'll believe you."

Travis scowled.

"What the hell was all that with the ball bats?"

Travis's scowl deepened. He fingered the fraying top of the desk chair he stood behind.

"One more report of you acting like a thug, Travis, and you're gone."

Travis nodded.

"You can go work for the mayor."

Travis nodded.

"I'm serious."

Travis nodded. "That all?"

Sheriff Goddard looked at the dumb young buck he had for a

deputy. They were all wasted words. Every one of them. "Yeah," he said.

Travis opened the office door and there stood Clover, looking particularly dainty in a little yellow flowered cotton dress that looked new. Sheriff Goddard was surprised and pleased that he had not spoken ill of the girl's mother in a loud enough voice that could carry beyond the door. "Miss Clover," he said.

The girl stepped gingerly out of Travis's path, not looking up at his face, keeping her eyes on the sheriff. "Please come in," he said, then edged Travis out the door and shut it behind him.

Clover nervously looked around. Steve pulled out the chair Travis had been fraying and she sat immediately and lightly on the edge of the seat. "How can I help you?"

"York's not going," she said simply. "I thought I ought to come and tell you before . . ." She cocked her head in the direction of Travis, whose shadow could still be seen standing next to the frosted-glass door. He was listening.

"You did right," Steve said. "What's York saying?"

"No reason for him to go. His ministry—you know—the usual."

Steve nodded. He'd heard it before. "How set is he?"

"Real set," she said, "but I don't know about his health, Sheriff."

"I know. That's a concern to all of us."

"Anyways, he told me this morning that he ain't going, and he said that you'd understand more than anybody."

Steve nodded. "He's right. Unfortunately, I'm in the middle here. If it were up to me, I'd just give York that property and wish him well for the rest of his days. Unfortunately, that isn't the case."

"They'll fight," Clover said.

"York said that?"

"Sly did. Just now. York didn't argue."

Fight, Steve thought. *What the hell does that mean? What do those three guys think they can do against the police department, the railroad and the mayor's office?* "Thanks for coming by, Clover. I appreciate this advance notice. It gives me a little negotiation leverage."

"Don't let them get hurt, okay? They're just guys. They're good guys. Just . . . misguided."

"Nobody's going to get hurt," Steve said, and ushered her out of the office and around Deputy Travis, who stood steadfastly in their way and tried to make eye contact with Clover as they maneuvered around him.

Clover didn't fall for it, but he caught Steve's stern eye, put his tail between his legs, and went to his desk.

Steve saw Clover to the door, then went back into his office and closed the door.

Kee-rist, he thought. *There's going to be a goddamn international incident over this.* He ran his fingers through his hair and tugged hard. Then he stood up, grabbed his hat and went down to try to talk some sense into the boys.

Mayor Milo Grimes shook his head as he read the newspaper account of the murder down by the train tracks. He clicked his tongue as if he were scandalized by the news, the clicking mostly for the edification of his wife and daughter. "We're going to clean up that eyesore," he announced.

"What eyesore, honey?" his wife, the fit, coiffed, manicured, pedicured, tanned, tennised and frequently massaged Susie Marie, asked.

"The hobo dump by the tracks," Milo said. "Now there's been a murder down there."

"Animals," Susie Marie pronounced. "Are you coming to the club this afternoon?"

"I've got a late meeting," Milo said.

Susie Marie pouted. "You haven't been to the club with me in over a month, Milo. You're ignoring your constituents."

"This weekend," he said as he folded the paper. Then he stuffed the last crust of toast in his mouth, washed it down with the last swallow of cold, over-creamed coffee, and stood up. "Things good for you, Sunshine?" he asked his sullen daughter.

"Fine," she said.

He kissed her on the top of her head, patted his wife's shoulder, and said, "I'll be home late."

"Have a nice day," she said.

Milo knew she'd have a nice day. She'd burden their already-to-the-limit credit cards, then she'd go for a facial and a tanning and a swim and a tennis lesson, maybe a massage, and as soon as she was tight and tan and squeaky clean, she'd fuck some young kid at the club until he couldn't see straight, then she'd come home and make dinner for their daughter.

Of course Milo didn't go to the club anymore; there wasn't a single room there that he could be in or event he could attend without counting at least another half dozen men who'd had his wife. And the list grew on a weekly basis. It was humiliating, but he didn't have time to deal with it. Not yet. An unfaithful spouse was the least of his worries at the moment. She'd get her comeuppance sooner or later, but getting rid of her was going to be a tricky maneuver, so he had to make sure everything was in place beforehand. He couldn't afford—not legally, not financially, not politically—to act in haste in ditching the perfect political wife, whore that she may be.

Nope, he had bigger troubles, and they began with the dead guy by the train tracks and they ended with the easement that the city had granted to the railroad on a ninety-nine-year lease that was up for renegotiation. The land that York was camping on was in limbo, being in no particular jurisdiction at the moment—not the city's, not the railroad's. And the railroad guys were making noises about renegotiating the lease instead of moving the whole line three miles east, and if they did that, then Milo Grimes was in deep shit. Because he had already sold the property to his Golim Corp and, through his Golim Corp, had sold the land to a Japanese development firm for a very handsome profit. Enough to pay for Susie Marie's lifestyle plus.

The environmentalists were all for the railroad moving, of course; turning old train tracks into bike paths was the new green thing to do. It would be a good thing for the city to get that ugly noise of a train out of the middle of town, especially since West Wheaton was too small to warrant a stop. So the train was a noisy nuisance, and it took up valuable real estate, but nobody knew just exactly how valuable besides Milo Grimes, and it was his business to make sure that nobody else found out just exactly how valuable it was, either. He wondered if somehow he could get rid of this problem and the wife problem at the same time.

Hmmm. Now there was an idea, he thought as he climbed out of his Mercedes at City Hall.

"Good morning, Mr. Mayor." Kathleen, his secretary, greeted him as usual, with a warm smile, a hot cup of coffee and a sheaf of pink message slips.

"Those railroad papers ready?" he asked.

"Yes, but the meeting's been cancelled."

"Says who?" He snatched the *While You Were Out* slips from her hand, thunder rolling in his head.

"Mr. Ashton's secretary called about ten minutes ago." She set the coffee cup down on a coaster on his desk.

"Resched?" he asked, shuffling the messages. He couldn't find the one from Ashton, although there were two from Oshiro.

Kathleen shrugged.

"Lease is up the day after tomorrow," Grimes said, looking at her as if she had the answers.

She shrugged again.

"What kind of game is he playing?"

"Raise the rent?" she said as a helpful suggestion.

"Yeah, thanks," he said, *you useless cunt.* "Get him on the phone, willya?"

"Right away." She turned and left, and Grimes couldn't even enjoy the view of her retreating backside. Ashton had to sign off on the renewal so the sale could go through as planned, with a double-escrow closing. That way Golim Corp need never be recorded as an interim owner. The property went directly from the city to Oshiro according to the recorded documents. If there were a delay, or if the railroad decided to renew, Milo Grimes could kiss his ass good-bye.

The intercom buzzed, but instead of answering Katheen, Grimes punched the blinking light. "Mr. Ashton!" he said, too loudly, too brightly.

"No, Milo, it's Steve Goddard."

Shit. Grimes looked at the phone and then at his office door as if both AT&T and Kathleen were in traitorous league, determined to ruin him. "What's up?"

"Two things. The first is that the ID on the dead guy is a Wayne Haas—two a's—most recently of Las Vegas. His fingerprints came up as a small-time hood with lots of debt, too many girlfriends and loose, small-time connections to the wrong kind of people. Did time a few years ago for fraud. Coroner hasn't done the autopsy yet, but he's looked the body over. Blunt instrument to the head, multiple fractures and contusions consistent with getting whacked on the head and pushed off a train."

"So?"

"So York and the guys had nothing to do with it."

"Meaning?"

"York's not leaving, Milo, and I don't think we should make him."

"Excuse me?" Grimes felt his blood pressure rise ten percent. "You don't think we should make him? *You don't think?*"

"He's old, Milo. Give him a month and he'll go to the county home of his own accord. The rest will disband, I'm telling you. But if you force him out over this death—"

"You're telling me?" Ten more blood-pressure points. "You don't tell me anything, Sheriff. I tell you. The railroad is about to renegotiate the lease on that piece of city property, and they're reluctant to do it with that little hepatitis breeding ground down there. That lease is very important to the economic security of our town, not to mention your cushy salary, Sheriff. So you just stop telling me what you do or do not think, and start doing what I pay you to do."

"With all due respect—"

"Fine," Grimes said as his face began to fill with superheated blood. "Never mind. *I'll* get that snake pit cleaned up and don't you get pissy about how I do it." He slammed down the phone and then stared at it for a long moment. AT&T *was* out to get him.

He looked at his watch. There's no telling where Deputy Travis was, but he would be the one to fix this problem. Grimes picked up the deceitful telephone and dialed Travis's home. He'd leave an urgent message.

But the machine didn't answer the phone at Travis's house, and neither did the deputy. A woman did, and Milo Grimes would know that beige voice anywhere. "Susie Marie?" he said incredulously.

There was a long pause, a click and a dial tone.

"Goddamn," Milo Grimes said softly and sipped his coffee. He went over the telephone number he'd dialed, and yes, he'd called Travis's house. Milo hadn't dialed his home or her cell phone by mistake. He took a deep breath, sat back in his chair and steepled his hands in front of him. He didn't want this to hurt him, but damn it, it hurt his pride to think that his slutty wife was screwing every young thing in West Wheaton. Didn't she even have enough respect for him to be even a little bit discreet?

Apparently not.

The familiar fantasies of revenge began to float up in his consciousness, but that wasn't good. It wasn't good for business. Revenge had no place in the handbook of politics, marriage, or business. He'd like to take that secretary of his, that Kathleen, with the sweetest little ass he'd ever seen, for a ride until her brains exploded, but that would hardly constitute revenge. That would just be a dead-end fuck. Kathleen would get attached or worse, Grimes would pay the cost somehow, and Susie Marie wouldn't care. Nope, no revenge. Revenge, while it would be sweet to just squeeze the throat of that two-timing little whore of a wife, would be a bad thing for Milo and his future, not to mention his daughter. *No,* he thought, and took a deep breath, *there needs to be a way I can use this information to my advantage. Knowledge is power.*

The problem was, of course, that Susie Marie knew that he knew.

But Deputy Travis didn't, and she wouldn't be the one to tell him. Travis probably wouldn't be able to get it up if he knew that everybody—the mayor in particular—knew he was screwing the city's first lady, and Susie Marie wouldn't want that, not one little bit.

Grimes leaned forward and punched the intercom button. "Kathleen, page Deputy Travis for me, will you?"

If he couldn't interfere with Travis's performance in one way, he'd interfere with it in another. Meanwhile, he and Travis had a secret they could keep together.

"So it turns out," Clover said to Denny, "the railroad doesn't own this land after all. Sly was wrong. They've got a lease on it. It belongs to the city."

"Who cares?"

"Listen, this is important," she said, and smoothed her new dress down over her knees. "The city can't throw you off land that is leased by the railroad. It's like the city coming in and throwing somebody out of your apartment. They can't do it. It's your apartment, and you can have whoever you want in it. The railroad has to evict you."

"So we don't have to worry about Deputy Dawg? He was here with railroad guys, though, those were the ones with the ball bats." Denny leaned in close and whispered, "You look so good in that dress that I can almost taste you."

Clover pushed him away.

"How do you know this, Clover?" York said. He splashed more coffee into his broken, handleless mug.

"I went back to city hall to look up the records. If we're going to fight, we have to know who we're fighting. Or who to negotiate with. And it isn't the sheriff, or the mayor, or the railroad goons, because the lease on the land is up tomorrow and it hasn't been renegotiated yet. At least the new lease hasn't been filed in court."

"I don't know if that's good," Sly said, wearing a brand-new teal golf shirt. "The enemy is camouflaged and can snipe from a tree at two hundred yards."

"It's very good," York said. "It means that the sheriff has to protect us from violence."

"There's no protection from violence," Sly said. "You have to report the violence after it happens in order for the police to do something. They provide no protection at all."

"He's right," Denny said, wearing a new shirt, new jeans, new socks, new shoes, and new leopard-print underwear that he intended to show Clover right soon. Sooner than soon, if she didn't stop looking so adorable. The dress he picked out for her was perfect. Absolutely perfect. He was very proud of his shopping excursion. Everybody looked spiffy.

"I want no violence," York said.

"That part won't be up to you," Sly said. "Those who are violent, that's their way. So listen, I have a plan. And it means we need another of those slingshots, Denny. Maybe two more, if Clover will work with one."

"Back to Walmart," Denny said. "No problem."

"Self-defense, York," Sly said. "We're not attacking anybody. We're just living here."

York nodded, then lay back on his cushions and turned his face away from them. The meeting was over. Everybody had their assignments: Clover had to put out, Denny had to steal two more slingshots and the shot that went with them, Sly had to devise the strategy, and York had to reconcile himself to the whole ugly business. Nobody had an easy job, except maybe for Clover.

"Who was on the phone?" Travis asked as he stepped out of the steamy bathroom, a dingy towel around his waist.

"Telemarketer."

"You shouldn't answer the phone," he said as he adjusted the volume on his radio. "I'm supposed to be patrolling."

"I've got something for you to patrol," Susie Marie said, then opened her legs and showed him that she wasn't wearing panties under her short tennis skirt.

"Ain't that pretty," Travis said, and pulled off his towel. "Makes my tongue hard."

"Clearly that's not all it makes hard," Susie Marie said with a giggle, then lay back on her elbows and shimmied out of her skirt. Travis picked up a pretty pedicured foot and kissed the arch, then slid his lips up her calf, up her thigh. "I love giving you these tennis lessons," he whispered. They locked eyes, for a moment. He loved the way she looked in heat. Lips slightly parted, brow slightly furrowed, thousand-yard stare. He palmed her fur and began to massage in slow circles.

She collapsed backward onto the bed.

"Gimme those tits," he said, and she began to unbutton her cotton blouse, exposing erect nipples that pushed hard against expensive lace.

"Good," he said, and kept his eye on them as he licked his lips and made himself ready to send her into the zone.

Then his pager began to beep.

Susie Marie gasped and slammed her legs closed.

"What?" he said, irritated at the interruption. "Come back here." He parted her knees and kissed her belly. "Come to me," he whispered. "Come for me."

The pager beeped again.

Susie Marie rolled away from him, right to the edge of the bed, sat up and began buttoning her blouse.

"Hey," he said.

"I can't concentrate with that damned thing going off all the time," she said.

He looked down at his zinging erection and wondered if she'd at least give it a little good-bye kiss.

She stood up and grabbed her skirt.

Guess not. He gave it a sorrowful mental farewell, got up and walked to his pants that had been flung over the chair. He fumbled for the pager that was hooked to his belt.

The mayor's office.

Travis wasn't very smart, but neither was he stupid. "The

phone," he said.

She zipped her skirt and sat in the chair, on top of his uniform pants, to put on her tennis shoes.

He grabbed her wrist. "He called here and you answered the phone."

"Let go of me," she said.

"Fuck," Travis said, and sat down hard on the bed. "I'm screwed."

"He doesn't care," Susie Marie said as she stood up and finger-combed her hair.

"I care," Travis said.

"Fuck you," she said, grabbed her purse and walked out, leaving him feeling very naked indeed.

After a few minutes, the pager sounded again. Travis picked up the phone and dialed the mayor's private number. He hoped there was a chance the mayor hadn't recognized his own wife's voice. Fat chance.

Regardless, there was no place for Travis to hide, so he listened to the phone ring, his heart hammering.

Luckily, the mayor had other things on his mind. Things that interested Travis—maybe not as much as pussy—but coming in a close second. And when they hung up, Travis was almost convinced that the mayor knew nothing about Travis's involvement with his slutty wife.

Whew. Close call, Travis thought, and began to dress.

Morning drive-time radio woke Brenda. She cracked an eye at the clock and knew that work was not for her today. She was too depressed.

She slapped the snooze alarm and picked up the telephone. Nobody would be in yet—she could call in sick and leave word on their answering machine.

"This is Brenda," she said after the beep, her voice sounded husky with sleep, but could be mistaken for sick. "I've got a skull-crunching migraine so I won't be in. I'm unplugging the phone and going back to bed. I'll be in tomorrow." Her voice sounded convincing, she had to admit.

Not even the prospect of a day off raised her spirits. She even had second thoughts. If she stayed home, she'd likely mope and cry and eat ice cream. If she went to work, she might mope, cry, eat less and come away with a paycheck to boot.

Too late.

The radio clicked on again with an advertisement for Gretta's, West Wheaton's finest family restaurant, specializing in homemade pies and trucker-sized breakfasts.

A trucker-sized breakfast was exactly what she needed, Brenda decided, and hauled herself out of bed.

An hour later, she had the morning paper. And since the place was packed—due in large part, she imagined, to their advertising agency—Brenda sat at the counter.

Just as Brenda got her first cup of coffee, the man next to her departed, and a lone woman took his still-warm stool a moment later. She smiled tentatively at Brenda. Brenda smiled back. This woman looked tired. She looked more than tired, she looked worn out.

Someone worse off than me, Brenda thought. *Now that's a comfort.* "Share the morning paper?" she offered.

The woman smiled again and shook her head in polite refusal. "Too tired to read," she said. "Coffee, food, bed. Just got off work."

"Oh," Brenda said. "I just called in sick. Coffee, food, and something to keep me from slitting my wrists."

The other woman stared at her and then they both laughed. "I'm Eileen," the woman said and held out her hand.

Brenda shook it. It was hard to fix an age on Eileen with her makeup, dyed hair, and pucker wrinkles from smoking, but she guessed Eileen wasn't a whole lot older than she was.

"I work in the bakery," Eileen explained. "Three to ten. I took off early today. I'm beat."

"You start at three o'clock in the *morning?*" Many times, Brenda wasn't even in bed yet by three A.M.

Eileen gave her a wry smile in return.

They each ordered hearty breakfasts, and Brenda perused the front page while Eileen sat hunched over her coffee. When the food came, Brenda, feeling more hungry for companionship than eggs, sausage, home fries, wheat toast and apple sauce, spoke again. "What is it, do you suppose, with men?"

Eileen barked a harsh laugh as she spread marmalade on her toast. "If you expect nothing, you'll never be disappointed."

"I get disappointed anyway," Brenda said and popped her yolks.

"Yeah," Eileen said. "Me, too."

They ate in companionable silence, two discouraged women taking comfort in the fact that they were not alone, if even for a half hour. When finished, Eileen pushed her plate away and pulled her coffee closer. "I'm regenerated," she said.

"Want to do something?" Brenda asked. "The day looms . . . empty."

"Sure."

The two women paid their tabs and then walked out of the diner and into the hot West Wheaton sun. As if choreographed, they both reached into their purses and put on their sunglasses. Brenda, apparently leading, turned uptown and Eileen followed. "So," Brenda said. "Tell me the latest with your man."

"He's not my man," Eileen said. "That's the problem."

Boy, Brenda knew that one.

"He's too young, and I'm too old, but the sex is great. What about you?"

"Well, at least you get great sex. I don't even get that. I met a great guy, I mean a really great guy, but he has a girlfriend. I can't get him out of my head, though."

"Forget him."

"Yeah." Brenda stopped and shaded her eyes as she looked into the front window of the town's priciest shoe store. "Cute, those strappy little sandals."

Eileen agreed. "I haven't bought cute shoes in years."

"Yeah," Brenda said. "Me, neither."

"I think the guy I'm screwing has the hots for my daughter," Eileen said, then turned her head and kept walking uptown.

Brenda jogged a couple of steps to catch up.

"He's all wrong for me, and he doesn't treat me very well, but it's like I'm addicted to him. When he's touching me, when he wants me, I feel like the queen of the universe. Then when it's over, I feel dirty again."

"Give him up, Eileen. You can do better."

"Yeah," she said, and sniffed.

"In fact," Brenda said, "having nothing is better than having that."

"Yeah." Eileen pulled a wadded-up donut-shop napkin from her purse and blew her nose, but kept walking.

Brenda realized the truth of her words. Having nothing was better than having that. Forget Denny, she told herself. Having nothing was better than having him. He's too young, and he wouldn't know how to treat me right. *And* he's spoken for.

But like Eileen, Brenda knew she had all that stuff straight in her head, but not in her heart. She couldn't wait to run into Denny again. She just wanted to take a look into his eyes, to make certain that there was nothing there, that there could be nothing there. He was her only hope for a boyfriend, and that made her sound and feel desperate and horrible. But at least she hadn't had sex with him. Jeez, poor Eileen. She was stuck on this guy, and it was all the worse because she couldn't keep her hands off him. And he was too chicken shit to cut her loose. She knew that kind of guy. She hated that kind of guy, the kind that wasted a girl's life, using his empty promises that came sometimes with and sometimes without words.

They walked on uptown, but the day stretched before them, like the vast empty warehouses of the future.

Sly felt the trouble coming on inside his head, but thought that this time he could control it. He knew it was because of the dead guy. Seeing another dead guy after all these years brought memories up to play on the inside back of his skull, and they weren't good memories. Dead guys and weapons. He pulled the slingshot out of his back pocket and put it in his hand, metal resting on his wrist. He pinched the leather and pulled back on the surgical tubing, aiming it at an exploded thistle head. He let go, the tubing snapped with a satisfying sound, and before he could stop himself, he said, not loud, but loud enough to wake York, "Take that, you gook."

And the fire in him continued to rise. He felt it, and didn't like it, but he knew that soon he would start to like it and then the trouble would start.

"You okay, Sly?" York asked.

York knew. York knew everything. Sly looked over at York and wondered if he'd take a bullet for York, or if York would take a bullet for him. Maybe. Maybe not. Hard to figure the allies when they're not wearing the proper uniforms. "Yeah," he said in answer.

"You out of money?"

"Yeah," Sly said. He knew what York was saying. That if he got a job and got some pride going again, he could maybe stop the trouble before it started. But that wasn't how he felt at the moment. He would much rather have those railroad guys come on down and try to evict them.

"Maybe you could go get me some kind of tomato juice?"

"Tomato juice?"

"Yeah. Got a hankerin'."

"Okay." Sly stuck his slingshot under his bedding and walked up the path toward town. Tomato juice. He wondered if they'd have anything like that over at the mission. He could use a shower, too, while he was out. Clean body, clean mind, clean kill.

There was a new guy at the front desk of the mission, and he wanted to give Sly a hard time, but Sly was in no mood, and it didn't take long for the guy to figure that out. "All I want," Sly said, slow and careful, "is to take a shower and get some tomato juice. That's it. Now just exactly what the fuck is your objection to any of that?"

"None," the guy said, and Sly walked on by him, grabbed a clean towel off the pile and headed for the showers.

But what he saw in the mirror caught him up short. He saw his father. Sly hadn't seen his father in thirty years, but he saw him right there in the mission mirror, wearing that polo shirt with the multi-colored shark embroidered on it. His hair was long and greasy stringy and gray, and his beard was out of control, and his teeth were going, but it was his father, no question. No doubt about those being the haunted eyes of Sylvester's dad.

Sly wanted to rip his eyeballs out. Instead, he got a firm grip on his emotions. *Save it,* he told himself. *You'll need all that later on tonight.* Then he stripped down and stepped into a steamy shower. He used a fresh razor blade from the box and gave himself a shave, then took a pair of scissors and a clean comb and whacked off his hair. The cut was uneven, probably especially the back, but at least it was short and it would be another year or so before he'd need another haircut. All the while, he avoided looking at his own eyes.

Then he brushed his teeth with a new toothbrush out of the box, and when he was fresh and clean from top to bottom, he looked at himself in the mirror.

He had become his father. He had become the man he hated.

The trouble was seeping closer, Sly could smell it. But it was still far enough off that he remembered York's tomato juice, snagged a can of it from the kitchen, and left the mission. He tightened his right fist over and over again, liking how his muscles and tendons looked when they were tense. He liked the feel of the tension. He wanted to hit something. He wanted to hurt, to punch, to smack, to damage.

He was ready for a kill.

Denny came home while Sly was gone, to find York shredding newspaper. York shredded newspaper into his lap when he worried about something, and he had a fair pile going over his knees.

Denny's head hurt like he never believed a head could hurt. That pool-cue crack had probably done some permanent damage inside. When he looked at anything light colored or shiny, he thought his eyes would explode. If he moved his head too fast, he thought he was going to throw up. Every step down the path made his teeth jar, and with every jar of the teeth, someone took a sledgehammer to the back of his head. He just wanted to give York the things he'd stolen from Walmart, then lie down and die.

But that wasn't going to happen, because York was shredding newspaper. That worried Denny a lot more than any railroad goons. When York wasn't right, the world wasn't right, and York clearly wasn't right.

"York?" he said, then emptied his pants of stolen booty.

"Sly's in trouble," York said, and the way he said it, Denny knew exactly the type of trouble he meant. It had been a long time. A long time they had lived in peace and quiet down there by the tracks, but the combination of dead guy, railroad hassling—and probably the full moon, if York's theories held true—added up to something about to spurt, and of course it had to be Sly.

Denny had never actually seen Sly be the legendary way he got, but he'd heard, and what he'd heard hadn't been good.

"My head hurts, York," Denny said.

York just reached for another sheet of newspaper and began tearing it into long strips.

"Where is Sly?"

"Gone to get me some tomato juice."

"How do you know he's in trouble?"

"I can sense it, is all. He needs us now. He needs to know he can count on us."

"Shit. He knows that." Denny saw shooting lights when he spoke.

"He needs to be reassured."

"Okay," Denny said, and then lay down on his blanket and put a new, clean pair of socks over his eyes to block out the light. In spite of the pain in his head, he liked the store-bought smell of those clean, new socks. He wished it was evening. The sun was hot and blazing down at him from directly above. That didn't help the sickening pounding in his skull. "Got any aspirin?" he asked, but York didn't answer. Clover would be the one with aspirin, not York. York didn't have anything. *Jesus Christ,* Denny thought to himself as he squinted at a new round of poundings. *I'd sell my soul for a couple of aspirin.* It was even worse than before, now that the world was dark and silent and he could see and hear the pain more clearly.

He lay as still as possible, feeling his head rock with every beat of his heart, and wished he was lying naked on some suede sofa in a cool, dark room with a beer in his hand and his head in Clover's lap, while she played with his hair. If he concentrated, maybe he could get himself there. He almost could, if it weren't for the sound of newspaper being ripped into strips.

At the moment, dying seemed like a step in the right direction.

York kept his fingers busy while he tried to think of himself as a resident of an old-folks' home. Could be that the good lord was thinking it was time for York to spread out with his ministry. There would be more people to reach in a place like that than there were here in the weeds. Personally, he thought that those who came down to the train tracks needed his particular type of ministry more than those who lived Christian lives and ended up brainless and tended, but it was not up to him to judge who were the spiritually thirsty. He'd go to a home if God wanted him to, and it appeared as if that's exactly what God wanted.

There would be no fighting the railroad guys and the mayor. Denny was down for the count, Sly was missing in action, Clover, bless her heart, was off doing girlie things, exactly the way she ought to be doing them, and York felt as though a regular bath and regular meals and maybe a little arthritis medicine now and then might do him some good. Yep, perhaps it was time for York to retire.

But he didn't want to. He'd still stand fast; he wouldn't go willingly. They'd have to take him by force, but he wouldn't resist much. He took another Sunday edition off the stack of brittle newspapers that served as a wall around his room and flopped it into his lap. It was damp from soaking up years of winter rain and smelled wonderfully moldy. He began to shred the pieces that didn't either crumble or crisp in his hands. He'd miss that smell.

He tried not to think about Ed, and what would happen to him if he didn't have a safe haven every now and then, and of

Chris, and all the other young'uns who needed his type of direction. He could see Ed, too drunk to get up some hot California morning, dried to a husk by afternoon. He could see Chris messing with drugs, messing with those fast girls looking for babies, messing with crime and police and a continual stream of jail cells.

And Sly? Well, Sly would move on down the line, and he'd be all right. He'd keep doing what he'd been doing all his life, being angry at everything, and that anger would see him through. Denny, too, always seemed to be able to land on his feet. Clover had a good head on her shoulders. No, it wasn't the home team that York fretted over. It was those faceless, nameless ones the lord steered his way who needed his old-fashioned talk. And he needed them.

That was the bad part.

"Hey, York?" Denny's voice cut through the noisy daytime silence.

"Yeah?"

"Who do you suppose killed the dead guy, anyway?"

Good question. "Don't know," York said, and got busy again with the shredding the newspapers. Who killed that dead guy and why? And why weren't the cops looking in that direction instead of at them?

Good questions. Very good questions.

"And now," Milo Grimes said to the shamefaced deputy standing in front of him, "if you think you can keep your dick in your pants for the next ten minutes, we've got some things to talk about." Grimes enjoyed making this little weasel squirm. He had use for him, and when this ugly situation was complete, he'd dispose of the worm. It would be his great pleasure. Maybe he'd put paid to both this little creep and Susie Marie both. Together. The thought made his lips draw up in exquisite distaste, and he had to clamp down on his emotions in order to deal with the task at hand. "Okay now," he said to Travis. "Sit down and listen very carefully to what I have to say. If things go well, they go very well for you, understand?"

Travis didn't, but he nodded. He was amazed he still had a job. He was amazed he still had his balls. At the moment, he couldn't think that anything could ever go better for him than to sit in front of the mayor, career and body still intact, and with the taste of Susie Marie still on his tongue.

And then he started to get the gist of what the mayor was asking of him. Not in plain English, of course, that wasn't his style, because that would be prosecutable. No, what the mayor was asking was far worse, and would leave him holding the bag.

The mayor stopped talking and looked at him, and Travis realized he was waiting for an answer. The answer was going to have to be either yes or no. The answer was either going to be to save his job and jeopardize his soul and trust that the mayor wouldn't blow the whistle and send him to prison for the rest of his sorry life, or to clear out with a black mark on his record and his tail between his legs.

Then the mayor smiled at him, and like the dog that wagged his tail as it gulped down poisoned meat, he smiled back and nodded.

They shook hands, and Travis left the mayor's office. That's when Travis realized that Mayor Grimes had no reason at all to go to bat for him. Travis couldn't implicate that suck-face Grimes, because he had no proof. Unless and until he could get proof, he'd just let the mayor think he was on his side, but he wasn't about to wear gray for the rest of his life just for screwing that slimeball's tarty wife. Nope, he didn't have to do anything he didn't want to do, he just had to wait until he had a little insurance policy against Grimes selling him out.

And with that decision, Deputy Travis felt in control again.

The day just got a little bit brighter.

He jumped into his cruiser and went to the station to check in with the sheriff.

Clover always sang to her plants when she watered them. She thought they responded positively to the quiet energy. She was pleased about all the baby spider plants that hung down from the mother spider plant. It had grown enormous under her careful tending. She knew she ought to clip the little ones off and let them start lives of their own, but that was hard for her, maybe because she'd rather not have been clipped off her own family. She had a Boston fern that she misted twice a day, and four different-colored Christmas cacti crowded into one big pot that bloomed in glorious profusion every holiday season. On the railing in the back were thirty different cacti, all in identical little terra-cotta pots. Each had a name, each had a personality, each had a flower in its own time. In her bedroom she had a philodendron that snaked across the floor, and in the kitchen, she had an oxalis. A four-leafed clover. The little leaves opened every morning and closed every evening, and it bloomed with little white flowers almost continuously. Clover found many metaphors for life in her plants. Sometimes she pinched them back when they were getting too far ahead of themselves, sometimes she decorated their pots, sometimes she just found comfort in their company. They weren't heartbeats in her little cottage, but they were friends and roommates nevertheless. They certainly communicated in very strong, vivid language. And their needs were uncomplicated.

"You ought to open up a damn plant store," Eileen said as she opened the back door and helped herself in.

"Hi, Mom," Clover said, stroking the leaves of a baby spider descendant and then setting the watering can down in the kitchen sink. "Want a baby spider plant? It'd add a little life to your place." Clover knew that sending one of her babies to her mom's house meant a slow, dehydrating death, but then, maybe not. You never know.

"Nah. I'd just kill it. Plants are meant to be outside, know?"

"Well, you can come over here and enjoy mine anytime."

"Came to show you my new shoes." Eileen hadn't polished her toenails in a month or more, so the bright-red polish was scraped and uneven, and grown out from her cuticles. Her new pink shoes were high-heeled sandals and looked to Clover like torture devices for her feet.

"Are they comfortable?"

"They were on sale." Eileen sat down in a kitchen chair and took them off. "Hell, no, they're not comfortable. I already got a blister, I think." She examined her foot while Clover filled the teakettle and put it on the little stove to heat. "Got any polish?"

Clover fetched clippers, nail file, polish remover, cotton balls and a light-pink nail polish from the bathroom. They sat at the little table in companionable silence and polished their respective toenails. The pink Clover chose was a perfect match for Eileen's new sandals. Then Clover poured them each a cup of tea, took one of her mother's wearied hands and began to file her fingernails.

"I turn forty next week," Eileen said.

"I know."

"My hands look like it."

"You should moisturize them before going to bed."

"What about my face?" Eileen barked a harsh laugh, rummaged for a moment in her purse for a cigarette, then put the pack back inside. Clover didn't allow smoking in her place.

"You should moisturize your face, too."

"You got some moisturizer for my future? Some kind of spot-removing cream? Some kind of a wrinkle remover? Some kind of something magical from the pharmacy that will make me believe, or even pretend that I even *have* a future?"

Clover gripped her mother's fingers tighter to keep her from pulling them away in agitation, and kept filing. "You have a future," she said calmly.

"Yeah," Eileen said, "but it ain't pretty. Especially if it includes pink nail polish."

Clover smiled up at her, and Eileen, in a rare moment of honest affection, smiled back.

"Pink is good. Give me your other hand."

Eileen obeyed, and Clover continued filing.

"Who did you go shopping with?"

"I met somebody in the diner at breakfast. Brenda. I like her. She bought shoes, too, but she bought those ugly cloggy things that are so much in fashion these days."

Brenda? Surely not the same Brenda. "A new friend. That's good."

"Yeah, well, I don't know about that. Maybe. We'll see."

"Know what I'm going to do today?"

"Can't wait to find out."

Clover finished filing, sat back and shook the nail-polish bottle, listening to the BB inside rattle around. She refreshed the hot water in their cups, then took Eileen's left hand and began to paint her nails. "I'm going to find out who killed that guy. The dead guy. The guy who was pushed off the train."

"Oh, baby, don't go there."

"I have to, otherwise York and Denny and those guys will get evicted."

"It's only a matter of time anyway."

"York doesn't have much time. He needs to live out his life down there. If I can figure out who killed that guy, they'd have no reason to move York to a home."

"They don't need a reason, Clover. That place is a nuisance. There are laws."

"They're not doing any harm. If I can solve the murder, the focus will be off them."

"Hey, pink's not bad," Eileen said. "Another ten years and it might come back into fashion."

"Since when are you a slave to fashion?"

"A girl's got to keep up. Especially if she's almost forty."

"Is that bothering you?" Clover regretted the question as soon as she asked it.

"Nah. Be nice to have a man, but I think that train has derailed, speaking of trains and dead guys." Again, the harsh laugh, and Clover had to grip the fingers to hold them still.

She finished the final nail, and screwed the top back on the polish. "Ten minutes and we'll do another coat. Then you can't smoke for two days."

"Why?"

"I don't know. Maybe after two days you wouldn't want a cigarette."

"Brat." Eileen blew on the wet polish.

Clover smiled.

"How are you going to find out who killed that guy?"

"I'm going to start with Deputy Travis," Clover said. "He'll know who the guy is, or was, and I'll just take it from there."

"You're a pistol," Eileen said, and put out her hand for another dose of pink.

Brenda threw the shopping bag with her new shoes in it onto her bed, stripped down to her underwear, brushed her teeth, got a cold beer from the fridge and then flopped on the couch. It was hot and she was tired and feeling a little gritty from her day shopping with Eileen, who didn't seem to need much help feeling gritty.

Brenda rolled the cold can around on her forehead and face, remembering Denny and the pool-cue lump on his forehead, and how he lay right here on her couch and slept. She was heartbroken that he'd gone before she got up in the morning. She was still heartbroken over it, and she wasn't exactly sure why. He wasn't her type; he was a bum who lived down by the tracks. Was it because he already had a girl, and she felt the competitive urge? Was it because she was so desperate that she'd throw her heart at any damaged guy she picked up off a barroom floor?

Or was it because some other, higher, greater force was urging her onward? There were no coincidences in the universe, Brenda was convinced, and the cosmos had thrown her and Denny together in a way that was for some purpose, no matter how small. Maybe it had merely been for her to rescue him. Maybe their purpose wasn't fulfilled yet. She certainly could not get him out of her mind. Maybe she'd have to go down there again and have a chat with him. Maybe she could get him away from his girlfriend for a few minutes.

And then what, Brenda? And then what?

She shrugged. Maybe their destiny had nothing to do with romance or love. Was he the type of guy she'd be happy to bring home to introduce to her mom? Not hardly.

Maybe it was just lust.

Brenda grinned, gave herself a moment to picture being in the shower with Denny, soaping him up from head to toe, his slippery hands all over her, then falling, soaking wet onto her new bedspread for a good, youthful, enthusiastic hump. Then she popped open the beer and took a long, startling drink and shifted her thinking to Eileen. *Man oh man,* Brenda thought, *I don't want to turn out like that.* Eileen was crusty and bitter, with smoker's wrinkles pointing the way to her thin lips. But she was funny and fascinating in kind of a husky-voiced, repulsive way. She had a perspective on life and love and age that was completely foreign to Brenda. They'd never be good friends, but they could probably enjoy each other's company now and then. Like today, for example. They'd found a good shoe sale. Brenda sipped her beer and wondered what outfits she could wear those new shoes with. Not many, but, hey, they'd been a bargain.

She sipped her beer, but her traitorous mind kept sliding back to thoughts of Denny and his lost-little-boy face. He was no bargain, but for some reason, she had to see him again. And now.

Before she could help herself, before she could think it through like she knew she should, before she knew what she was doing, she checked herself in the mirror, briefly and from a distance, slipped back into some comfortable shoes, grabbed her purse and keys, and went outside. Consciously readying herself for whatever she might find, or whatever he might have to say to her, Brenda walked toward Denny as if some internal compass had set her course direction. She had no idea what she was going to say to him when she got there.

She was still working on her opening line when she got down to the head of the path, and met, head-on, a tall, gray-haired man. They made eye contact, and Brenda slowed and stopped, and so did he. It was as if they were each waiting for the other to pass so they could head down the path.

Brenda smiled. "Go ahead," she said.

"I'm going down there," the man said.

"Me, too."

"Why?"

"To see Denny."

The man squinted at her, and Brenda wasn't sure she liked that look, but she looked him squarely back. He looked familiar.

Just as she realized that, he spoke. "You're the one who nursed the whack on his head."

"Yeah," she said.

"I'm Sly," he said.

"I remember you now. You got a haircut. I'm Brenda. Is Denny okay? Sometimes a whack like that can be a problem later."

"C'mon down and let's take a look."

Brenda followed Sly down the path through the blackberries, aware that he kept looking back to make sure she was coming down competently. He must have noticed those ridiculous sandals she'd had on last time. About broke her stupid neck coming down here in those.

"Denny!" Sly bellowed, startling Brenda. "Got company!" It was good, him announcing a visitor. She didn't want to take anybody by surprise. It was always good to call first.

Denny stood up, wavering on his feet, a pair of white socks in his hand. Brenda might have stepped right on him; she didn't even see the camp. It seemed to be sunken into a maze of short walls made of—seemed like bales of newspapers—that made it invisible from far away.

"It's a girl, York," Sly said as he passed the old man, and Brenda stepped into the hardpan ground of their home.

"Brenda," Denny said, wincing. "Hi."

He was in trouble with that whack on the head, Brenda could see that before she got to him. One eye was swollen and almost completely black, and the bump on his head was like an eggplant. "Wow," she said. "You can't be feeling too good."

He sank down to his knees, and then sat back on his bedding. "Nope," he said. "I'm for shit."

"I'll take you to the emergency clinic, if you want," Brenda said, jangling her keys. "They don't charge you if you can't pay."

"Nah."

"You might have, you know, like a cracked skull."

"Nah. I'll be okay. I just need to let it work itself out."

"They'll give you something for the pain," Brenda said. "You must have one splitter of a headache."

Denny nodded. His whole body rocked back and forth with the nodding motion, and then he held his hand out to her, his eyes closed. "Help me up?"

She braced her foot against his, then grabbed his hands and helped him to his feet. He kept his eyes closed, and even so, she saw him wince with the pain of the movement. "I'm taking Denny to a doctor," she announced to nobody, or to everybody, and then he put his arm around her shoulder and they started awkwardly back up the hill on the path that was only wide enough for one. Denny leaned on her heavily, and she wondered if he had his eyes open at all. He was one damaged dog. Brenda congratulated herself on following her instincts. This guy needed to have some medical attention, and right soon.

She successfully pulled them both out of reach of the blackberries that snagged them with every step. When they got to the top of the hill, Brenda turned and looked back down at the train tracks, and there stood Sly, standing hip deep in weeds, or so it appeared, although he was probably standing in what served as his bedroom. He was watching them; he had probably watched them all the way up the path. He looked different to Brenda. He was clean. His hair was freshly cut, his face clean-shaven of those gray whiskers. He looked tall and thin and almost fit. He was almost handsome. If he'd put on a few pounds to fill out his cheeks, it would make his hawkish nose a little less obvious. Then he'd be right nice-looking.

"Watch out for the curb here," she said to Denny. She guided him into the street, then stopped thinking about Sly at all and concentrated on the task at hand.

The emergency clinic wasn't busy and they took Denny right in. Brenda picked at her cuticles, then looked at a few children's magazines, and then paced back and forth for a while. She doubted they'd give him anything more than a Tylenol until they ran a bunch of tests, but that was okay, too. She didn't have anything better to do than wait for him, but she wished she had brought something to read.

Then the nurse opened the door and crooked her finger, and Brenda was ushered into Denny's curtained cubicle, where he sat with a cold pack on his head, warm blankets on the rest of him and an IV running into his arm. He had a paper cup of juice in his hand.

"They're going to x-ray my head," he said.

She nodded. He looked so vulnerable she felt like crying. Instead, she busied herself with bringing over a chair, and then she sat down and picked at the edge of one of those blankets.

"You were good to bring me here," Denny said. "These warm blankets, I gotta get some of these."

Brenda nodded. She wanted to hold his hand, but was afraid he might misinterpret the gesture. Or, in fact, he might interpret the gesture rightly.

"I might could use your help with Sly," Denny said, his eyes closed.

"Sly?"

"He's headed for a bad time, we think. You know, inside his head."

"How could I help that?"

"Just be nice to him, you know, like you are. Maybe take his mind off himself for a little while."

"You trying to get rid of me?" Brenda regretted the words the minute they were out of her mouth, yet she couldn't help herself. His words stung. "You trying to line me up?"

"No," Denny said, opening sick eyes and looking at her for emphasis. "You're a good friend." He closed his eyes again. "Sly needs a friend, too. A new friend, somebody . . . not one of us. That's all I meant."

"Okay. We'll see."

"Thanks. Thanks again."

Brenda lifted the cup of juice out of his relaxing grip before he spilled it. A moment later, he was snoring softly. She sipped the juice and watched him sleep. She didn't know how she could be a friend to Sly, but if Denny asked her to, she'd try. It sounded kind of weird.

Be careful, girl, she told herself. *Don't get too mixed up with these guys. And do not forget that Denny already has a girlfriend. A young girlfriend, someone close to his own age.*

Yeah, yeah, she told herself, and finished the juice.

Athena Goddard wiggled into her panty hose, cursing the whole time. The last thing she wanted to do was go to this damn meeting. Wearing a dress and panty hose, no less. She had work to do in the garden, and was looking forward to digging in the dirt and transplanting a whole flat of impatiens. The tomatoes were ready for canning, and the cukes were perfect pickling size, and here she was, dressing up to go hobnob with that slut Susie Marie Grimes.

"This is the last year," she said to herself in the mirror as she started with the foundation makeup. She hated the way the stuff smelled, and she hated the feeling of it on her skin, but she knew that being the sheriff's wife brought with it some social obligations. She couldn't go to the palatial home of Mayor Grimes, wearing her gardening clothes. It was bad enough she didn't dye away the gray streaks in her hair. She wasn't really cut out for this type of stuff, but she did it for Steve.

She stroked on the blusher and eye shadow, highlighted her eyebrows just a little bit, and then applied mascara. She'd go to all the fund-raisers Steve wanted her to go to, but this was absolutely the last year she'd serve on any committees. She'd done her duty. She'd paid her dues. She was finished. She'd rather work on the 4-H fair, or something hands-on with the kids. Not this socialite crap.

She slipped into her dress, belted it, stepped into her pumps and surveyed the impression. Good. This was the last meeting before the event, and this would be a good time to give notice. She grabbed her purse and keys and headed to Susie Marie's house.

The meeting was in full swing when Athena got there. She unapologetically helped herself to coffee, heavy on the cream and sugar, and took a seat that allowed her the sweeping view of West Wheaton. The Grimes mansion was up on the hill overlooking Milo's domain. It was a stunning view on an achingly beautiful day. While Athena would someday like to have a house with a view like this, the plastic-perfectness of the rest of the place reflected a little bit too closely the plastic-perfectness of Susie Marie. This was a nice place for a house; too bad Milo and Susie Marie got the site.

Athena and Steve would have a completely different house on this hill. Earthy, with lots of wood and quilts and a big pot-bellied stove instead of the glassed-in, never-used gas fireplace at the end of the decorator-perfect, never-used living room. She'd have a magnificent garden, up here with all the sunlight, and there would be profusion of color everywhere. Milo and Susie Marie had red-cinder landscaping with junipers. The whole place, in the hands of the Grimeses, was about as functionally sterile as it could get. Pity.

"Hi, Athena," Susie Marie said. "We were just talking about the entertainment. That's your committee, right?"

"Right," Athena said, and launched into her report of what was going to happen at the local celebrity auction, which this year, would benefit the local Special Olympics. Athena had no passion for the Special Olympics, and had voiced her suggestion for a different charity, but had been overwhelmingly outvoted. Another reason to get off the committee. She was certain Special

Olympics was a good thing, it just wasn't her thing. She'd not only get off the committee, but she'd get out of this stupid women's group altogether. The extension office was starting to donate labor, materials, seed and education to lower-income folks to help them start their own vegetable gardens. Athena was far more suited to that type of project. Watching rich women bid against each other for dates with the handsome local radio personality wasn't her idea of fun.

"And," she finished, "this is going to be my last year on this committee. I have too many other commitments, and I don't want to give anything but my best to any of them. Unfortunately, something has to give, and I'm afraid it's going to be this project." She looked around. "Obviously, there is no lack of support for this fund-raiser, so I'm sure it will be easy to find my replacement."

There was polite applause, and a queer look from Susie Marie, and then the meeting went on. Athena tried to listen, but instead, she enjoyed the view and the relief she felt with giving up the responsibility.

While most of the women stayed after the meeting to gossip and probe into the mayor's financial situation via his loose-lipped wife, Athena made her apologies and a quick exit. Susie Marie saw her to the door, and as they stood on the outside, Susie Marie pinned Athena with a predator's stare. "Sorry you're leaving the committee," she said, "but I understand, considering the circumstances."

"Circumstances?"

"I know it's not official yet, but you need to know that you've got one hell of a fight in front of you. Milo and me, we've got our allies."

"What?"

"Steve, running for mayor."

"Steve's not running for mayor." Athena had no idea what

Susie Marie was talking about.

"Not if he's smart, he's not. But smart isn't one of Steve's better qualities, is it? Not like the size of his dick. Now *there's* quality."

Athena was so appalled she didn't even think to slap the little twit. Instead of standing there with mouth agape at Susie Marie's horrifying innuendo and lack of couth, Athena just turned and walked away, her face red hot, her guts on fire.

She got into her car, and vowing not to even mention it to Steve, before she was halfway down the hill, she had her cell phone out of her purse and was speed dialing his office. When he answered, she didn't waste any time. "Steve, just tell me two things."

"Honey? Are you all right?"

"Are you going to run for mayor, and have you ever had sex with that stupid Susie Marie?"

There was a pause on the other end, long enough for Athena to dive into it and begin to wither. She couldn't breathe.

"The answer is no to both questions," he said.

Tears spurted out of her eyes as if pressurized. She pulled off to the side of the road.

"Why would you ask me those things?"

"I'm sorry. Susie Marie said—"

"Why don't you come by here—better yet, why don't you meet me for coffee? I'll buy you a piece of pie. You sound like you could use a piece of pie."

Athena hiccupped and nodded, then drew in a ragged breath and smiled. "Okay."

"Gretta's. Five minutes."

"Steve?"

"Hmmm?"

"I love you more than you could ever know."

"Me, too," he said, and then hung up.

Athena felt stupid for doubting him, but felt very good about having the type of spouse she could be stupid with.

She clicked off the cell, put her car back on the road and headed for the diner. Gretta made the best pies in the county. And homemade pie was, without question, Athena's one dietary temptation. This time of year, there'd be blackberry. When she saw Steve, she'd ask him what he thought Susie Marie was up to. She couldn't even hazard a guess.

Clover saw her mother off, changed into a sundress and sandals, and put on a pink lipstick to match the fresh polish on her toes and fingernails. Then she picked up her purse and headed for the police station. It was only a couple of blocks, but the afternoon was hot, and before she got there, she dashed into Gretta's for a cold lemonade and to freshen herself up before approaching Deputy Travis.

She was sitting at the counter when Sheriff Goddard and his wife came in. They sat down at a booth, had a little chat with Gretta, refused menus, and then held hands over the Formica table. Clover was charmed. She had always liked the sheriff, but had never met his wife, had only seen her. Clover turned away on her counter stool and thought for a moment. Maybe she could get the information she needed from Sheriff Goddard and not have to deal with Deputy Travis. She knew what the deputy would have in mind. He'd want a favor for a favor, and she wasn't about to make any such deals with that creep. No, this would be much better. She'd wait until Mr. and Mrs. Sheriff spent some time together, and then, as if she were walking out after lemonade, she could stop by their table and initiate a little conversation. Maybe she could turn that around to the questions she needed to ask about the dead guy.

But then maybe the sheriff couldn't answer those questions. It was an ongoing investigation, right? Why would he want to tell her anything?

It was a bad idea. She should go with the original plan. Deputy Travis.

Clover's spirits took a tumble, and she sipped her lemonade right down to the ice cubes.

"Clover?"

She turned and saw the sheriff standing behind her. "Sheriff. Hi."

"My wife and I were just about to have a piece of pie. Would you join us?"

"Oh, no, I wouldn't want to intrude . . ."

"I'm inviting."

Clover smiled shyly. "Well, okay." She picked up her empty lemonade glass and followed the sheriff to the table, where he slid in next to his beautiful wife, and Clover sat facing them. Clover felt young and inexperienced and completely inadequate. Mrs. Goddard looked completely put together, even though her makeup was a bit smudged at the corner of one eye.

"Hi," she said, and held her hand out over the table. "I'm Athena."

"Clover." Clover shook the cool, smooth hand with closely cut, conservatively polished nails. Athena wore no jewelry except a plain gold wedding band. Very classy. Even her name was classy.

"So," Sheriff Goddard said, "what's going on with York and the boys?"

"They're preparing for battle," Clover said. "They're armed."

Gretta set down two pieces of pie, two cups of coffee and a fresh lemonade.

"Armed?" Steve asked.

"Wrist rockets and ball bearings." The smell of the warm pie made Clover's mouth water. "Is that blackberry?"

Athena nodded and signaled Gretta. "I'll get you a piece."

"They're expecting trouble from the railroad guys. And Deputy Travis. Tonight." Clover watched a look pass between the Mr. and the Mrs. and wished with all her weight that she had a spouse she could share looks like that with. Knowing looks that required no words. "But I have to tell you, Sheriff, none of this has anything to do with Denny and York and Sly. It's all about the dead guy, right? Who killed him? Shouldn't there be an investigation into that instead of how to get York and those guys out of there? They're not hurting anybody. They're just living down there. What's the problem all of a sudden?"

"I'm on your side, Clover. I think York ought to be left alone to live out his life down there. But you and I are the minority. They're breaking the law by living down there, and this murder has brought them to the attention, to the *glaring* attention, of everybody in town. People can't go on ignoring them the way they have in the past."

"I know that," Clover said. "York said he's not ready to go die in some old-folks' welfare home, and that's exactly what'll happen if he goes there."

"I know."

"It isn't fair."

"I know."

"It's the stupid mayor's fault. Can't you do something?" Gretta set the pie down, but Clover was no longer interested in it. "What if we solve the murder? Hey, yeah, what if we solve the murder? Isn't that what this is all about? Couldn't things go back to the way they were before?"

"Things can never go back to the way they were before," Athena said.

Clover took a long look at Mrs. Goddard, whose eyes were fixed on the untouched pie before her. She didn't look up, and Clover didn't know what she was talking about. In a flash of calculations, Clover figured that the Mrs. wasn't talking about York and the guys, but Clover better act as if she were. "Maybe not," she said to break the weird silence. "But things could be better, and not worse. What's better for the mayor isn't necessarily better for the guys."

She cut her pie and waited for somebody else to say something.

"Well, I think you're right about solving the murder, Clover. That's what we're doing, of course, working on that murder case. But I'm afraid it isn't going to help your cause."

"Got leads?" she said around a mouthful. Man, that pie was good. "How come the blackberries around here aren't sweet like this?"

"Not enough rain," Athena said. "Blackberries like lots of water."

Clover thought about the blackberry brambles by York's place. That would be a good source of vitamins, minerals and fiber for the boys, but the berries were always bitter and hard.

The sheriff put a forkful into his mouth, too, and the Mrs. picked the top crust off hers. "No leads yet," he said, trying to speak politely with his mouth full.

"Train records? Know who was on the train? Investigate the dead guy's background? Gambling debts? Jealous husbands?"

Mrs. Goddard smiled.

"Whoa," the sheriff said. "You've been watching too much television."

"But that's what it's about, isn't it? Motive, method, and opportunity? We know the method, we can see the opportunity, but what about the motive? Find that and you'll find your killer." Clover scarfed another big bite of pie and let her words hang in the silence. She felt foolish for presuming to give the sheriff a lesson in detective work. "I'm sorry, Sheriff. Like you don't know that stuff."

"Your enthusiasm is good, Clover," the sheriff said, and the Mrs. looked up, smiled, and actually put a bite of pie in her mouth.

"Well, I don't know much, but I know I want to help. If you need me to help, Sheriff, I will. Those guys are my friends. And I'm afraid for them tonight. Do you have somebody who can go down there and protect them?"

"Not really. The land belongs to the railroad, and they have a right to evict trespassers."

"But the land *doesn't* belong to the railroad. That's the whole point."

Steve watched her carefully as he sipped his coffee. "It doesn't? Who does it belong to?"

"Seems like nobody at the moment. I don't know. The lease to the railroad has expired. They're renegotiating it, but until they do . . ."

"But who owns it?" Athena asked.

"Maybe the city."

"Maybe?"

"Well, it looks like the city owned it and then sold it to the railroad. Then it looks like the railroad sold it back to the city, or to some Golim Corporation, I guess, who leased it back to the railroad. But now the lease is up."

"The railroad sold a lot of their land when they hit hard times. They raised a lot of capital, and it seemed like a good idea at the time," Steve said. "But now they're having trouble renegotiating all the leases all the way down the line. It could be years before that's all settled in court. This Golim Corp probably wants to suck blood."

"Who owns Golim Corp?" Athena asked.

"Exactly!" Clover said, so excited she couldn't sit still. She wiped her mouth on a napkin and slid out of the booth. "I've got to go," she said. "Thanks for the pie. I'll let you know what I find out."

"Feeling better?" Steve asked Athena, after they watched Clover skip out the door.

She nodded.

Steve moistened the corner of a paper napkin in his ice water and handed it to her. "Your mascara is smudged at the corner of your eye."

She took the napkin from him and kissed his finger.

"I would never cheat on you," he said.

Her mouth screwed up in that female grimace of pain, the one that said that tears were on their way.

"Never."

She put her hand over her mouth to hide those stretched lips, squinted her eyes shut and nodded at him.

He took her hand again, the one with the napkin still clutched in it, and stroked her thumb. "And I would never do anything like even *consider* running for any office other than sheriff without talking with you about it first. I swear to God, Athena, there has never been a word spoken about it, not around me, not in my office, and certainly not by me."

She nodded and sucked in a ragged breath. "Susie Marie . . ."

"Consider the source."

Athena spit out a harsh laugh in spite of herself. Steve took that as a sign and followed the thread. "I mean, really, Athena. *Susie Marie?*"

She laughed again, and then dabbed the damp napkin at the corners of her eyes. The storm had passed, and Steve breathed a sigh of relief. This woman was his whole life. If he had the power, he'd always make her laugh rather than make her cry. He decided that his mission in life, from here on out, would be to make her laugh as often as possible. He picked up her hand again and kissed that perfectly manicured thumb. "You'd make a perfect First Lady, you know. Of West Wheaton."

She jerked back her hand and gave him a look.

"Kidding," he said. "Unless you want."

She shrugged. "Maybe," she said playfully.

Her smile set the world right. Now he could go back to work and deal with the mess swirling around York and those guys. And really. Who did kill that guy?

They finished their pie and coffee, Steve saw her to her car, and gave her a long, lingering kiss before closing the door firmly and seeing her off.

Then he jumped into his cruiser and made a beeline for Milo Grimes's house. He had a few things to say to Susie Marie, and there was no time like the present.

Denny felt much better with a prescription in his pocket and a few of those pain pills in his bloodstream. His skull had not been cracked, but they figured he had a pretty severe concussion. Rattled his brain. He could believe it. Brenda was waiting for him when he came out of X-ray, and she sat with him while the doctor talked to him and then as the pills took effect. He probably wouldn't have gone to the clinic on his own, and was very happy that she took the initiative to take him there.

The pills didn't make him woozy like he thought they would. They seemed, in fact, to give him a little energy, now that he didn't have to struggle against the pain. She bought them a couple of burgers on the way home, and Denny wolfed his like there was no tomorrow. He could have eaten another half dozen of those ninety-nine-cent treats, but she was buying and he still owed her for the steak dinner, so he couldn't exactly ask her for seconds.

They didn't talk much; they didn't seem to have much to say to each other. Not much in common, he guessed, and he was a little uncomfortable being seen with her in public when Clover could wander on by at any moment, since this was her day off. But Brenda was being a pal, and she hadn't touched him, and he was keeping his hands to himself, so Clover couldn't be anything but grateful to Brenda for tending to him the way she had. Clover should have been the one taking him to the doctor. But Clover was young, and probably didn't have the kind of instincts Brenda had. Brenda was older. Wiser. More worldly.

Brenda walked him to the top of the path and then said goodbye. He wanted her to come down and talk with Sly—maybe a little female company would settle his soul down a little bit—but she seemed kind of agitated and eager to get back to her day. She'd certainly wasted enough of it on him, so he didn't press the issue. "Thanks," he said. "I mean, really."

"No problem. Glad you're okay."

He kind of held his hand out to shake it, then kind of dropped it just as she kind of put hers up, and the end result was that their fingertips touched just a little bit. Then they both smiled at the ground and moved off in their own directions. Denny was glad the encounter was over.

He was feeling much better until he got down there and saw the enormous pile of shredded paper around York and saw Sly pacing back and forth like a cat. The two of them were talking in low tones, and Denny's day took a turn toward the dark. He didn't want any part of this. Brenda and the emergency clinic had almost made him forget about their eviction troubles, and the confrontation that the deputy and his heavy friends had promised. Denny had the slingshots and lots of ammo, but what kind of defense was that? None. It was stupid kid stuff.

Denny closed his eyes and stood still for a moment, looking for the pain in his head, but it seemed as if there was a giant vacancy where the pain used to be. *It will be back,* the vacant spot promised, *but for now, live with the echo of it in your mind.*

For the first time in a long time, Denny wished that life were different. He wished he'd made different choices. He wished he had a future that he could spend on Clover and eventually a bunch of kids. He wished he had an education so he could hold his own in a conversation with people he admired. He wished he had a place to go every day where his brain could be stimulated by conversation about important things, like those people at the clinic. Those nurses and doctors and orderlies and the X-ray lady all had lives with meaning.

"You okay?" Sly asked, busting Denny's wishful thinking.

"Yeah. They x-rayed my head and told me to go home. Gave me some pain pills."

"Anything good?"

"No buzz. But no headache, either."

"Where's the redhead?"

"Brenda? She went home. What are you guys talking about?"

"You got two girls?" Sly was very interested in Brenda, Denny realized. He should have insisted Brenda come down and just hang out for a few minutes.

"Nope. Brenda's just a friend."

Sly shook his head, and squinted his eyes suspiciously at Denny. "No such thing," he said.

Denny ignored him and lay down on his blanket. That same pair of clean socks was still there. He put it over his eyes to block out the sun, which was lowering in the sky, but still bright as hell. Night was approaching, and with it came danger. Denny didn't know what was going to happen that night, but he had a feeling it was going to change a few lives. That would be just fine with him. He felt ready for a change.

Denny, at twenty-eight years old, had been living at York's place for six years. He left home in a white heat after his stepdad had chased him around the living room with a lamp base. Denny had lifted some cash from his mom's purse, just a little bit for a little bit of dope to smoke and some beer to go with it. It wasn't the first time, but apparently it was the last straw. Denny had no doubt that Stan, big hulking stupid geek that he was, could easily crush his skull with that lamp, so he shouted some things at his mother that he immediately regretted, and ran out of the house. He'd never gone back. He'd never called, either. Not something he was proud of.

He thought of his mom sometimes, and hoped she was well. He hoped she'd gotten rid of Stan and found herself a nice guy who treated her right, who had a good job and could provide some of those luxuries a good woman of her age deserved. He'd hate it if she turned out like Clover's mom, used up and bitter about everything. A guy like Stan could make that kind of thing happen.

Denny bounced around for a while, scamming this and scamming that, mostly scamming on women and their generosities until he learned the fine art of commercial theft, and the finer art of hopping freights. He'd heard about York's place—it was legendary among rail rats—and one night when he was sick with some kind of a fever, he got off the train and followed the tracks down to York's. York threw him a blanket, brewed him up a cup of beef bullion, and Denny had been there ever since.

Denny's life hadn't been so great, but he'd never spent more than one night at a time in jail, and he lived free and had a girlfriend and a bedroll of his own. His dad had abandoned them when Denny was still in diapers, and his mother worked hard to provide him and his overachieving brothers with a good house and good nutrition, and he'd kind of shit on her at the end.

Seems like men did that to her. First his dad, then him, and Stan was no prize. But that was her life, and not Denny's, and he didn't have any control over her choices. He wished he did, not that he was any genius at making life decisions, but he wished her well in his heart and in his mind. He thought of her in the long dark of the night when he was the loneliest, and he vowed to send her a postcard. But then the sun came up and life became a completely different story that took up all his time and all his concentration, and he forgot about her until the next time he was awake in the night, listening to the darkness play music upon his guilt.

If he was smart, he'd go home, make his peace, get a good job, or maybe go back to school. Become a regular member of society.

He longed for it, but he couldn't exactly imagine it. He didn't even know how to start.

"Mr. Ashton, please, Milo Grimes calling." Milo couldn't even sit at his desk, he was so agitated. He stood behind it, having kicked his big black leather chair out of the way, and tapped the end of a pen on the desk. He wanted to drive the pen right through the desk, but he restrained himself, because the desk and the pen both had been very expensive.

"I'm afraid Mr. Ashton isn't in the office today," said the secretary on the other end. "May I take a message?"

"I've left messages," Milo said, feeling the reins of restraint slip through his fingers. "I have deadlines. Where is he? Where can I call him?"

He heard her cover the phone with her hand and then background voices. Then another voice came on the line. "Mayor Grimes?"

"Yes."

"This is Eva Long, Mr. Ashton's personal assistant. Mr. Ashton had a heart attack yesterday afternoon. He's in intensive care at the cardiac unit in the hospital in Sacramento."

This was bad news indeed. "Who's taking over his duties?"

"Well, nobody at the moment. We're in a little bit of turmoil here until we can figure things out."

"Well, figure this out," Grimes said. "Ashton has papers to sign and the deadline is tomorrow. We have business to transact, dammit, business that won't just sit still while he takes a little vacation in the hospital." He paused, his blood pressure skyrocketing, but there was no response. *"Are you listening to me?"*

"Yes, Mr. Grimes," Eva Long's cool voice replied. "I'll be sure to tell Mr. Ashton that you send your best wishes for his speedy recovery."

Grimes slammed down the phone. "Jesus Christ," he said. The city council was meeting the next morning at ten A.M., and he had several things to accomplish before then. First, he had to get Ashton's signature on Oshiro's papers, because in a weak moment, a *rare* weak moment, Milo had included Ashton in the deal that Golim Corp was putting together with Oshiro. Ashton would make a ton of money by doing nothing but cooperating. Apparently, he couldn't even do that.

Then Milo could assure the city council that the property had been sold, the railroad line was going east, it was all a done deal, signed, sealed, delivered and legal, so nobody would feel obligated to go poking around. Otherwise, the damned railroad still had an option to renew, and if Ashton's second in command took that option as a safe way out, as a way to buy a little time while somebody did a little investigating, Grimes would lose everything—*everything*—in one swell foop, because he'd already sold the property to Oshiro, who had a mall to build. Second, he had to get that dump cleaned up down by the tracks. Third, he had to get Steve Goddard to arrest somebody for the murder of Ashton's flunky, which got Ashton's attention and convinced him to get on board with Milo's plan. And fourth, he had to do something about Susie Marie and her bedroom Olympics, although that didn't necessarily need to be done before the council meeting.

But the sale had to be a done deal before the council meeting, because it was on the agenda.

He called his secretary and asked her to send some cubic zirconium earrings to both the escrow officer, who was finessing the simultaneous closings on the land, and the city manager's wife, so the manager would keep his trap shut during the council meeting, and make sure the earrings got delivered before the council meeting. A little grease for the important wheels. "Gold settings," he told her. "I want them to look like real diamonds." Then he called to make certain that Fletcher was taking bulldozers down to York's dump in the morning. The receptionist at his construction company came back within minutes saying the job order had been processed, and the appointment was confirmed. Six A.M.

That, at least, was a good thing. York and his cronies would be gone, and his creepy little rat hole would be nothing but freshly scraped soil and a dump truck full of trash. The city mothers and fathers would be loving all over him for that, and that was nothing but votes in his ballot box come November.

He turned his big chair around, sat in it and tried to think what he could do to fix the Susie Marie problem. She'd pushed it in his face until he could no longer avoid dealing with it, damn her.

"Got luggage?" the bus driver asked as Clover stepped down off the big bus. She shook her head no, the driver closed his door and pulled away. She pushed open the doors of the Bonita train station and stepped into its cool, cavernous interior. She'd never seen so much gray granite. She thought she could even hear her breath echo. One old woman wearing a red suit, with matching hat and white gloves sat on a burnished pew with a small suitcase at her feet. A teenaged boy slept on another bench, his head on his backpack and his sleeping bag covering him. There was an overflowing trash can next to the vending machines. Other than that, the place seemed deserted. Nobody was in line at the ticket counters, which had long black ropes to keep the crowds orderly.

She walked up to the front counter. "Hello?" she called, and a man came out from the back, wiping mustard from his mouth with a napkin. He was in his late twenties, maybe early thirties, and very cute. She felt herself perk up a little bit. He wore his blondish hair cut short and he was blue eyed and clean-shaven and looked fit and muscular in his gray uniform with the red piping.

"Hi," he said.

"Hi." She looked down and twisted a little bit, unsure, suddenly, of how to proceed. "I have a little problem."

He sat on a stool and leaned toward the glass. "How can I help you?"

She looked up and saw him smiling at her, and that made her blush. She felt giggly and childish, and was surprised at herself for feeling like that. But this guy was really cute. He looked like a surfer. Like a surfer aerobics instructor. "Day before yesterday a guy was killed on the Western Express," she started.

He pulled back. "Yeah, I know," he said.

"The police been here about it?"

"No, but they talked to railroad security and some executives in Sacramento. I heard about it."

"Nobody came down here to investigate?"

He shook his head.

She noticed that his silver nametag said Mr. Warrenton. "Should I call you Mr. Warrenton?" and then a giggle escaped her before she could stop it.

He leaned back toward the glass again. "Depends. Are you buying a ticket?"

She shook her head no.

"Then you can call me Trey."

"Tray?"

"Trey. As in the Third. I'm the third, you know, after the junior? Nicholas August Warrenton the Third."

"Wow."

"Trey."

She smiled, then got back to business before she got herownself derailed. "Friends of mine are being accused of the murder," she said, "even though everybody knows they were just standing by the tracks when the guy got pushed off the train. I was hoping to find out who killed that guy so they could stop getting hassled."

He smiled. "Yeah, you and the cops and the FBI and everybody else."

"Don't you think it would be a good thing if you and I figured it out?"

"And how would that happen?"

"I don't know," she said. "Maybe if we looked at a passenger list . . ."

"Sorry," he said, and pulled back again into a more professional posture. "That's private information."

"I know," she said. "But what could it hurt for me to look at it? I'm nobody. I might recognize somebody's name is all."

"You think you might know the killer?"

"No. But I don't know what else to do. York'll die if he has to live in some old-folks' home, and they're going to evict him, the stupid mayor and his idiot Deputy Dawg. Denny'll leave because he's got no place else to go, and I don't know what'll happen to Sly, he's not quite right in the head sometimes, you know, Vietnam." Clover felt her face grow hot again, and a ball of emotion that she hadn't allowed herself became lodged in the back of her throat.

"Whoa," Trey said. "Hold on, now. This isn't worth getting worked up over."

"I'm just trying to save them," she said, and she heard the little hic in her voice when she said it.

Trey looked beyond her at the empty lobby. "Come around back here," he said, and nodded toward the baggage door, then got off his stool to go meet her.

Clover couldn't believe her luck. She walked around and was there when she heard the electronic lock click open and he held the door for her. She slipped in, and into the back room where a half dozen suitcases and some freight boxes waited.

"Sit here," he said, and she sat on a big rolling cart and waited for him.

A minute later he came back with a piece of computer printout paper and said, "You never saw this here, okay? You'd get me fired."

"I promise," she said, and accepted the paper. It was just a list of names and symbols she didn't understand, so she concentrated on going down the list of names. Right in the middle was Norman Cheston. Norman Cheston? She knew a Norman Cheston. Clover had gone to high school with Sylvia Cheston, and she had an older brother named Norman. A gang banger. Now there was a possibility. She kept going down the list, but saw nothing else that was familiar.

She handed the paper back to the cute guy, and put her finger on the name Norman Cheston. "What about this guy?" she asked.

Trey looked where she was pointing. "Got on in Sacramento, got off here in Bonita," he said. "It's pretty common."

"He lives in West Wheaton."

"Train doesn't stop in West Wheaton, so there's a bus. Lots of people go to Sacramento for, you know, doctor appointments, or dentists or something like that, shopping, financial stuff, and they take the train."

"Huh."

"You live in West Wheaton?" he asked.

"Yeah."

"You seeing anybody?"

"Sort of."

Trey looked down. "My luck."

"What are you doing here in Bonita?" she asked.

"I'm just here for a while, working on my seniority. This is a good gig, working for the railroad. I can transfer to anyplace, work a while, transfer again, and I get unlimited travel for myself on my days off or for my vacations, and there's good benefits, too. Problem is, I'm stuck in Bonita for a year, and there's pretty much nothing going on."

"Yeah, no kidding."

"You could come visit me again."

She looked up at his shiny clean face with his white teeth and his clear blue eyes and a little something twanged in her heart. "Maybe I will."

He stuck his head out the door, and looked both ways before he held it open. "Remember, this is our secret," he said.

She nodded, and swore to herself later that as she passed by him, he'd sniffed her hair. She would indeed come back to visit him, but first, she had a busy afternoon ahead of her, and time was getting short.

Steve Goddard pulled his cruiser into the circular driveway of Milo and Susie Marie Grimes. He radioed to dispatch exactly where he was and that he didn't expect to be there more than five minutes. He got out, leaving the engine running. If somebody stopped by, Milo Grimes, for example, he didn't want anybody thinking he was boinking the mayor's wife on the mayor's own sheets. He was there for one short verbal exchange and that was it.

He pushed the doorbell and heard it chime throughout the cavernous house. Then, while he waited, he looked around at their manicured grounds, at the beautiful view of the hills and the sky. It was quite the location. Mr. Mayor didn't score this kind of a place on mayoral salary, that's for damn sure.

Susie Marie opened the door, wearing a white tennis dress. Her hair was done up in a ponytail and she looked ready to hit the court. On the floor in the foyer was a gym bag with a pink towel folded neatly on top of it.

"Hi, Steve," she said brightly, batting her eyes in complete innocence. "What's a big hunk of a guy doing coming over to visit me in the middle of the day?"

"You know exactly why I'm here, Susie Marie. You keep your insults to yourself."

"Ahhh," she said, nodding coyly. "Mrs. Sheriff got her feelings hurt, did she? Poor thing."

"Leave her alone, Susie Marie. You and I both know what happened between us was over long before high-school graduation. And I'm not running for mayor. What the hell is that about?"

"Milo needs some . . . stimulation, let's say," Susie Marie said with a suggestive flip of her head. "I thought if you ran for mayor, it might be just the thing for him. Somebody had to suggest it sometime. I know thoughts like that don't just float around in your pretty little head."

"Fuck off, Susie Marie," Steve said. "I mean it."

"Now you're hurting my feelings."

He walked back to his cruiser, got in, put it in gear, and drove around the horseshoe drive. She was still standing in the doorway, leaning against the jamb when he turned out onto the road. He could see her in his rearview mirror. He wasn't quite sure, but he thought she blew him a kiss. What a skank. The thought of him throwing his magnificent Athena away for a tumble with Susie Marie was laughable. He picked up his radio microphone to let dispatch know that he had left the premises, and it hadn't even been five minutes.

But just because she was skanky didn't mean she wasn't dangerous. She'd showed a little of her true self to Athena, and Steve knew he had to watch those two, Susie Marie and her weaselly little husband.

Sheesh. Maybe he *should* run for mayor. It would be an improvement, having a little honesty in the office.

"So what do you want me to do with this?" York asked. He held up the wrist rocket and little plastic bag full of steel peas.

"I don't know," Denny said. "Sly told me to get it for you."

"First thing, I don't engage in no conflict," York said. "Second of all, I can't see nothin'."

Sly came down the path, feeling jumpy and anxious. He walked right up to Denny and before Denny could ask him about the slingshot for York, Sly said, "What the hell are you doing with two women when I don't even have one? And what about York?"

This took Denny by surprise. "Hey, wait a minute. Those women have their own minds, and in fact, Brenda liked the looks of you."

That stopped Sly cold. This was not news he expected to hear. He didn't really expect anything from his confrontation with Denny—he just felt like confronting someone about something. "Really?" he said.

"Really. I think if you play it cool, she might come around to see you, you know, the way Clover comes to see me."

This sounded suspicious to Sly, like Denny was bullshitting him, setting him up, putting him off, salving the wound, keeping the peace. Conspiring to put him off his guard. And yet, he couldn't help but be intrigued.

"But, listen," Denny went on, "York can't use no wrist rocket tonight. You and I can, but what's he going to do? He doesn't want to fight."

"I got an idea about that," Sly said, and walked Denny over the pile of railroad ties, stepping on shreds of yellow plastic crime-scene tape that had been left, and they sat down together, by where the dead guy used to be, and Sly told Denny his new idea, and what Denny had to do to make it happen.

Denny liked it, and once they had their plan thoroughly thrashed out, they told York, who agreed. Then Denny went five-finger shopping to score their one last piece of warfare equipment. *This,* Denny thought, *was going to be a night to remember.*

"We're going to kick some governmental ass," Sly told York as Denny scampered up the path.

This will all be over soon, York thought. *The moon will go back to a normal size, I'll be dead and that'll be good.*

Golim Corporation, as Clover discovered at City Hall, had a post office box in West Wheaton, and was owned by a dozen other corporations. They all had California addresses, but Clover had never heard of any of them. Wait. Fletcher Corporation. Was that the same Fletcher Corporation that picked up the trash every Monday morning and handled the little blue recycling bins? They had to be local.

She checked the address on record, and sure enough. West Wheaton. So Fletcher was part of Golim Corp. Who owned Fletcher?

She went back to the records desk and asked a few more questions of the clerk, and took another big black tome to the reading table.

Closed corporation, no information of ownership on record.

But Milo Grimes was the corporate treasurer. Well, hell, that made more sense than anything else she'd come across all day.

So Milo Grimes probably owned Fletcher, and Fletcher was part owner in Golim Corp. For all Clover knew, Milo Grimes owned Golim Corp. There was some sort of notation in the ownership records, and it looked as if something were incomplete.

This was all too complicated. Clover could give this information to Steve Goddard, but for now, maybe she ought to concentrate on solving the murder.

She knew a guy named Norman Cheston, and she was going to go pay him a visit and see what he'd been doing going to Sacramento on the train. Maybe he saw something.

She borrowed the city clerk's telephone book and telephone and gave her old friend Sylvia Cheston a call.

Brenda went back to her place, her head full of Denny and Sly. She could not believe how intrigued she was by those guys living down there like that. There was something about it that made her want to take them books to read, or make them pillows for their comfort. They had kind of a weird little place but it was kind of cool, too. But what the hell did they do when it rained real hard? Wasn't life sucky beyond imagination when that happened?

She wondered if they ever had roast beef to eat, or a pumpkin pie.

She took off her shoes and rubbed the sore spots on her feet. They were nothing compared to the sore spot on Denny's head, poor guy. She turned on the stove and started to heat some water for a cup of tea, and then turned it off again. Those guys kept a fire going all the time, and a raggedy old bent-up coffeepot set on some kind of a grate. That was their hot food. Coffee. That's all they had to keep them warm.

Something about all that wasn't right, and didn't set right with Brenda. She had her hands full just trying to keep her bills paid, keep her own head above water. She didn't have anything left over for charity cases, and yet . . .

If what Denny said was true, they were all going to get evicted that night. Denny, as much as she was attracted to him, had Clover, his girlfriend, as he so mildly pointed out. York, well, he was an old man, and they'd have to put him somewhere, but what about Sly? Where would he go? What would he do?

Maybe she could offer him something. A couch to sleep on for a couple of weeks or something.

Brenda fired up a cigarette and sat at her kitchen table, thinking about him. She hadn't done much of any consequence with her life. Maybe it was time for her to do a good deed. Maybe she ought to go down there and get acquainted with Sly a little bit, and if it worked out, she could offer him a place to stay until he figured out what he was going to do. He'd no doubt want to stay in West Wheaton and see to York, but he'd need a job, and all that was hard to find without a telephone, a warm meal, and a place to sleep. Maybe she could do that for him. *It would be a nice little bit of energy to throw out into the universe,* she thought. *Secure a little good karma.*

She washed her face and her feet, then put on some more-sensible shoes to go down and talk to him, but as she did that, she had a few second thoughts.

Brenda knew she didn't always make the right decisions, particularly about men. She was a little too gullible, and a little too generous, and that usually got her hurt and sometimes worse. Maybe she ought to bounce this idea around with one of her girlfriends. Living alone can skew one's thinking.

Maybe she'd pop by Eileen's place on the way. Eileen would certainly have an opinion about what Brenda was about to do. Perhaps Eileen's take on it would be more balanced. Perhaps not, but regardless, Brenda wouldn't be making a stupid decision blind. Nope, if she was going to be making a stupid decision in spite of girlfriend counseling, she'd only have herself to blame for it.

Stealing the hand-held spotlight was more difficult than Denny had anticipated. They didn't have one at Walmart, so he had to hitchhike all the way to Bonita and go to the sporting goods store there. That place was crawling with security, so he had to be damn clever. But clever was his profession, and he got away clean, the big damn light safely stashed in the Walmart sack he'd brought folded up in his hip pocket for the purpose.

Rides were hard to get going back, so he spent some time walking, some time thinking, and some time practicing with his slingshot and roadside pebbles. It didn't take him long to get the feel of it, and he could hit the five on the speed-limit sign with no problem at thirty yards. And of course, he wasn't going to need no thirty yards come nightfall.

Denny had a lot to think about, and he didn't like it much when he had too much solitude on his hands, because that gave him time to think about it.

He thought about Clover, and Brenda, and York, and Sly, and the pending situation with Deputy Travis and the railroad guys. He thought about the dead guy, and how Clover wanted to tell his family, and that made him smile. There wasn't a better soul anywhere on the planet than the one inside that Clover. And her outsides weren't so bad, either.

Denny let his mind wander as he shuffled down the side of the highway, and his mind went to a sprout of a growing hunger inside him, something that told him to make something of himself, to do better. He'd like to keep Clover around for a long time, and do good by her, but he knew deep in his soul that he'd end up disappointing her, and he'd hate that. She was too good. Too good for him. Maybe if he got to the place where he stopped disappointing himself, then he could see his way clear to a fine girl like Clover, but that was a long ways down the road. He knew he'd never get there if he never started, and he didn't see himself starting anytime soon.

The heaviness on Denny's chest started to throb with the pounding of his head, and his fingers went to the knot on his forehead that still hurt. He fumbled a pain pill from his pocket and stuck it in his mouth, wincing at the bitterness of it, and then stuck another in there to follow it. One for his head, one for his innards. He was a little bit afraid, York tearing paper and talking about dying, and Sly pacing and talking about perimeters and enemy incursions and such. He had to be clearheaded if anybody was going to be. He couldn't afford to go to pieces when the shit hit the fan. He couldn't take too many pain pills—he fumbled another one out and stuck it in his mouth—and he couldn't let the guys down.

But life was going to change, no matter what happened that night. People didn't ride the rails much anymore—it was too dangerous. Camps like York's place were obsolete. York was obsolete. They'd all have to move on, and that, Denny knew, was what was eating at both York and Sly. And maybe that was his problem, too. More of the same? Find another place like York's and settle in? Lose all his teeth, get some itchy skin disease and rot? Or what?

A black rusty pickup truck with some kind of cages in the back pulled off the side of the road and stopped. Denny trotted on up to it, made eye contact with the old Mexican guy who was driving, and said "West Wheaton." The Mexican nodded and pointed his thumb back toward the truck bed. "Can I sit in the front?" Denny asked. "I'd like to charge my battery here"—he held up the sack—"in your cigarette lighter." The Mexican looked squinty eyed for a moment as if he was thinking, or trying to figure out what Denny was saying, then he pointed with his chin back toward the truck bed. Denny sighed, walked to the back, loaded himself, settled among the cages—chicken cages, they were and very recently vacated as evidenced by the fresh chicken shit and multitude of feathers—and he was on his way home.

It would be nice to ride in the front of the pickup someday, he thought. Or to have his own pickup and give Mexican hitchhikers a ride. Could that ever happen?

Not likely. Not in this lifetime. Denny slammed the lid down on that familiar longing before it consumed him the way Sly and York were being eaten alive by their demons.

Athena Goddard put on her gardening gloves and surveyed the vegetable garden. For the first time in a long time she had no taste for digging in the dirt. She always got this feeling this time of year, when everything was thirsty and hot, but knew that it would go away once she lost herself in the cool soil and the plants. She longed for the cold nights and the crisp air of fall. She wished she could look forward to a forgiving blanket of snow to cover these beautiful raised beds and let them rest while she took a long winter break in front of the fire with a lap robe and cup of hot chamomile tea with honey and a fast-paced novel with lots of sex. Those were the memories of her mother, the memories of her youth in South Dakota. Then she got caught up in the fast lane of beauty pageants, college, and marriage to a young criminal-justice student. They moved to the job, and she embarked upon a career as a sheriff's wife, started their family and started the perpetual garden. The perpetual dirt under her fingernails. The perpetual work.

Athena was ready for a rest.

The tomatoes were blushing, and growing heavier, so she decided she'd start the day's work with tending them, pruning and propping them up as needed. The beans were full on, so that would be a major part of the evening meal. She'd end her day in the garden harvesting beans for dinner.

As soon as she got to work with the tomatoes, pinching off the little yellow flowers so the plants wouldn't set more fruit, but would ripen what was already there, Athena's thoughts roamed back to Susie Marie, Steve, and that nervy little Clover. There were no thoughts to be wasted on Susie Marie. West Wheaton wasn't a big place, and Athena wouldn't run her life to avoid Susie Marie, but that was the last person Athena was interested in seeing again. Ever. Athena suspected that Steve'd had a fling with Susie Marie at some time in their past, but Athena wasn't worried. Steve had never shown himself to be anything but faithful. A perfect man, a model husband and father, but maybe not quite smart enough to go head-to-head with Milo Grimes. Milo was not only smart, but ruthless and wily, so Athena hoped that Steve really wasn't thinking of running for mayor. Ruthless and wily could be dangerous. Sheriff was a good thing to be, and perfect for Steve, especially in West Wheaton, where up until now, graffiti was the worst crime committed.

Steve would make a good mayor if he didn't have to face Milo Grimes in the election. He had the right kind of heart and a populist view. Athena knew she'd make a great mayor's wife. If there was anything being a beauty queen had taught her, it was how to live appropriately in the public eye. Something Susie Marie had never learned. Neither had her disgusting husband. Regardless. Athena didn't strive for the public eye; she didn't crave it—she didn't even want it. But if she had it, she would do a good job. She knew that for certain. She'd use her station for good purpose.

Then there was that little Clover. Wasn't she something? Athena knew Steve would like to have had another child, maybe a girl, but two children had been enough for her. Maybe that's what Steve saw in that Clover. Athena knew what Clover did for those tramps down by the railroad. Maybe Athena could help channel Clover's altruistic endeavors into more productive avenues. Hell, Clover should be in school. She should be going to the community college over in Bonita. She should be bettering herself, she was certainly attractive enough. She could land herself a fine husband if only she tended to herself a little better. Shaved her legs, plucked her eyebrows, put on a little makeup.

The thought made Athena smile. Perhaps Steve wasn't the only one who felt cheated out of a daughter. She knew that Clover had a mother, but not much of one. Maybe Athena could make a difference. Maybe Clover would like to come help her in the garden someday. She could take some of the leftover produce to the guys down by the tracks.

Oh. No, the guys wouldn't be down by the tracks after today. They'd be somewhere else. Well, that would be the perfect time for Athena to extend the invitation to Clover. Take her mind off other things.

Take Athena's mind off other things.

Athena attached the soft-sprinkle watering wand to the end of the hose and carefully gave each tomato plant a healthy drink.

Whenever Travis thought about what he had to do later, at sundown, down by the tracks, he got a sick feeling in the pit of his stomach. He was afraid that his little indiscretions with Susie Marie had queered his immunity. In fact not only queered it but stamped "PAID IN FULL" on it, and stapled it to an invoice for services rendered. The mayor knew about them. Of that, Travis had no doubt. What the mayor would do about it remained to be seen.

And that was the thing that scared Travis the most. If one of those bums got hurt real bad, Travis would be the one they'd string up, because those railroad guys, they had no names. They were just thugs.

A man is known by the company he keeps, his grandmother's voice rang loudly in his head. So he was a thug. He knew it. And he also knew that his time in West Wheaton was growing short. And he knew that his time as a deputy was even shorter, his little dalliance with Susie Marie was probably over, and Eileen was the only thing that kept his ego going, and only if he saw her in very dim light indeed.

He needed to get himself some space and to think through what was going to happen down there by the tracks.

He knew what the mayor wanted him to do. The mayor wanted him to beat those three bums within an inch of their lives, but Travis didn't know how much they could take. The old blind one, he couldn't take much, that was for sure.

He also knew what the sheriff wanted him to do. The sheriff wanted him to leave well enough alone, and not hang with the railroad thugs and their strong-arm, baseball-bat tactics. The sheriff was a good man, with a good heart and a good mind, and if Travis were at all smart, he'd listen to the wisdom of Steve Goddard. But that wasn't going to happen, because Travis owed the mayor, and the mayor also put a few folded hundreds into Travis's jeans, and that never hurt, either.

And he knew what he himself wanted to do. Travis wanted to kill those fucking bums, bash their skulls in, smash their bones to dust, just because he wanted to smash something.

He was pretty sure that come sundown, nobody was going to get his wish. And that might be a good thing.

Travis pushed the door open to the sheriff's office men's room, secured a stall and sat down. He put his face in his hands and tried to figure out how to put a throttle control on the situation so it wouldn't scream out of control and get people seriously hurt. He didn't know how to do that, even though he was an educated lawman. Threats weren't going to work again; they hadn't worked the night before. They'd made the threats last night, they had to follow through tonight, but Jesus Christ, he didn't want to. Not in the tiniest least little bit. And he resented the mayor for making him. And he resented Susie Marie for putting him into this particular position.

He checked his watch. Five o'clock. Way too many hours until dark. He stood up, flushed the clean toilet, and exited the stall. He smoothed down his hair in the mirror, and then went to punch out. Maybe he'd drop by Eileen's come twilight. Maybe this time she'd induce him to stay with her for a while, and he could lie in her nasty, swayback bed, arms behind his head, eyes staring up at the stained ceiling while she snored vodka breath next to him and he envisioned the railroad guys taking those baseball bats to those defenseless bums. And he could be completely innocent of the whole mess.

Or would he be innocent? By not being there, he didn't prevent it, right? Is that complicity?

It was. He knew it was. He was up to his eyeballs. The only thing, then, was for him to show up and minimize damage. He could do that.

As he walked past the sheriff's office, he waved good-bye, and was dismayed to see the sheriff, phone to his ear, hold up his hand, and then wave him in.

Crap. Travis opened the sheriff's door and stood there, head barely inside, and waited. He didn't want to go in. He didn't want to have a long conversation.

Sheriff Goddard motioned for him to come in and close the door.

Shit. He did as he was told.

The sheriff finished his phone conversation and hung up. "Going to be no trouble at the tracks tonight, right?" he said.

Travis shrugged. "Not that I know of."

"You're sure," the sheriff said. "I've heard of a little planned assault down there."

Travis almost asked him who he heard it from, and almost asked him who was planning the assault, and then decided he didn't want to know the answers to either of those questions, so he just shrugged again.

"If you're in on this, Travis, I'm telling you, you're on your own. I can throw you in jail as easily as I can anybody else." He stretched out the *an-y bod-y else* part so it had a little rhythm of its own.

"Be no arrests down there tonight," Travis said. "Gotta run."

"Have a nice night," Sheriff Goddard said and turned to the stack of papers on his desk.

Clover walked up the front steps of Sylvia's house like she had a thousand times when they were in school. The house looked the same. Kind of an average place on an average street. Nothing special, but nothing dumpy like the old trailer Clover had grown up in. Sylvia's dad had a gas station, and her mom worked at the hospital over in Bonita. Sylvia still lived at home with her folks.

Clover felt good about having her own apartment.

Sylvia answered the door, and she looked just the same, too. It had been only a couple of years since they'd seen each other, and Sylvia gave the expected girlie squeal and dance before enveloping Clover in an all-consuming and very-well-padded hug. Sylvia smelled like nail polish remover, and the living room smelled like unwashed dog.

Clover got the impression that Sylvia didn't have many friends. They sat down on the broken, stained brown couch, where Sylvia had been painting her toenails blue, and chatted about classmates. Clover, who didn't keep in touch with anybody, knew lots more about them than Sylvia did. Clover worked in the donut shop, and she saw people periodically, and she got to hear things, too. Sylvia worked as a file clerk for an insurance company and didn't see anybody during the day except the file room, which was, as she put it, "nothing but a million paper cuts waiting to happen." Sylvia had put on weight, and her complexion was still bad. She had never been popular in school, but for some reason, Clover always liked her. She liked Sylvia's spirit.

Sylvia went to the fridge, walking carefully with toes up so as not to catch carpet fibers in the new polish, and came back with two Cokes, a box of saltines, two knives and a jar of peanut butter. "Snacks," she said, and set the whole mess down on the table. Then she peanut-buttered herself a cracker and stuffed it, whole, into her mouth. "Tell me about you," she said around it, then started filing her fingernails.

Clover talked about her job, and her mom, and a little bit about Denny. After about fifteen minutes, though, Clover found herself running out of things to say to Sylvia. The television was still on, and Sylvia's attention kept being drawn to *The People's Court.* Clover finally picked up the remote and clicked it off.

"Thanks," Sylvia said. "That was too distracting."

"How's Norman?" Clover dived right in.

"Norman? My brother?" Sylvia squinted her curiosity at Clover. "He's okay, I guess. Why?"

"Was he in Sacramento last week?"

"Norman? My brother? I don't think so. Why?"

"Is he here?"

"Norman? My brother?" Sylvia didn't seem to be getting the message. "No, he lives with his slut." She started applying a second coat to her right hand.

"So he could have gone to Sacramento without you knowing."

Sylvia shrugged, a frown on her face. "What's it to you?" she asked without looking up.

"Can we go see him?"

Sylvia stuck the brush back in the bottle and looked up at Clover. "Norman? My brother?"

Clover nodded.

"Why would you want to go see him? What's this about? You didn't come to see me after all, did you? You came to get information on my brother."

"I need to talk to him," Clover said. "Coming to see you was the bonus."

"Sure."

"Can we?"

"Can we *what?*"

"Go see him."

"Yeah, sure, someday."

"Now."

"This better be important, Clover, because you're starting to hurt my feelings."

"It really is important, and I'm really in a hurry. I promise you that in a few days, when everything is settled, I'll come by and we'll go have lunch. I'll show you my apartment. We'll go to a movie or something."

"Really? Don't say that if you don't mean it, because I really like you. I've always liked you."

"I like you too. I do mean it. I didn't know how much I've missed you until I saw you."

"Really?"

"Really." Clover said it and she meant it. She would like to see more of Sylvia. Sylvia could be fun, mostly because she could say things like "he's living with his slut," without blinking an eyelash. Saying something like that would never occur to Clover in a million years.

"Okay. Let me put my shoes on." Sylvia screwed the top back on the peanut butter, tested the fresh toenail polish, found it satisfactory, carefully slid her feet into sandals, grabbed her purse and said, "It's not far from here. Want to walk?"

"Sure."

Clover was happy to be out in the fresh air. She didn't know what she was going to say when she got face to face with Norman, but she figured she'd blurt something out. She'd think of something. For now, it was nice to just walk with Sylvia on a late summer afternoon.

"I'm thinking of moving to Hollywood," Sylvia said.

"Hollywood? That's not a very nice place."

"Better than this dump."

"What would you do in Hollywood?"

"Marry well," Sylvia said, then gave a harsh bark of a laugh. "Don't you ever feel like living here is going to keep you down? Don't you wonder if you'll be working at the donut shop all your life? Don't you want to see some of the world? I do, and I'm afraid that if I don't make a drastic move, that I never will. I'll marry some slob because it'll get me out of my parents' house and into one of my own and then I'll have a pack of kids and my body will be shot to shit and I'll have baby puke on me all the time and my life will be ruined."

Clover was not surprised to hear this kind of talk from Sylvia. Sylvia had always been discontented, even when a child, but the harsh take on her future was startling. Clover had not looked at her life in that way, nor did she want to. Clover was more of a day-by-day type of person, and only rarely did she think that was perhaps not the best way to maximize her potential. But *Hollywood?*

"I could move to Hollywood and become a high-priced call girl," Sylvia went on, "but already I'm getting too old to do that. And I'd have to lose a ton of weight." She kicked at a plastic car some kid had left on the sidewalk. "But that's how you meet the rich and powerful."

"You might meet them that way, but you aren't going to marry them that way."

"I could marry a porn mogul," Sylvia said. "They're not so picky."

Sylvia's self-esteem had taken a shocking and drastic nose-dive since they had graduated from high school. *Maybe getting out of West Wheaton would be a good thing for her,* Clover thought. *But maybe she ought to be steered toward a healthier place.* "How about Seattle?" she said. "Or maybe you could go over to Davis or something and go back to school?"

"What about you? Why aren't you in Seattle or in Davis?"

"I've thought about it. Right now I'm seeing a guy—"

Sylvia put her hand out and they stopped walking. "So tell me, Clover, does this guy of yours have a job?"

Clover smiled, looked at her feet, shook her head.

"Yeah. That's what I thought. Does he have a car?"

Clover shook her head again, then looked up at Sylvia.

"Exactly what I'm talking about, girl. You and me, if we don't escape this rat hole, we're going to be stuck with six screaming kids and a man who visits occasionally, just long enough to knock us up. Then he's out of there, leaving no money behind. We've got to make our escape before it's too late. It might already be too late for you. You're probably already knocked up."

Clover knew it could be true. She never missed a birth-control pill, but she also knew that they were not fail-safe.

"You're probably right," she said. "I'm going to give it some thought."

"We could be roomies. We could get an apartment together, say in Beverly Hills."

"What about San Francisco? Or Portland, Oregon?"

"Ick. Cold. Rainy. Foggy. Let's go where the beautiful people are. Venice Beach."

"I'll think about it."

"It could be great," Sylvia said, and there was a little lilt in her step after that, as if talking about the reality of it made it automatically happen. "I think I'll start my diet."

Clover nodded and they kept walking, past the nicer of the low-rent neighborhood houses, to a ratty area of town, where fences leaned, dogs barked, porches sagged, and screen doors hung half off their hinges.

"Here we are," Sylvia said. "The coke whore's lair."

They clomped up the front step, avoiding the big hole in the porch, and Sylvia opened the front door. "Hello?" she called. "Christine, are you here? Norman?"

The inside was dark and stank like moldy produce. The living room looked tossed, but that's probably the way it always looked. Empty wrappers from cookies, cakes, and other sweets were thrown in a pile in the corner along with a half dozen broken children's toys. There was a speckled mirror square on the table with a piece of a fast-food drink straw laying across it, and empty beer bottles on the nasty, stained and littered carpet. The couch was a horrid green, covered with what looked like laundry.

"Jeez, what a dump," Sylvia said, and started folding the things on the couch. It wasn't laundry: it was a tangle of sheets, afghans, blankets and old bedspreads. All old, all torn, all stained. Clover grabbed the end of a wrecked yellow chenille bedspread and helped Sylvia fold it. "Norman, are you here?" she yelled again, then went into the kitchen while Clover folded a couple of blankets, and came out with a cardboard box. She started throwing trash into it.

Just as they were getting the place looking better, the toilet flushed, and the two girls looked at each other. Someone *was* here. The door opened, and a skinny, bare-chested Norman lurched through the door into the living room. His eyes were vacant and his beard was at least three days long.

"You're thrashed," Sylvia said to him.

"Hey, sis," he said, and landed on the newly folded stack of linens on the couch, sliding it into disarray.

"You wanted to see him?" Sylvia said to Clover. "There he is, in all his drugged-out glory." She threw more beer cans into the box in disgust.

"What?" he said, and reached for a beer can, shook it and threw it at Sylvia when he found it empty. She picked it up from the floor and put it into the box.

Clover saw the raw needle marks in the crooks of his elbows, and her stomach took a turn. "How do you get the money to do this to yourself?" she asked before she could stop herself.

Norman ratcheted up a wily smile. "Friends in high places," he said. "Hey. Where's Christine?"

"Where are Christine's kids?" Sylvia asked. "They live here in this rat hole with you two creeps? I'm calling Child Protective Services."

Sylvia dropped the box and disappeared into the back, presumably to check the bedrooms for children, sick or dead or worse.

"Been on the train lately?" Clover asked.

Norman was busy running his finger over the surface of the mirror tile. "What's it to you?"

"Nothing. Just saw your name on the train roster, from Sacramento to Bonita the other day, and thought you ought to know that somebody is about to hang you out to dry." It was a bold move, but Clover had nothing to lose.

Norman's head snapped up and he fixed her with a cold stare for as long as he could maintain it, and then he blinked, stretched the muscles of his face and went back to scouring the mirror for errant grains of cocaine, which he rubbed on his gums.

"Big prison time, Norman," Clover said, "killing a guy for hire."

"Shut the fuck up," he said. "You don't know anything about it."

"I know enough. I know you killed that guy, beat him up. Look at your knuckles."

Norman looked at the back of his hands like he'd never seen them before. They were skinned and bruised.

"And you got enough money for it to drug yourself all the way to hell. Somebody's going to jail for that, you know, and it isn't going to be the person who hired you, unless you tell who that was."

"Nobody knows."

"Hell, Norman, even I know, and I'm nobody. Wait until the police get hold of the train's passenger list."

"You shittin' me?"

Clover shook her head slowly.

"Fuck me," he said softly. Then he stood up, grabbed a shirt from the floor and put it on. "I gotta get out of here."

"What'd he pay you?"

"Shut up."

"Just tell me, Norman, and I won't say anything to anybody. If they sniff out your involvement, they'll have to do it by themselves."

Norman buttoned the two buttons that were on his shirt, and ran his hand over the front of it. He dipped his fingers into the front pocket, and pulled out a tiny plastic bag full of white powder. "Ha," he said. "There you are, my pretty."

"Tell me, Norman," Clover knew she was beginning to whine. "Innocent guys are going to get blamed for what you did."

"Cry over it," he said, and disappeared back into the bathroom.

Clover followed him, and watched in fascinated horror as Norman put a rubber tube around his arm and tried to slap up a vein. He gave up on one arm and tried the other.

Then he cooked up the smack in a spoon over a candle stub on the window ledge and sucked it into a syringe he kept on top of the medicine cabinet.

"Was it somebody from Fletcher? Somebody from Golim? Who the hell was it, Norman?" she was yelling at him by the time he found a not-so-recently-used vein in his foot and poked the needle in. "Deputy Travis? The railroad guys?"

"Milo Grimes," Norman sighed as the plunger went in and his head fell back against the filthy window next to the toilet. "Paid me good. And I got proof."

Clover turned around and bumped into Sylvia who had been watching over her shoulder. "Jesus fucking Christ," she said, then burst into tears and ran out of the house.

Clover caught her and got her to stop a block away. She tried to comfort Sylvia, but Sylvia would not be comforted. She was hurt and angry and scared and heartbroken to see her brother like that, and there wasn't much Clover could say or do that would help her through the experience.

"Let's go back and make sure he's okay," Clover said. "Maybe we could get him into bed or something. Tidy the place up a bit."

"I don't want to go back there," she said. "I've got to talk to my folks. We've got to get him into treatment or something. He's going to die! See what I mean, Clover? We've got to get out of here. You and me, we've got to escape before this place takes us down with it."

"I'm going back," Clover said. "I'm going to make sure he's all right. C'mon. Come with me."

With slow coaxing, Sylvia eventually took a step back toward the house, and then another, and a few minutes later, they were walking in the front door.

But it was too late for Norman. He was dead on the toilet, saliva dripping in a long stream from his chin to his chest, the needle still stuck in his foot. Clover went to the neighbor's to call 9-1-1 while Sylvia stood in the living room and screamed.

Denny got out of the pickup truck, waved his thank-you to the Mexican farmer, then walked down past the path to Yorktown, all the way to the county motor pool. He thought about going down to check on Sly and York, but he didn't have the stomach for it. Those two guys were losing it, and Denny had to stay focused if he was going to survive the night.

The motor pool was only a couple of blocks away, and there was a place in the chain-link fence that a skinny guy like Denny could shimmy through. Used to be when it rained at night, Denny and Sly would bundle up York and walk him up to the motor pool, where they'd all three get a good dry night's sleep in one of the county vans or trucks. But it had been a long time since they'd done that. Now they just threw tarps over themselves and dug little trenches around their sleeping blankets so the runoff wouldn't soak them.

They got soaked anyway. Good thing they were where they were. They'd never survive up in Seattle or someplace like that where it rained a lot. Or the Midwest, where the climate was always out to kill ya.

Denny made it through the fence. The motor pool had already closed for the night, so all he had to do was find an unlocked truck. It wasn't hard. The county guys thought that the place was secure because there was a fence around it. They hardly ever locked the trucks, and sometimes they even left the keys in the ignition.

Denny climbed up into a big pickup truck and with teeth and his pocket knife, opened the stiff plastic that enclosed his new light and its recharging cord. Then he plugged the cord into the cigarette lighter. He didn't know how long it would take to charge; probably not long.

It was a good time to take a nap. The pain pills he'd taken earlier were making it hard for him to keep his head up, so he lay down on the seat in the truck for a short nap.

"You gotta stop ripping those newspapers, York," Sly said. "You're about to make me crazy." Sly felt like his skin was the wrong type of material to keep his innards under control. It didn't stretch enough; he felt way too big for it. It itched. He could not remember feeling this restless. *It's like Christmas Eve when you're a kid,* he thought, *only a bad one. This is like Christmas Eve in hell.*

"Blood on the path," York said.

"What?"

"Blood on the path. Blood will be shed tonight. I seen it all in a dream."

"Not your blood," Sly said. "Not mine, neither."

"Full moon," York said, and ripped another long piece. "Anything can happen."

"Their blood, York. The enemy's blood. They're the aggressors. Their oppression will not last."

"Help us, Lord," York said, and ripped another strip. "Help us be on the side of righteousness."

"We're on the side of righteousness," Sly said, jumping to his feet and starting to pace. Action gave momentary relief to his anxiety. "Ain't nobody more righteous than those who live free and do good. Like us, York. That ain't something you have to worry about, righteousness. We're righteous, all right. You especially."

He stopped pacing and went to York, knelt at York's side, and gently removed the newspapers from the old man's hands. "Listen to me, York. About tonight. Silence is what we need. Absolute silence. I'll give you the command by touching your elbow with my foot. I may have to rearrange you a little bit. Let me do that. But don't talk. Don't say a word, okay?"

York took a deep breath that ended in a little strangled cough. "Yeah," he said. He pushed the strips of smelly newspapers off his legs and said, "Help me up."

Sly knew that York was as agitated as he was, only York didn't have enough energy for it. "You ought to sleep this afternoon," he said. "Tonight's going to be busy."

"I'll sleep when I'm in my grave," York said, and shook the cobwebs out of the veins in his legs. "That'll be soon enough. Help me to the latrine."

Steve was just straightening his desk before going home when the call came in about a drug death. He had no idea where Travis was, so he had him paged, grabbed his hat and keys and went to see for himself. On the way, he called Athena on his cell and told her he was going to be late.

He was surprised and a little disconcerted to find Clover standing in front of the house, talking with another girl. A uniformed police officer was standing next to them.

"What are you doing here?" he asked as he walked up.

"This is Sylvia," Clover said, and Steve looked into the swollen eyes of a young woman who looked like she belonged in this part of town.

"My brother—" Sylvia choked out and then started to shudder and sob.

"Who found him?"

"We both did," Clover said. "I called nine-one-one."

"Good girl," Steve said. "What happened?"

"Can't you tell?" Sylvia wailed.

Steve looked at Clover. She raised an eyebrow and shrugged her shoulder. "He was shooting up."

Steve nodded. "Stay here," he said, then went inside. Two more uniforms wearing latex gloves were inside. It wasn't pretty. They spoke for a few minutes, and then Steve went back outside.

"Did you see him do that?"

Clover nodded. "But, listen, Sheriff, more important. He was the one who killed the dead guy. He pushed that guy off the train."

"What?" Sylvia was having no part of this. "No way. My brother may have been a drug addict, but that's not his fault. No way did he kill anybody. Clover, I can't believe you said that. No way!" She squared off against Clover. "You bitch!" She took a swing, but Clover ducked, and Sheriff Goddard grabbed her wrist. "Settle down now," he said.

"Don't you ever say anything like that about my brother again!" Sylvia shouted.

Steve held her fast. "Sylvia, we have to phone your parents. Where are your parents?"

With something new to focus on, Sylvia relaxed and gave the uniformed cop her parents' phone numbers. Then she started to cry again, and Steve let her sit in the backseat of his cruiser and handed her a box of tissues from the trunk.

He went back to Clover.

"Now what?"

"He said that Milo Grimes paid him very well to beat that guy up and throw him off the train. Said he had proof."

"Milo Grimes?" Steve wasn't a bit surprised, but he had to act not only surprised, but shocked and doubtful. He didn't know if he pulled it off.

"That's what he said." Clover kept looking past him at Sylvia.

Steve turned to see what she was looking at. Sylvia was giving her the evil eye. He turned his attention back to Clover.

"There she goes," Clover said.

Steve turned around again, just in time to see Sylvia running down the middle of the street, thighs waggling in her little shorts, sandals clapping on the asphalt. "That's okay," he said. "You're sure he said Milo Grimes?"

"I'm sure. Look at his hands. They're all beat up. And he had plenty of money to put into . . . you know, his arm. His foot. Whatever, it was too much." Clover looked at the ground and kicked the dirt driveway with the toe of her sneaker. "His name was on the train manifest. He took the train from Sacramento to Bonita that day. He was on the Western Express with the dead guy."

"Are you kidding me with this stuff? Are you some kind of Nancy Drew all of a sudden?"

"Nope." Clover looked up at him and smiled an adorably crooked little smile that was half naughtiness, half proud of herself. "I just can't let York and those guys get punished because of something they didn't do."

In front of the uniforms and everybody else, Steve couldn't help but give her a hug. "You're amazing, Miss Clover. Miss Clover, girl detective."

She pushed him away and said, "Now. Now that we know that York's guys couldn't have done it, can't they stay?"

Steve let out a loud breath. "Sorry, kiddo. That ship has sailed."

"There's nothing we can do?"

"Sorry."

Clover nodded, her self-satisfaction gone. "I'm going to go."

Steve nodded, thanked her one more time, told her he'd be in touch, so be sure to be available, and then went into the house to make sure procedure was being followed to the letter.

He better call Athena to tell her to forget dinner; he'd catch a burger. When he left here, he had to talk with Milo Grimes, and that might take a while.

Travis kept a bottle of Southern Comfort under the seat of his car. He knew it was against the law, but since he was the law, he didn't think it was such a big deal. It was for times just such as this.

He reached under the seat while stopped at a stoplight, retrieved the bottle, unscrewed the cap and took a long pull. It was like alcohol syrup. Sickening in a way, and yet oh-so-delicious. "To Janis," he said, which is what he always said when he took his first drink of Southern Comfort. He'd heard that it was Janis Joplin's favorite drink, and he'd loved her ever since he was a kid and got his first look at her on the *Pearl* album cover. He took another drink, screwed the cap back on and wondered what he was going to do to keep his mind off what he was going to do later.

Eileen.

He didn't like the thought of it, because she was so old, and so boozy, and stunk like cigarettes all the time, but she was a surprisingly good lay. Maybe that's what he needed to take the edge off. He'd give her a shot of Janis Juice, then he'd give her a bigger shot of Travis Nectar, and he'd be good to go tonight.

He turned left from the wrong lane of traffic, cutting off a geezer in a Mercedes, gunned it and headed for the trailer park.

But when he walked up the stairs, bottle in hand, he heard voices inside. Female voices. He wasn't sure what to do for a moment, so he hesitated, and the door opened.

"Hi," Eileen said, and she looked kind of good, kind of fixed up.

"Hi." He held up the bottle.

"Ooh, Southern Comfort," she said, and held the screen

door open for him. "C'mon in."

Another woman sat on the sofa. She had red hair, like Eileen's, only it was softer, not fried on the ends. She was younger, too, Travis could see, and they each had a drink, and it didn't take long for him to see a few other possibilities in this situation. *Yep,* he thought, *this just might take my mind off things for a little while.*

"Brenda, this is Travis."

"Hi, Travis," Brenda said. "I've just been hearing all about you."

"I'm better in person," he said, and handed the bottle to Eileen. "I'll take a stiff one, babe," he said.

"Me, too," she said and gave him a kiss on the cheek.

"Later," he said, gave her a swat on the butt, and sat down on the couch next to Brenda.

"Didn't expect to see you today," Eileen said, and handed him a jelly glass half full of booze. "What with your moonlight job tonight and all."

"Got antsy waitin'," he said, and took a sip. He eyed Brenda's tight T-shirt and all that was inside of it.

"What do you do?"

"Travis is a deputy sheriff," Eileen said with obvious pride. "Tonight he's gonna clean up that hobo camp down by the train tracks."

"You are?"

Travis nodded and inched his hand over toward Brenda's shoulder.

"How are you going to clean up that camp?" Brenda wanted to know. She looked at Eileen, but Eileen was looking at Travis with stars in her eyes. *This guy is way too young for her,* Brenda thought. *Way too young.* And she didn't like the way he looked at her boobs, either. Especially right in front of Eileen. This guy was an ass.

"Me and some friends are just going to go down there and persuade them some."

"How?"

"We got our ways. Now why don't you tell me a little bit about yourself?"

"You going to hurt anybody?"

"Not unless they ask for it."

Brenda moved away from Travis, who was leaning closer to her. "They're harmless guys," she said. "I don't think you ought to hurt them."

"If you don't want me to, I won't," he said. Then he looked up at Eileen. "You told Clover to steer clear, didn't you?"

Eileen nodded.

"Clover?" Brenda said. "You know Clover?"

"Clover's my daughter. Do you know her?"

Brenda stood up. "I gotta go."

"No," Travis whined. "We were just getting cozy."

Eileen didn't like that at all. She took Brenda's glass and said, "Thanks for stopping by. Let's get together next week."

"Yeah. Okay. Bye."

Brenda left and Eileen sat down next to Travis, but he'd lost his taste for her. He wanted somebody younger. What he really wanted was Clover, and the fact that she didn't want him was a thorn in his brain. Eileen snuggled up to him, but he was no longer in the mood. When Brenda left, she took all the interesting possibilities out of the evening that stretched long before him. He downed his drink. "Fill me up," he said.

"I'll fill you up now if you'll fill me up later," she said with a naughty look.

"We'll see," he said, and realized he'd need a lot more booze in a lot bigger glass if he was going to be able to make that happen. He felt helpless, lost in a downward spiral. The only thing he could do was anesthetize. He took the glass of Southern

Comfort that Eileen held out for him, then pulled her down onto his lap. He felt safe in her nasty little trailer for some reason, and since he had nowhere to be until dark—about ten-thirty—he could relax, at least for a while. Eileen had the kind of muscle control that could take his mind off of the activities ahead. He needed it.

West Wheaton is way too small a town, Brenda thought as she drove down toward York's place. Clover was Eileen's daughter. Eileen was doing Travis, the guy who was going to trash Denny and the guys that night. Whoa. Too weird.

She parked her car a block away on the street above, decided that carrying her purse made her look like a hooker, so she put her keys in her pocket, fluffed her hair, and locked the car.

Halfway down the block, she was surprised, or wished she was surprised, to see Clover approaching the top of the path from the other way. Brenda waited for her at the top of the path. While she waited, she watched Clover walk and tried not to be envious of her young, lithe body and the absolutely unself-conscious way her hair swung. She was adorable, even without makeup and styled hair. She could be fixed up a lot with just a touch of eye shadow and a razor cut on that hair that glowed with highlights Brenda had to pay good money to have put in her own hair. Brenda was no competition for this. Actually, Denny was a loser, and both she and Clover could do better.

"Hi," she said as Clover approached.

"Hi." Clover acted feline and wary. "Is Denny here?"

"I don't know," Brenda said. "I just got here."

Clover stopped and looked at her with a soft expression that nevertheless demanded an explanation for Brenda's presence.

"I heard there's going to be some trouble down here tonight."

"Oh?"

"I just came to warn the guys."

"They already know," Clover said.

Brenda nodded. "Think Sly's down there?" she asked.

"Why?"

"Think they need some help? I mean they're going to leave, right? Don't you think they need some help? Where are they going to go?"

"Why are you so interested?"

"It isn't Denny, if that's what you're worried about," Brenda said. "I'm not after him. I just helped him out when he was hurt, is all."

"And we're grateful."

Brenda was getting frustrated with this conversation, or lack of it. She wanted to do something, and she didn't know what. "I just saw Travis over at your mom's place, and got worried about the guys, that's all. I don't think Travis is . . ." She didn't want to bad-mouth Clover's mother's boyfriend—or whatever he was—but she'd already started the sentence and didn't know how to finish it.

"Such a nice guy?" Clover said.

Brenda nodded, looked again away from Clover's clear-skin face and down at her own dusty shoe.

"He's an ass," Clover said. "What was he doing at my mom's? How do you know my mom?"

"I met her at breakfast a few days ago. I like her."

Clover seemed to like that. She emitted a small smile. "She needs friends. Good friends. Is Travis—what was *he* doing over there?"

"Drinking," Brenda said. She'd leave the rest for Eileen to explain. "Listen, I just came to help if I can. I'm no trouble for you."

"C'mon," Clover said, and lightly tripped down the path. "Let's go see who's here."

But what she found didn't please her at all, and didn't lighten the load on her mind for the approaching evening.

York sat in a cloud of mold dust amid an enormous pile of shredded newspaper, his hands busy tearing more of it into tiny strips. His legs were covered, and there was a shoulder-high pile all around him. Clover had seen him like this before, and it was never good. Sly paced back and forth, making an occasional violent gesture, as if arguing with another half of himself. Denny was not there.

"Daddy?" She knelt next to York and scooped moldy, crumbling paper from his legs. "Daddy?" she whispered. "You all right?"

"Clover, bless your heart," York said. "Thank you for coming. There's going to be blood tonight. I seen it in a dream. Blood on the path. I don't want no violence, girl, you know I don't. And I don't know what to do next. Maybe you better take me to the shelter, hon. I don't want to be a party to nobody getting hurt."

"Nobody's going to get hurt, York," Clover said. "I found out who killed that guy, and the sheriff's with him right now. He's dead. Killed himself with drugs. I don't think there's going to be any problem down here tonight. They're going to make you clear out, but that won't be until probably tomorrow. You don't worry about it."

"I seen it," York said, and his rough hand gripped her arm. "I seen it in a dream. You don't mess with a full moon, girl."

"I'll take you home with me if you want," she said, "but I've talked with the sheriff. Tomorrow we'll find you a nice place to live."

"I'd like to die under the stars," York said, his pale, sightless eyes taking on that faraway look that frightened Clover. She knew that his health was bad and knew that one day she'd come down the hill and find nothing left of him but his shell, but she wasn't ready for it.

Not now, not ever.

Clover looked over to see that Brenda was talking quietly with Sly, and her presence seemed to have calmed him down. Clover sat down on the ground and held York's hand, hoping that she could have the same comforting influence. "Know where Denny is?" she asked.

"No," he said, and his hands reached for more newspapers to shred, but Clover just held his hand and stroked the wrinkled, spotted back of it.

"These things are all mildewed and rotting," Clover said. "Breathing this dust can't be good for your lungs."

"Blood on the path," York said.

"Where's Denny?" she asked.

York shook his head.

She stood up, scooped more of the stinking newspapers away from him and then went over to where Brenda and Sly were having an earnest conversation. "Know where Denny is?" Clover asked without waiting for them to acknowledge her.

"Went for supplies," Sly said.

"What kind of supplies? When?"

"Self-defense supplies," Sly said too loudly, loud enough for York to hear. Then he lowered his voice. "We're going to war tonight."

"I don't think so," Clover said, and told him about Norman.

"That doesn't cut any ice with Deputy Dawg," Sly said, and Clover figured he was right about that. "He and those railroad guys, they've got a case of the red ass, and they're thinking they're going to evict us tonight. They're wrong."

Clover saw Brenda put a calming hand on his arm, and while he didn't shake it off, he didn't much acknowledge it, either. Clover had to take a mental step back and see the two of them as they were, standing in front of her, instead of looking at Brenda as a rival for Denny's affections, and at Sly as a bum and a bad influence. They kind of looked right for each other, in some weird way. Their ages matched a little closer, and since Sly got a haircut and shave and cleaned up a little with a new polo shirt on, they looked like they could be right at home, strolling through the park together.

Except for that wild look in Sly's eyes. His eyes were dark and mysterious, and at the moment they were dangerously unreadable. Clover had seen him off and running; Denny had told her even worse stories. Denny said when Sly went into this military mode, he shouted orders and talked in code in his sleep. Every now and then, he'd peer over the edge of his little bedroom surroundings, suspicious-like, and Denny said he knew that Sly was deep asleep, but his eyes were open and looking around for gooks. Eerie.

Well, whatever it was, it was Sly's problem, not Clover's. She had enough to worry about with Denny, and he wasn't even here. Maybe he'd found someplace else to be for the day. That would be good. "Okay," she said. "I'm going. Tell Denny I'll be back later."

"War is not for women," Sly said, and gently pushed Brenda away from him. "You both go on. Come back tomorrow for the body count."

"No conflict," York yelled.

"You may not want it," Sly yelled back, "but you got it."

"Blood," York said, and shook his head. "Blood on the path, god*damn* it." Then he pointed his face at the late-afternoon sky and apologized to God.

Clover stopped at York on her way out, put her hand on the old man's shoulder. "I'll be back for you, York," she said quietly, "and I'll help you get to somewhere nice. It's too late today, but we'll get you settled someplace warm and wonderful with nice hot food and good warm baths, okay? Tomorrow, okay?"

"Go on home, Clover," York said.

"Okay, York? Tomorrow, okay?"

"Okay."

"You going to be all right tonight? You just stick to no conflict and they'll have no beef with you. Tell them I'm going to take care of you tomorrow, okay?"

"Go on."

"I love you, Daddy," she whispered to him.

His old weathered hand patted hers. Then he cleared his throat and shooed her away.

"Brenda?" Clover called.

Brenda finished up her conversation with Sly and joined her, and they single-filed up the path, Clover leading the way.

"I'm scared for them," Brenda said.

"The sheriff will take care of things," Clover said, and just as she said that, Steve Goddard's cruiser stopped right at the top of the path.

"They're expecting trouble tonight," Clover said as soon as Steve got out of his car, "from Travis."

"And Travis is expecting to deliver it," Brenda said.

"York said he'd go with me to a nursing home tomorrow," Clover said, "but it's too late today to do anything for him. You can keep them all safe, can't you, Sheriff?"

"You two girls go on home," Steve said. "I'm going to talk with York."

"Please don't let Travis hurt them," Brenda said, and Steve gave her a queer-enough look to make her feel out of place. Then she realized that the sheriff certainly wasn't going to *encourage* Travis, and she felt stupid for saying anything at all. She tugged at Clover's sleeve. "C'mon," she said, and they walked up to Brenda's car while the sheriff disappeared down the path and was lost from sight in the blackberry brambles.

Clouds blew in from the north, and with them came a chill wind.

When Milo Grimes's staff left for the day, he didn't even say good-bye. He just sat in his big swivel chair and listened to the silence.

The shit was coming down.

What a day.

First Ashton died, leaving Milo holding the bag. He wanted to give Oshiro's money back and just weasel out of the deal, but Oshiro got pissy and refused. Then Norman stuck a needle in himself and went straight to hell, but not before giving some stupid girl some stupid information about Haas, Ashton's flunky, which implicated the fine Grimes name. Then Steve Goddard showed up to rub his nose in it, ask too many questions. Travis and the railroad guys were moot and obsolete, and probably out of control at this point anyway. His wife was a slut, and the city-council meeting was in the morning, and sure as shit, they were going to nail his butt to the wall. Fraud. Racketeering. Aggravated murder. The whole scam would come out at the meeting in the morning.

Milo had troubles. His troubles were so big and so bad that he didn't even want the bottle of Jack Daniel's he had in his desk drawer. Instead, he was thinking about the .32 he had in the other desk drawer.

He had watched one of those police programs on television the other night while listening to Susie Marie snore. He realized that somebody's life just stopped when they went to jail. Nobody feeds the dog, nobody makes the mortgage payment, nobody checks the phone messages. Life for that person just stopped. Susie Marie could never figure out his convoluted finances. She had no way to pay the bills. She'd end up broke and on the street. Somebody else would be going through all his stuff.

Somebody else would be fucking the maid on his expensive Oriental rug.

Somehow, he'd always thought he'd be able to keep the scam rolling, keeping his butt just far enough ahead to keep it from rolling over him. It was a game. His life's work. Now it seemed like all his well-conceived plans had morphed into a heat-seeking missile, zeroed in on his ass. If the shit came down, it would come down heavy and immediate. He'd be living his life one day and the next minute he'd be in a prison jumpsuit, eating in a chow line, trying to keep his ass from being violated by some enormous sadist, and priorities would instantly change from buying a thousand-dollar suit for the election-night victory speech to learning to play the harmonica.

He'd never survive. He'd never be able to do it.

He'd never even survive the perp walk, handcuffs and press and all. Would Susie Marie stand by his side and be in the courtroom every day of his trial? Never. Not for a moment. It would interfere with her tennis lesson.

It would interfere with her finding a new husband to move into the house on the hill and take over the mortgage payment.

Maybe he could cop a plea. Maybe he could deny everything. Get a fancy, high-priced lawyer and go the distance with the legal system.

And what would he have when he was through? No money, no job, no status, no wife, no house. At best.

Prison at worst.

Life as he knew it, no matter what, would be over. All life as he had ever imagined it could be would be over. There would be nothing left.

There *was* nothing left.

It *was* over.

Milo was too old to start again, especially with a cloud as big and black as this was going to turn out to be. He had hoped that he could liquidate everything and jump out of the public eye, his cushy retirement safe and secure in some offshore account before the shit hit the fan, and then he could just lie on the beach while some bikinied beauty peeled his grapes.

Timing was everything, and he'd missed it. He couldn't leave now, his finances weren't ripe. He wasn't ready.

He was fucked.

His options were few. The most likely of the bunch would be to skip out with enough cash to start over somewhere else. It wouldn't be easy, but hell, nothing he did was ever easy. It wasn't his choice, but he seemed to have screwed himself out of his choices. He'd get a new set of ID and a new name, manufacture himself a fresh history and start over. Maybe in Baja. Maybe in Ecuador.

Regardless, he wouldn't prolong the agony. He'd see how the city-council meeting went and take it from there.

That settled, he opened one drawer and pulled out the bottle, spun off the cap and drank down a hefty slug. It burned good. He followed it with another.

Then he opened the other drawer and left it open, the .32 snub-nosed revolver just lying there waiting, loaded and looking mean.

"There's going to be blood shed here tonight, Sheriff," York said.

Steve Goddard pulled an old plastic bucket up next to where York was sitting, his milky eyes wide open yet focused inward on his vision. Steve sat down and put a hand on York's shoulder. "Now listen to me, York," he said. "You and me, we go back a long ways. Remember when I used to come down here to visit you when I was just a kid and you'd talk me out of smoking cigarettes?"

York pulled on a piece of newspaper and began to tear a long strip off the edge of it. Steve gently took it from his hands. "I grew to trust your judgment," he said. "You've always been square with me, and square with Denny and Sly and the others who have come and gone, down here over the years."

"Lord knows I try," York said.

"The lord does know," Steve said, "and so do I. And so does the rest of the community. But now we've got a little situation, and I need you to trust *my* judgment. We've got a bad situation in the government in West Wheaton, York, and it's going to take a little time to cut out the cancer. But I'm going to do it. I'm the law man in this town and I'm going to make it happen. But things like that don't happen overnight."

York nodded.

"Tomorrow, Clover and Brenda are going to take you to a place to stay for a little while, until we get this all worked out. Sly and Denny will have to find places of their own. I think Clover and Brenda are going to help with that, too."

York nodded, squinting his eyes shut in dread. In pain. Steve saw moisture squeeze out between his lids and he hoped those weren't tears of grief, but just the seep from watery old-man eyes. "Tonight—" York began.

"You leave tonight to me. Nothing's going to happen down here tonight because I'm going to be up there on the street in my car. If anybody comes down here, they're going to have to come by me, and that ain't going to happen."

"I seen the blood, Steve."

"Could be Denny gets a nosebleed."

York nodded, but Steve could tell he wasn't convinced.

"Sly and Denny, they have a plan." York kept his voice low because Sly was pacing back and forth, close enough to hear.

Steve kept his voice low, too. "That's okay. Let them have their plan. Nothing will come of it, because nobody's going to come down here, except maybe me. And none of you better ambush me."

York managed a small smile at that.

"Okay, then," Steve said as he stood up and brushed off his uniform pants. "All we have to do is survive this one night and we'll be fine. Okay?"

York nodded.

Steve approached Sly with his hand held out. Sly took it and shook it, the intensity in his deep brown eyes a little frightening to Steve. "Everything's going to be just fine tonight," Steve said. "I'll be watching."

"We're on high alert," Sly said.

"Good. Let's you and I keep the perimeter safe."

"Roger that," Sly said.

Steve took a last look around. It was the last time he'd see this place that had been a home to York for generations of young visitors. Tomorrow the bulldozers would come, erase this place, and life would never be the same.

He walked up the hill, got into his car and took a deep breath. He had a couple of hours yet before nightfall, and he had to go visit Milo Grimes. Then he'd stop at the diner, get a bagful of dinner, a thermos of coffee, and sit and wait to make sure peace was kept down here by the tracks.

"So what are you going to do now?" Brenda asked Clover as they walked up the hill and into town.

"I don't know," Clover said. "Maybe go over to my mom's and see if I can persuade Travis to leave the guys alone."

"Bad idea," Brenda said. "He's drinking. You know about talking to drunks."

"No, what?"

"Trying to reason with a drunk is like trying to blow out an electric lightbulb."

Clover smiled for Brenda, but she didn't find that amusing. It was too true; she'd known that about her mother. "Then I don't have a plan. I'll be too nervous to sleep tonight. Maybe I ought to go get a phone book and make some lists about places to call in the morning for York."

"I could help."

Clover nodded. "I wonder where Denny is."

"Maybe we could go have some dinner or something, make some lists, and then come back and see how the guys are doing. Denny ought to be back by then."

"Good plan."

They walked along, headed automatically for Gretta's, when Brenda surprised Clover by asking, "Think Sly ought to come live with me?"

Clover didn't look up, for fear her astonishment would show. "How well do you know Sly?"

"Not very well."

"He's—" Clover tried to find the words to describe her feelings about Sly. She liked him all right, and didn't want to dissuade Brenda from giving him some much-needed help, but she didn't want Brenda to get herself into trouble by having good intentions, either. "He's troubled," Clover said. "Real troubled. Vietnam vet, you know. Some of those guys came back not quite right. Heck, Brenda, you know he ain't right in the head to be living down there with Denny and York."

"Well," Brenda said. "What about that? What about Denny?"

Clover smiled a little, shy smile to herself. "He ain't the marrying kind, that's for sure. I don't know. He's got those eyes, and that smile, and I get all gooey inside when he talks nice to me."

She straightened up, stopped dead in her tracks and put a halting hand on Brenda's wrist. "I won't be having kids with Denny, that's for certain. He's not in my future for the long term. But as long as he's there, and I can feel good about taking care of those guys a little bit, I'm happy with him. It's fun having a boyfriend, but one of these days—well, one of these days he'll be moving on down the line." She shrugged. "Maybe tomorrow."

A little fist grabbed her heart when she said that, and she knew it was more than a possibility. In fact, Denny was already missing. He could already be gone.

"One thing's for sure," she said, starting to walk again and trying to disguise the little catch in her voice. "He won't be moving in with me. Neither will Sly. York could, but I can't take proper care of him. You best think clearly before you hook up with the likes of Sly."

"Prospects are slim," Brenda said with a similar catch in her voice, and Clover's capacity for wisdom took a monumental leap as she saw herself as not quite Brenda, not quite Eileen, but somewhere in the same latitudes, and in just a few short years, too. She didn't like the vision. Maybe it was okay that Denny took off without saying good-bye.

She pulled the diner door open and held it for Brenda as the air-conditioning blew out to them. She had that familiar hot ball of emotion at the bottom of her throat that seemed like sadness, seemed like grief, but was always temporary. She'd survive Denny, and she'd survive Denny's abandonment. *Hell,* she thought with a stab at levity, *maybe that'll save me from abandoning him.*

She wasn't hungry, but she was happy for the company. They sat down and looked at their menus, trying not to look at each other just quite yet. The big clock on the wall said it was eight-fifteen.

As Steve came through Milo's office door unannounced, he saw the mayor slam both his desk drawers closed. Steve was hot, and while he wondered briefly what it was Milo was hiding, it was probably more of the same. More of Milo Grimes. Hiding his shame, the little shit.

"Saw your light on, Milo, thought you might be working on your presentation for tomorrow's council meeting."

"Don't you knock?"

"This is my door," Steve said, the righteous indignation rising within him. "I pay the taxes around here, you don't."

Milo sat back in his chair, giving Steve an even bigger feeling of power and strength. He didn't particularly like it, but he was going to give it full rein. He'd never done that before, and if there was ever a good time to try it, this was the time.

"This is my office, my desk," Steve said. "My chair you're sitting in. And this is my goddamn town. I don't like you, Milo Grimes, and I don't like your way of doing business. I don't like what you've done to my deputy, or what you're about to have done to those guys down there by the train tracks."

"Murderers," Milo said. "Filth."

"Bull. Shit." Steve said it low and slow and put his palms down on the desk and leaned over toward Grimes. "York's been down there for forty years without so much as a nuisance complaint. *You* had that guy killed and thrown off the train for some damn reason. Norman spilled his drug-riddled guts before he stuck the final needle in his vein. Said you paid him enough to kill that guy to fry his brains."

Milo shook his head no and held out his hands to ward off the onslaught.

"Don't you tell me no, you weaselly little fuck. You've pissed me off for the last time, Mr. Mayor, and I've about had it with you and your little tart of a wife. Your self-serving little regime has ended in West Wheaton. I'm here to give you notice not to leave town. You're under suspicion for murder."

"You're out of line, Sheriff."

"My ass, Mayor. I'll get all I need for a grand jury, and I'll do it by this time tomorrow, or you can have my badge for your collection of plundered goods." Steve stood tall. "This time tomorrow you'll be in jail."

"Well, until that time comes, I'll thank you and your mouth to leave my office, and take your attitude with you."

"Come special election, this will be my office. See you at the council meeting. Wear short sleeves," Steve said, "the handcuffs will be more comfortable." Steve spun on his heel and left the spacious mayoral office, leaving the door open behind him. He could hardly believe what he had just said, but he'd said it, and at the moment, he'd meant it. He had West Wheaton's best interests at heart, and he would indeed run for Grimes's vacant seat once he was safely in prison. Assuming Athena approved, of course.

He got down to his cruiser, his heart pounding, sweat popping out on his forehead. He'd been a sheriff for a long time, but he'd never sounded off like that before, especially not to his boss.

No, he thought, *the taxpaying citizens are my employers.* He was just supposed to *answer* to the mayor. But those days were over. If he was right, Grimes would be in prison before he could do any more damage, and Steve would have proved true to the trust of the citizens.

He felt good about himself, if a bit hopped up on adrenaline. He thought about his plan of going to Gretta's and getting a sandwich, and decided instead that he might want to check in on Athena. She ought to know what happened in the past couple of hours, just in case the mayor or his troublemaking spouse decided to give her a call. Or worse, stop in to see her.

Besides, he realized with a twinge of wonderment, he needed to tell her about him overpowering the mayor and doing it so righteously. He wanted Athena to be proud of him, and he knew she would be.

He put the cruiser in gear and pointed it toward home. It was nine-fifteen. Dusk had fallen, but in these long summer nights, it wouldn't be dark for a while yet. Travis and the railroad guys wouldn't do anything until the dark was thick enough to hide in.

It was the first time in his life that Travis couldn't get it up. He blamed it on the booze, he blamed it on the stinking trailer, he blamed it on Eileen's aging face and the fact that she stunk like cigarettes and tasted worse, he blamed it on the activities about to take place down by the tracks later that night. His mind was elsewhere. His concentration was off.

But that didn't help. For the first time, he couldn't get it up. He knew it happened to other guys, but it had never happened to him. He lay back, watching Eileen work with her hands and her mouth, her ratty red-fried hair bobbing up and down as she tried to suck some life into his poor dick, and it only made him mildly nauseous. He pushed her face away and turned over on his side away from her. He ought to put his clothes on and get ready for tonight. He was to meet the railroad guys at ten-thirty at the motor pool gate. The cheap little alarm clock on Eileen's wall said nine-thirty. He had an hour to kill.

Coffee, maybe, at Gretta's. He ought to be sober. More sober than he was.

" 'Smatter, baby?" she said as she crawled over onto him.

He pushed her off, then sat up. She ran her claws lightly down his back, and he had to admit he liked that. "Got anything to eat?"

"Not much," she said. "I could make you a sandwich. Or fry you an egg, maybe."

He thought of her kitchen sink and thought better of it. He stood up. "I've got to go to work."

"I was hoping you'd stay," she said.

He looked down on her, and in this light, from this angle, she didn't look half bad, actually. He wondered if he could maybe get Thor to find a little interest there. He could certainly use the distraction.

Then she stuck a cigarette into her mouth and he changed his mind. "I was hoping you'd blow off that little job you had tonight and stay here with me instead."

"Can't. Need the money."

"You can't need the money. You've got that cushy civil service job with benefits. You sure don't spend your money on me. Where does it all go?"

He wanted to tell her to shut up, but he didn't. He silently dressed, tied his shoes, and walked out into the darkening twilight. He ought to have said good-bye, he ought to have kissed her, she worked so hard to get him going, he ought to have said thanks, see you soon, but he didn't have the stomach for any of it.

He didn't have the stomach for his future. Not his immediate future, not his long-range future. He didn't have the stomach for much, and he sure didn't have the stomach for worn-out Eileen. He heard her yell something to him as he was walking out the front door, but the only word he caught was "Clover." He knew her heart was in the right place about Clover, and that was a big point in her favor.

But maybe he could find somebody else from here on out. He always felt dirty when he was through with Eileen. Maybe that's what his dick was trying to tell him.

He parked in Gretta's parking lot and checked the cash in his wallet.

He found ten bucks, stuck his wallet back in his pocket, and went in to get a bowl of soup or a sandwich or something that would take the edge off the Southern Comfort and the taste of Eileen's cigarettes. He caught sight of himself in the reflection of the glass door and resolved to get to the gym. Tomorrow. He'd drop a few pounds, tighten up the abs, find himself a decent woman and maybe think about settling down. Give up these midnight jobs for the mayor. Start feeling good about himself again.

But, shit, it was hard. He couldn't afford his trashy little lifestyle as it was. How was he going to attract a decent woman?

Maybe he'd fluff up his resume and send it on to the police station over in Sacramento. That might be the best thing. Maybe after tonight, the mayor would give him a good recommendation to go with it.

He pushed open the door and smelled the fried grease. It added to his discomfort, but he choked it down, sat at the counter and felt a tired smile come across his face when Veronica greeted him. Veronica set a cup of hot coffee in front of him, and he doused it with sugar and cream while he ordered.

He ate the beef barley soup and a whole basket of crackers, and when that was finished, he was feeling better and it was ten o'clock. Maybe he'd get to the meeting place early and wait. Maybe the whole thing could be over with early and he could go home and sleep for a couple of days. Call in sick and stay in bed. Maybe he'd just quit. But on the heels of that thought was the thought of that stack of unpaid bills on top of his refrigerator. One of these days he'd have to go through them and see what needed to be paid.

Meantime, he thought, as he pushed the bundle of envelopes out of his mind, he had work to do.

He paid the tab, flirted a little bit with Veronica, although she was way too old for him, and got into his car. He took a deep breath, said out loud, "Let's get this over with," and revved the engine a couple of times before putting it in gear and slowly backing out of the diner parking lot.

★ ★ ★ ★ ★

Brenda and Clover watched him go.

"He never even saw us," Clover said in wonderment.

"This isn't a very big place," Brenda said.

"Don't you look around to see who's in a place when you first go in? Especially a place like this?"

Brenda nodded.

"I mean in case you've got friends sitting in a booth, and you might want to join them?"

Brenda nodded.

"Everybody looks around. Everybody always looks around in the donut shop, too."

"Maybe he doesn't have any friends."

"He's got other things on his mind," Clover said, and again she wondered where Denny was and what was going to happen to them all as a result of this approaching night. "I've got to take care of York in the morning," she said to Brenda. "I think I'll call in to work and tell them I can't make it."

"I did that today," Brenda said. "I better not do it tomorrow, too."

Clover nodded. "You need to get home?"

"Yeah. I hate to, but it's after ten already. I ought to get some sleep. You going to be all right by yourself?"

"Sure," Clover said, but she had no idea what she was going to do to occupy her mind. She couldn't even ask Denny to call her when it was all over. "It's getting dark."

They paid their tab and walked out together, said their good-byes, almost but not quite engaged in a hug, and Brenda went one way while Clover went the other.

Clover headed for home, knowing she ought to be there and be safe, and wait for word. It was going to be hard. She could make her list of places to call in the morning for York. She could paint that picture frame she'd been wanting to decorate.

Maybe she'd get out some glue and put some beads on it, too. Or the shells she'd picked up last time she went to the beach. Maybe she could occupy her hands with that project while she thought about Denny and tried to make it all right that he had up and scampered away. It was hard for her to believe it one way, but in another way, she'd been expecting it.

By the time she got home, the streetlights were on, it was pitch black, and she was glad Denny was gone. He was going to suck her youth away. It was time she found a nice guy she could have babies with, somebody who had a car and a job and a future. She was certain there were guys like that out there, she just had to open her eyes. Denny had put blinders on her, but now the blinders were coming off, and Clover was on the prowl for a man.

It hurt kind of good, the feeling, and she laughed through the couple of tears that squeezed out of her heart and fell off her eyelids. A new life, a new adventure.

Denny woke up when he heard the car door slam and for a moment he couldn't figure out where he was. He squinted and looked around. Dark. He moved a little bit and realized he was in the front seat of a car. Truck. He moved his head and felt the enormous ache that came with the colossal knot on the front of his forehead. He moved to touch his forehead and found the spotlight in his hand. The cord was plugged into the cigarette lighter.

Jesus. It was dark. He'd fallen asleep under too many pain pills. Who knows what could have happened down at the tracks. Deputy Dawg may have beaten York to death by now, and it would have all been his fault.

He sat up, but as his mind began to clear, he searched mentally for the sound that woke him. It had been a car door slamming. Somebody else was in the motor pool. He had to be careful.

He unplugged the light, slipped it inside his jacket, zipped up the jacket and slid out of the car as quickly as possible, then shut the door quietly to minimize the interior light. Then he crouched by the rear tire, listening to the night, listening for voices. Nothing. Just the sounds of the night.

Then, the crunch of footsteps. Denny ran in a crouch as quietly as he could until he could see who was illuminated under the security light at the front gate. It was the deputy himself.

Good. Denny ran the other way, found the breach in the fence and scampered through, headed hell-bent for home, trying to ignore the pounding in his head, which felt with every footfall as if his cranium would fly apart. He checked to make sure the slingshot was still tucked into the back of his jeans, and he didn't stop running until he hit the top of the path.

"It's me," he called as he walked down. He didn't want Sly ambushing him at the bottom.

"Where the fuck have you been?" Sly asked.

"I got the light, and it had to get charged up," Denny said.

"Jesus Christ," Sly said. He was relieved that Denny hadn't deserted them, but the fact that Denny was back didn't help their situation all that much. They hadn't trained. He'd practiced with his slingshot a few times, agitation building in him to the snapping point, but now the time was at hand.

"Deputy's at the motor pool," Denny said.

Sly nodded as if he knew something. "Douse the fire," he said. "Everybody assume their positions."

The two of them got York up amid a flurry of rotten newspaper powder, and had him sit on the overturned bucket right at the bottom of the path. "Maintain absolute silence," Sly whispered. Denny smothered the small fire with dirt and let the starlight illuminate the camp. The eastern horizon glowed with imminent moonrise.

"Full moon's coming," York said.

"Shhh," Sly said.

"Full moon's going to have its way with all of us."

"Quiet."

They maintained their silence, York sitting on the bucket with the light in his hands, Sly and Denny on either side of him, wrist rockets at the ready. They knew that it wasn't going to be long before the ambush, and all three of them wanted it over quickly.

"Ready?" Sonny Topolo called out to Travis as they pulled up in the van. "Leave your car."

Travis slid open the side door and got in.

"Here's the plan," Sonny said. "We're cleaning out that place tonight. Everybody goes. They either go to the hospital, to the morgue, or down the line. Tomorrow morning the dozers make a park down there. Everybody clear?"

"Morgue?" Travis didn't like the sound of that.

"They make trouble, we're just defending ourselves."

Silence.

"Everybody okay with that?"

"Hell, yes," the guy in the passenger seat said.

Travis felt himself shrinking inside his skin.

"You? You there in the back?"

"Yeah, I guess, sure, okay, let's do it."

"All right," the driver said, he put it in gear and they headed out.

"I gotta go, baby," Steve said to Athena.

"Nooo," she moaned, and threw a well-formed leg over his hip.

He rubbed the outside of her thigh, and then around to her muscular butt, up the small of her back, and he felt her wiggle a little bit under the caress, but his mind was already on other matters.

"Mr. Mayor?"

"Stop that now," he said, and tried to push her leg off him.

"Can I start thinking of what my social programs are going to be when I'm First Lady of West Wheaton?"

"Yes, you can."

"What about when I'm First Lady of California?"

"Whoa. I'm no politician, Athena. You know that. I'll run for mayor, because this is where we live, but when the term is up, we'll retire and I'll help you in the garden."

"You'll help me in the garden?" She raised up on an elbow and looked at him. "Really?"

"Really."

"What if you run and don't get elected? Then will you help me in the garden earlier?"

"I'm done with you, woman."

"Obviously." She pulled her leg back and rolled over, her back to him, hugging a pillow. "Come home, use me, abuse me, and then leave again like a thief in the night."

"I'll be back for another round."

"In your dreams, cowboy."

She lay quietly, listening to him dress, thinking again, for the millionth time at least, that she was the luckiest woman in the world. She loved how he made love to her, and she loved how he came home to share information with her, his triumphs and his defeats in life. She loved how when he was triumphant, his first thought was to come home and make love to her, and whenever he had experienced defeat, he came home and she always wanted to make love to him. And so it went. Life was good. Better than good. And soon he'd be mayor.

He kissed her on the cheek, and she looked up just in time to see him wearing a short sleeve sweatshirt and jeans, not the uniform she expected to see him in. "You okay?"

"I'm going to see to York tonight," he said. "I want to make sure nothing bad happens down there. I don't trust Travis."

"I love you," she said.

"I love you, too, babe," he responded.

"Honey?"

He stopped and looked back at her from the doorway.

"Be careful."

"Always," he said, and headed out.

As soon as Sly heard the van pull up and stop at the top of the hill, he knew who it was and what they were coming for. "This is it," he whispered to Denny and York.

"Where are the cops?"

"Fuck 'em," Sly said. "Can't count on nobody but ourselves." He turned to Denny. "Aim low, boy. We don't want to get arrested for putting eyes out. Ready? Lock and load," and with that, he and Denny both loaded their mouths with ball bearings, and each put one in the leather of their slingshots.

York, sitting on a bucket at the bottom of the path, tensed, his hand on the spotlight trigger. He knew the signal, that Sly would tap him on the elbow when it was time for him to turn the light on, but they should have practiced this. It was too important to be flying by the seat of their pants.

He heard the van doors slam, heard men's harsh whispered voices, felt the heavy footfalls as they came around the van and then started, single-file, down the path, momentum carrying them a little too fast.

York's heart started to pound until he couldn't get enough air through his nose. He opened his mouth to breathe. He wished he could see. He wished he could see the full moon, wished he could see the faces of those he was about to illuminate.

He felt the tap on his elbow. He pulled the trigger.

Nothing happened.

The light took a moment to wake up, but when it blazed, it lit the place up like a movie set. Even York could see the thick blackberries on both sides of the dirt path. Sly reached down and grabbed York's wrist and aimed the light right at the eyes of the first man to come down from the street, while Denny let fly with a ball bearing. It hit the first man square in the chest.

"Ow, fuck, what was that?"

"What?" The next guy bumped into the first guy who had stopped suddenly by the blazing light and the ball bearing in his chest, and they both stumbled a few steps closer. The second guy took a ball bearing to the nuts and brought his knee up in painful reflex, falling back on Travis, who was bringing up the rear.

Sly and Denny hit them with hot little ball bearings as fast as they could spit them into their hands and pull back on the surgical tubing rubber bands. They stopped aiming and just kept firing. In the brilliance of the surreal light, the three men were ambushed by stinging bullets like invisible bees bombarding them from unknown sources. Everything was eerily silent except their exclamations of pain and confusion. There seemed nowhere to go, no way to turn that would get them away from the light and the stings. And the goddamned blackberry brambles that grabbed at their clothes and ripped through their skin.

Sly spit a ball bearing into his hand, pulled back hard on the rubber, but it slipped out of his fingers before he could aim.

Travis elbowed his way past thrashing railroad guys, pushing both of them into the brambles. He was blinded by the light, but someone needed to be in charge, and since he was the law, he thought it ought to be him. He stepped around the cursing men—why was it so goddamned quiet?—and took one step too many.

Something white hot hit Travis on the ankle bone. "Ow. Fuck!" As he bent down to rub it, grimacing puzzlement mixed with fear, a steel pea released by Denny, aimed low, hit him square in the mouth. Travis heard the tooth crack and tasted the warm blood. He spit both into the dirt, and backed up the path. Blind with the startling light, he got himself caught up in the blackberry brambles with the two other guys, which grabbed his skin and tore his arms. "Jesus fuck!" he said, then turned and tried to run up the hill back to the van, but he couldn't see anything but floating globes in front of his eyes. He felt the railroad guys right behind him. He kept hearing the whiz of the dangerous missiles as they barely missed his head, hit the top of his ear, stung his neck, the back of his arm. The other guys were feeling the stings, too.

Travis finally stumbled to the street, just as a car came around the corner. He sat down on the curb and felt around in his mouth. There was just a jagged piece of tooth that hurt like holy hell in the space next to his left front tooth. What the fuck had just happened down there?

"Travis?"

Oh, great. The sheriff.

Travis heard the van doors slam, the engine roar to life, and the van pulled out, leaving him behind. Those railroad guys were chicken shits. He opened his mouth and spit more blood onto the street.

"You okay?"

"Fuck, no, I'm not okay," he said. "They ambushed us. They've got some kind of weapons down there."

Steve Goddard kicked the baseball bat that was lying on the street next to where the pathetic Travis sat with blood running down his chin and staining a streak on his shirt. "What's that? Not a weapon, is it? No ambush planned from this end, right?"

"Can you get me to the hospital?" Travis whined.

"Yeah. Are York and those guys all right?"

"Hell, yes," Travis said. "We didn't even get close. We couldn't even see them."

Steve smiled to himself, helped Travis up, and put him in the cruiser. And Steve had thought he was going to have to protect those hobos. As if they needed him. They were street people. They lived in the jungle. They knew how to protect themselves.

While there was no yelping and high fives down at York's place, the three men were silently pleased with the outcome of their plan.

Sly took the light from York and turned it out. The world went dark for a while, until their eyes adjusted. Then the big yellow moon began to show itself.

Denny helped York off the bucket and back to his bed, and once he was settled, Denny and Sly quietly elbowed each other with pleased congratulations. Denny was glad the light was out; it was making his head pound. He was glad it had never been aimed straight at him. Jeez, it was like the spotlight from hell.

"Did you hear those panties yelp?" Sly asked.

Denny smiled and nodded. "Yeah. It was great."

"Little girls with baseball bats," Sly said.

"They might be back."

"I'll take the first watch."

But Denny had slept the afternoon away, and the wild adrenaline of victory pumped through him. He put the rest of his ball bearings in his pocket, stuck the wrist rocket in the back of his pants, and sat on the bucket. He heard the van pull away, he heard the car eventually leave, and then he heard York's labored breathing, and that was the scariest thing of the night.

Steve dropped Travis off at the all-night medical clinic, but all that was wrong with Travis was that he got his pride hurt. It cost him a broken tooth, but that was no big deal. Easily fixed, probably not by the emergency-room folks, but in a few days by his dentist. Not so easily fixed was the thrashing he'd taken at the hands of an old blind bum and two weird rail riders. Even if nobody but Steve ever knew about it, Travis knew that Steve knew, and that could be enough to break a man like Travis.

York's little gang would be moving on down the line right soon, he figured, and so would Travis.

Hell, he thought, the mayor ordered bulldozers for York's place in the morning. He wondered if York and the boys knew about that. Of course they did.

Anyway, Steve didn't have the patience to deal with it at the moment. If he was called to go take care of the bulldozers in the morning, he'd show up there. Right now all he wanted was to shower himself clean of the grit he felt on his skin and get smooth and cool in the sheets next to Athena's warmth.

She was sleeping when he crawled in next to her, and it wasn't until then that he started to laugh. He didn't mean to laugh; the whole thing had seemed absurd, but hadn't been exactly funny until he was in bed with his beautiful wife, and then he started to chuckle, and that jiggled the bed and woke her. She turned toward him and cocked a sleepy eye at him and that made him laugh even harder, so hard he couldn't explain what it was that he was laughing about. He couldn't even choke out the words that York had kicked Travis's butt, but it was so hilariously funny that three men, armed with baseball bats, couldn't even see their assailants. And one of the boys had even taken out one of Travis's teeth.

Steve had to sit up, he was laughing so hard, and the tears

came down his cheeks, and he laughed with an abandon and a release of tension he didn't know he carried in his body, in his psyche, in his profession. He laughed and laughed until he couldn't laugh anymore, and by that time, Athena was up and into her robe, sitting on the bed, looking at him as if he was a madman, and he started to laugh all over again.

In the end, he told her, and held her, and kissed the top of her head, and they both smiled into the moonlight, knowing that at least occasionally, justice was meted out by some cosmic force.

Just before they drifted off to sleep together, Athena said, "I'll be a good first lady of West Wheaton, you know. Much better than Susie Marie," and Steve gave her a little squeeze.

Denny jumped up and had his slingshot ready at the first sound of footfalls on the tracks, but it turned out to be Chris, sleepless and restless and looking for York.

"York's had a stressful night," Denny said.

"What's the matter with him?" Chris sat on a timber and lit up a cigarette. York's irregular, raspy breathing was loud in the stillness of late night.

"He's old and he's sick," Sly said. "What the fuck do you think?"

"Hey," Chris said, not expecting to be attacked by the guys in the place he felt the safest.

"He's dying," Denny said, and then felt that heat of emotion crawl up his chest and into his throat. Nobody had spoken words like that ever before, and Denny didn't like the sound of them, not at all. He waited for Sly to correct him, but Sly was silent, kicking at something.

"Dying?" Chris said. "I thought York would never die."

"Grow up, kid," Sly said. "Everybody dies."

"What'll happen when he dies? Is he going to die now?"

"Shut up," Sly said. "Just shut the fuck up." Sly stopped kicking whatever he was kicking, and came over close to Denny, pulled up the bucket, and sat down. "Put that goddamn cigarette out if you're going to be around here," he said to Chris, who immediately ground out the butt, then scooted closer to the two men.

Sly's voice came out low and smooth in that do-not-misunderstand way of his, the way Denny assumed men spoke in combat. It was just above a whisper, yet it carried. Denny was pretty sure that it only carried to the ears of those Sly wanted to hear. Not as far as York. "Here's the deal," he said. "We're moving out in the morning. We ought to have evacuated by the time the sun comes up."

"York—" Denny said.

"Clover will come by for him," Sly said. "Don't forget the bulldozers. They'll be here at sunrise."

"You think?" This was all news to Denny. He'd thought that they were going to stand fast to defend their territory. That they'd live here forever. And now York was leaving him and so was Sly. He felt as if the rug were slipping from under his feet and all he wanted to do was swallow a few more of those pain pills that rattled in his pocket. His head was beginning to pound, his throat felt tight, and a new ache in his heart began to blossom when he thought about walking away from Clover.

"You," Sly punched Chris in the arm a little harder than was necessary. "You get your ass back to school, stop smoking cigarettes, and listen to what your parents tell you. Join the Navy. Go to college. Make something of yourself. York said that to you and he's right. He's right."

Chris snorted. "Let the government start a file on me?"

"Don't talk like that," Sly said. "That anger'll burn you up. Don't be forever fighting the government. Join it. Get a civil-service job and a pension. A wife and a bunch of kids. Or something. Shit, I don't know. Be happy. Be normal. Be what York said you ought to be."

"He's right," Denny said. "I'd have liked to finish school."

"You still could," Sly said.

Denny snorted. He was way beyond that. Books. Paper. Classes. Registration. Reading. Homework. He needed stability to do that. A desk. A reading lamp. A real bed. A car. He thought he had stability, but now he had to be on the next freight out and he didn't even know how to do that, it had been so long. The dream of his own apartment, or a dorm room, going to school, drinking coffee in the student union seemed to be bathed in golden light, a dream he knew would never come to pass. He'd wasted all those opportunities, and now it was beyond him. He was too old. "Get out of here," he said to Chris, and kicked at him. He wanted some silence, and some privacy. He was dealing with too many things; he didn't want to have to deal with a kid, too.

Chris got up and moved away, back toward the tracks, and Denny could see Sly stand up and walk with him. He heard low voices, and then saw the flare of a lighter as Chris lit another cigarette and made his way back down the tracks in the direction he'd come.

Denny pulled the pills from his pocket, rolled the little plastic bottle around in his fingers for a few moments, and knew that they weren't going to do anything about the pain he was feeling, so he set them down. He punched up his moldy pillow and put his head down on it, visions of a different life floating before his eyes. A life with a real bed, a real desk, a bathroom, a kitchen, a girlfriend.

Then he squinted his eyes closed real hard against that fantasy, and a tear leaked out of each eye as he did so.

The emergency-clinic doctor gave Travis a couple of pain pills and a bag of blue ice for his jaw, told him to see the dentist first thing in the morning and sent him on his way. He walked all the way home from the clinic, feeling more and more pissed off with every step. The goddamned mayor had set him up, had set them all up. Travis would never be the same in the eyes of Steve Goddard, maybe would never be the same in his own eyes, either. Somebody had to pay for that, even if he had to leave town and never come back here. He could get other jobs in other places.

He got to his house, walked in the front door and saw the pile of bills sitting on the floor where they'd come in through the mail slot. Man, oh, man, when it rained it poured. Everything was coming down on his head in a big way, all at once.

He went to the bathroom to look at his mouth. The tooth was broken and jagged, but it didn't hurt too much anymore. His cheek was red from the ice pack. He threw the blue ice into the overflowing trash bag in the corner of the bathroom, took another look at himself in the mirror, didn't particularly like what he saw, what with the blood down the front of his shirt and all. Travis decided he needed to see the mayor, and he needed to do it now, while the emotion was high, while he was feeling righteously indignant, while he could still say what he had to say, before the mayor broke him down further. Now was the time.

He pulled off his shirt and threw it in the corner, then grabbed a fresh one and put it on, picked up his keys and headed for the mayor's house. He'd get that sonofabitch out of bed and clue him in on the consequences of using people the way he did.

Clover woke and stared, disoriented, at the darkness. She was in the living room of her little apartment, on the couch, fully dressed. The corners of her mouth were sticky and her eyes were swollen from crying. She remembered now.

She got off the couch and went to the kitchen for a big glass of water. Then she took off her clothes and let them stay where they dropped on the floor. She climbed into bed, her heart aching over Denny. She was certain that he had skipped out on her and York just when York needed him the most. At least York and Sly had Sheriff Steve to protect them. He'd do a good job.

Clover didn't need Denny, and maybe it was a good thing that it all happened this way, because it was probably time. Denny wasn't good for her, and it was only a matter of time before she got pregnant, she knew it. No birth control was a hundred-percent effective.

But to have him sneak out like that was really low, and it hurt Clover's heart to think Denny was even capable of such a thing.

Perhaps he wasn't. Perhaps he got tied up in traffic. Maybe he got arrested. Maybe some blood clot burst in his brain and he died by the side of the road. Or was back in the hospital.

Perhaps. Perhaps she needed to think he'd run out on them all in order for her to have the courage to move on.

She curled up in her little bed, wearing only her underwear, balled her hands into fists and stuffed them up under the pillow, under her head. This would be the end of it for them, she resolved. No more Denny. No matter what happened down at York's place, she needed to move on.

In the morning, she'd go down there, get York and take him someplace. She'd bring him back here, if nothing else, while she found a place for him to live.

No more Denny.

The thought of never feeling his hands on her again brought up a hiccup, and another tear leaked out of sore eyes. Could she ever find another man who kissed like that?

Yes, she thought. Her new guy would kiss like that, after he brushed his teeth in his own bathroom sink. She squeezed shut her tear-duct faucet. He'd be better than Denny in every way. Especially after, when Denny's mind bounced around to something different immediately, her new guy would kiss her and caress her, and they would lie in a comfortable bed in soft sheets, not in some weed field. Nope. No more Denny.

Just York. And then she'd never go down there again.

Sick, grieving, but resolved, Clover closed her eyes and thought of York in a clean place with pretty nurses and good food. It settled her a little bit. Enough, she hoped, to keep her mind off Deputy Travis, Sly and Denny and what all was going on down there, and get to sleep. No more Denny. No more Denny. She whispered it to her pillow and she repeated it in her mind until she drifted off.

Milo Grimes missed the light switch the first time he tried to turn out the light in his office. He knew he was too drunk to drive, but since it was in the middle of the night—or, more accurately, midnight or later—there wouldn't be any traffic. Besides, he was the mayor. No self-respecting policeman would pull him over and give him a ticket. Certainly not Steve "my shit don't stink" Goddard. And not his ass-wipe deputy, either. This could very well be his last official act as mayor, this turning out the light in his office, .32 in his pocket, the Jack Daniel's in his left hand, the keys to his Mercedes in his right.

He made his way crookedly down the hall, out to the parking lot, awash with the silver light of the full moon high overhead, and into his car. He breathed in the smell of leather. It almost brought tears to his eyes, but he knew that was Jack Daniel's emotions, not his. He had but one thing left to do tonight, and that was to find a place where he could shoot himself in the head.

The office wasn't good. His secretary would find the gooey

mess, and that wouldn't be nice, although being nice wasn't exactly high on Grimes's list. But she'd unbuttoned her blouse regularly, and let him take a tiny lick, suck, and nibble, and that was worth a little respect. He didn't want to do it at home, because Susie Marie was going to have to sell the mansion sometime soon, and he didn't want her to have to clean up gore first. Maybe he could stage it as an accident. Or as a murder. Give Steve Goddard some real goddamn work. Maybe he should do it down by York's place and give the railroad guys a run for their money.

Fucking Ashton.

Fucking Norman! He could have killed that little pussy Haas all the way back in Sacramento! Why did he have to wait until the train got to West Wheaton, for Christ's sake? He's the one who screwed everything up. Good thing he was dead, or Milo would go over to his hovel right now and put a bullet in his skull. In fact, he'd like to go find his corpse in the morgue and put a bullet in his skull just for grins.

Note to self: Never send a junkie to do a man's work. Never again.

Milo snorted. Never anything again.

Maybe he ought to just drive out into the desert weeds and do himself in out under the stars. It might take a couple of days for them to find his body if he didn't leave a note somewhere, and that might be ugly, too. Not the best way for Susie Marie to remember him, after identifying his body all bloated and buzzard-pecked.

Shit. This was a lot harder than it seemed at first. Maybe he ought to just go home. Go home, take a little rest, sleep off the booze, and then with a clear mind, he could make a clear plan.

He wouldn't show up at the council meeting. He'd be dead by then and they could put that little item on their agenda. That was the best plan. He ought to at least stop by the house to tell

Susie Marie that . . .

Tell her what? That she had been a good wife? She hadn't. That she had made him happy? She hadn't. That she'd been good for his career? She hadn't. She'd been a runaround little gold-digger bitch, and he ought to just take her with him.

Oh man, am I drunk, he thought to himself. *I need to get home.*

With one eye closed in order to focus, he slowly moved the Mercedes out of the parking lot and weaved his way through West Wheaton's deserted streets toward his mansion on the hill that Haas had helped finance.

He should have left well enough alone and let his suspicions ride, the little jerk. He could have been useful over and over again, if he hadn't gotten so greedy and/or pious. Whichever it was, it had got him dead in Yorktown, and now Milo Grimes was going to have to pay that bill, too.

Brenda's eyes snapped open and she was instantly wide-awake. She looked at the clock. Two-fourteen A.M. Her first thought was that Sly was not the type of guy she could take home to meet her parents at Thanksgiving. Her second thought was that it was probably just exactly that type of thinking that had led her to her current pitiful life. She only saw her parents one day a year. It was probably time for her to stop using them as her yardstick. They weren't such great role models themselves.

She thought about Sly living in her apartment, sleeping on her couch—or her bed—showering in her bathroom, leaving wet towels on the floor. She thought about him getting a job. She'd get up every morning and make his lunch, and rub his sore muscles when he came home at the end of the day complaining about the boss. She thought about making a menu and fixing good meals. She thought about taking his dirty work clothes to the Laundromat, bleaching them clean and folding them just right. She thought about cleaning out a couple of drawers in her dresser for his things.

She wanted this thing. She wanted the family life. She wanted a man, and it wasn't all about sex. It was about making a life with someone. She could be, *would* be, a good, loyal, devoted woman to some man, and God knew Sly needed a woman to tend him.

She slipped out of bed and turned on the light. She walked through her small apartment, turning on the lights and looking at the whole place through what she imagined would be Sly's viewpoint. It was adequate. Maybe they'd move to a bigger place someday, when he got a job, but for now it was okay. Plus, there was always the safety valve in case it didn't work out. She didn't want to be stuck in a place she couldn't afford. She could afford this. She could afford to help Sly get on his feet.

She washed up the few dishes that were still in the sink from the day before, dried them and put them away. She threw the dishcloth into the hamper and hung a fresh one on the door of the oven. Then she showered and put out fresh towels, and changed the sheets. She did her hair, called in to work and left a message on the answering machine that she still wasn't feeling well and would be taking another day.

And then she sat down to wait for the sun to come up, so she could go rescue Sly from the bulldozers, from the weeds, from the train tracks, from his misguided and lonely freedoms.

Eileen's alarm went off as it always did at three A.M. She sat up, scratched around in her hair, and looked out the window. The full moon looked back at her and she rubbed her eyes, then realized that she'd gone to bed without washing off her mascara.

Full moon. Another month gone by. Another month older, another month frying donuts, another month for the same old worn-out, rump-sprung, elastic-gone panties, another month of the same stained uniforms, another month of too many expenses for the income, another month alone.

She looked up at that moon from where she sat on the edge of her bed in her tiny little trailer and wished she had the guts to drink in the morning. She could really enjoy a nice, refreshing martini at the moment.

But coffee would have to do. She lit a cigarette from her bedside pack and remembered that she'd forgotten to buy coffee filters. She'd have to use a paper towel again today.

"I'm going to buy this land and put up a monument to York," Sly said.

Denny snorted. He was feeling increasingly restless as York's breathing became deeper and more labored. His fingers toyed with ball bearings as he listened to Sly talk with an unusual calm and confidence, even though he was just talking bullshit. Buy the land. Sure. Put up a monument to York. Absolutely. What crap. Sly rarely held down a laborer's job for two days straight.

"Make it a park. For the kids, you know?"

"Yeah, they'll all get run over by the trains."

"No, they won't. It'll be nice. I'll make it nice. Brenda'll know how to do all that stuff. She'll help."

"You and Brenda and what taxpaying organization?" Denny knew that York was about to die, and he couldn't deal with it. He couldn't deal with it. He jumped up and shook out his sleeping bag, but the old seam finally let go, and feathers flew with the dirt and grit.

"Hey," Sly said. "What are you doing? Stop it."

Desperation gripped Denny. He couldn't stand it anymore. He wanted to stuff the sleeping bag into York's mouth and still that awful breathing. He wanted to call 9-1-1 and bring an ambulance down here to save him. He wanted to curl up into a little ball and have Clover rock him. He didn't want to deal with the bulldozers that would be there in a couple of hours, he didn't want to listen to any more of Sly's government conspiracy crap, he was sick of living in the weeds, in the dust, in the dirt, he was sick of the politics, he was sick of the low-down lifestyle. He was sick of having that grit in his nose and in his mouth and between his toes every damn day of his life.

He remembered having that six hundred some-odd bucks in his pocket, and ordering that steak and cold beer with confidence. He'd like some more of that feeling. He'd like to be clean, and to stay clean. He'd like—Jesus God—he'd like to go back to school and learn some new things.

Then he heard it, from a few miles south, the whistle from the train as it left Bonita. That whistle carried a long way on the clear air, and Denny heard it call him.

"I gotta go," he said to Sly. He threw the handful of ball bearings into the weeds, and taking nothing with him but the pain pills in his pocket, he ran up the embankment and started walking north on the tracks. When the freight caught up with him, he'd grab hold as it slowed for the curve and jump aboard. He wished he'd said good-bye to Clover, he wished he'd said good-bye to York. Oh, well. He kept walking. Behind him, he felt the vibrations of the approaching train. Ahead, he felt the vibrations of his future. Within each was the excitement of the new freight, the new experience, the new place, the new people, the boldness of the unknown. Within each was also the dread that nothing would ever change, that his whole life would merely be same shit, different day.

If that were true, then everything Clover had done, everything York had ever said would all be useless. York's life would have had no meaning.

It was inconceivable, but deep down, Denny thought it to be true. An old anger fired up in him that he hadn't felt in a long time, not since the last time he was hopping freights, before he showed up at York's.

He owed York. He owed Clover.

And the best way to repay them, he figured, was to get the hell out, and not rub their noses in the uselessness of it all.

He ignored the little sob that broke free from his chest, and started walking faster. The freight was coming and he was going to have to run to catch it.

When Milo saw Deputy Travis's car in his driveway, he figured something had gone wrong down by the tracks. The sky was beginning to lighten and the air was harsh with the heat of the approaching day. For a moment, Milo forgot his personal problems and worried about business. Deputy Travis probably screwed up the mission, and he was here to tell Milo all about it.

Well, Milo thought, *I'll listen to the young punk's confession, and then pull out my .32 and blow my brains out right in front of the kid. That ought to be good for a decade of therapy.* At least he'd make a difference in someone's life.

But the lights were off, and the kitchen was dark.

Milo knew, with a terrible certainty, what he was going to find in his bedroom long before he walked down the hall and pushed open the door.

Susie Marie lay with her back to Travis, wound up in that expensive sheet, sleeping. Milo couldn't see her face. Travis snored, lying on his back, the sheet down around his waist, his hairy chest and one muscular leg exposed, the bedroom reeking of sex.

Milo paused, the swirl of emotions weakening his knees. He felt indignant that he should be left to see this. He was hurt that Susie Marie would actually commit this act in his own bed. He was furious at Travis for cuckolding him, and he was lonely. So horribly lonely. There was no one in the universe with whom he could share his burdens. Nobody. Not his wife, not his employees, not the council, not the sheriff, not his mother, not anybody.

Milo Grimes was alone in the world.

"Hey!" he yelled. *"Wake the fuck up!"*

Susie Marie twitched, opened her eyes, saw him, gasped, pulled the sheet up to her chin and scooted up toward the headboard in fear. Travis continued to snore.

Milo felt himself weaving. He wanted to sit down, but to sit down would be to mitigate his power. He needed his power right now. It was all he had.

"Hey!" Milo said again, and kicked the foot of the bed.

Susie Marie nudged Travis with her freshly pedicured foot.

"What?" Travis said, rubbed his hands over his face, and opened his eyes. "Oh, jeez," he said when he saw Milo. He looked up toward Susie Marie with what appeared to be some type of apology on his face. "God, I musta fallen asleep."

"Musta," Milo said.

Travis sat up and reached for his clothes.

"Sit tight," Milo said, and pulled the gun from his pocket.

Susie Marie gasped with a satisfying little noise of fear. "Milo!" she said in a little mouse voice.

"Whoa," Travis said. "Hold on, now. This isn't something that's news to you."

"You prick," Milo said. He was astonished at the man's chutzpah, and pulled the trigger.

The bullet went through Travis's right lung and knocked him back onto the bed. Bright-red blood flowed from the hole and began to froth from his lips as he looked, wide-eyed, back at Milo.

"Nice shot," Milo congratulated himself. "Don't die too fast. The entertainment has just begun." He turned to Susie Marie, who looked like she was about to scream. "Shhh," he said, holding the short barrel of the little gun to his lips. "Shhh." He walked over to her side of the bed, and tried to ignore the stabbing pain in his heart as she cringed and shrank away from him.

Milo sat on the edge of the bed. He wanted nothing more than to lie down and go to sleep, but he had work to do first.

"The thing is, Susie Marie," he said, and then forgot what the thing was. Oh, yeah. "The thing is—" But the thing was too big to say. The loneliness, the guilt, the hurt, the lies, the years of deception that had permeated their lives. . . . It was all just too much to say, to deal with, to account for. Hell, she knew it. She was part of it. "Well, hell," he said. "You know."

She nodded, and he shot her in the same place. Right lung.

"Well, okay, then," he said, and stood up. He went to the foot of the bed, standing right before them, as if on stage. He had their undivided attention, or as much as could be expected from two bleeding, gasping, dying fornicators, and he discovered that he had no last words.

He put the gun to his head and pulled the trigger.

York dreamed of strings. Dark, thick, ropelike strings that wound around his chest, light, silvery weblike strings that floated up to the full moon, gossamer strings that bound his eyes, rubbery strings that hobbled his feet. He struggled with the strings, trying to break free, needing to breathe, but breath didn't come easy. *First, the wrists,* he thought, if he could only free his wrists, then he could pull away the rest of the bindings, but he was asleep, paralyzed in a dream, and he couldn't move his hands.

He struggled, his breath coming harder and harder, the bonds around his chest turning into steel bands, and someone was cranking down on them as if tuning up a barrel. He began to panic, feeling closed in and afraid. He wanted to yell, to tell whoever it was to stop, but his mouth was sleep-befuddled, and he had no breath to speak with anyway.

Then a cool hand was laid upon his forehead, and a sweet, light, rich voice spoke clearly into his ear. "Stop struggling," she said.

It was just that simple.

Clover's eyes popped open, and a sudden alertness was upon her. It was early dawn, a time of day she was all too used to seeing as she suited up and walked down to the donut shop. But today was her day off.

She gave herself a luxuriously feline stretch, and thought about what lay ahead. First, go down and wake York, then bring him home. While here, he could bathe and shave, while she made a few phone calls, then she could trim his hair. His chances of getting into a nice place would be better if he looked clean. Maybe then he'd take a nap while she went to the Goodwill to get him some new clothes, and then she'd take him to his new home. Someone would take him, and he'd go someplace nice, she just knew it. He was too important. He was too wonderful. He was her daddy.

That would probably take up most of the day, she thought, what with paperwork and all. But once York was settled in his new place, and she'd maybe read to him, and made sure he had a good meal in his belly, she thought she might have business down at the train station in Bonita.

Maybe. She had to consciously push aside thoughts of Denny, but she knew that if she didn't have to see him whenever she went to see York, she'd get over him fast.

Whatever. Denny was probably long gone anyway. She didn't have to think about him, she had things to do that were infinitely more important.

The birds were singing their morning songs, it wasn't too hot yet, and the day had purpose and direction. Life was good, Clover thought, and it was going to be a beautiful day.

ABOUT THE AUTHOR

Elizabeth Engstrom is the author of eleven books and over two hundred fifty published short stories, articles, and essays. Her most recent novel is *The Northwoods Chronicles.* She is a sought-after teacher, panelist, and speaker at writing conferences and conventions around the world. Engstrom lives in the Pacific Northwest, where she teaches the fine art of fiction and is always working on the next book. www.ElizabethEngstrom.com